THE DEATH OF MOISHE-GANEF

Also by Simon Louvish

The Therapy of Avram Blok

THE DEATH OF MOISHE-GANEF

A Levantine Tale

Simon Louvish

HEINEMANN : LONDON

William Heinemann Ltd
10 Upper Grosvenor Street, London W1X 9PA
LONDON MELBOURNE TORONTO
JOHANNESBURG AUCKLAND

First published 1986

SBN 434 43100 1

Filmset by Northumberland Press Ltd,
Gateshead, Tyne and Wear
Printed in Great Britain by
St. Edmundsbury Press
Bury St. Edmunds, Suffolk

"Do not fear the terror of the night,
Nor the arrow that flies by day,
Nor the pestilence that walks in darkness,
Nor the destruction that wastes at noon,
Though a thousand fall at your side,
And ten thousand at your right hand,
It shall not approach you . . .

". . . The Lord said to Jacob: Do not fear, my servant Jacob.
The Lord has chosen Jacob: Do not fear, my servant Jacob.
The Lord has redeemed Jacob: Do not fear, my servant Jacob . . .
How good are thy tents, Jacob: Do not fear, my servant Jacob.
Your laws are taught to Jacob: Do not fear, my servant Jacob.
For there is no sorcery in Jacob: Do not fear, my servant Jacob.
Iniquity has not been seen in Jacob: Do not fear, my servant Jacob.
The Lord has promised Jacob: Do not fear, my servant Jacob.
Pardon the sins of Jacob: Do not fear, my servant Jacob."

from the Jewish *Siddur*, or Prayer Book

Acknowledgment and Note

The spelling of the Yiddish word "ganef" in this book has been used following the Israeli pronunciation. This is also the spelling favoured by the YIVO Institute for Jewish Research in the USA. Other authorities, relentless rivals of the YIVO Institute, prefer an alternative spelling - "gonef" or "gonif". There is no agreed standard.

All the characters in this book are fictitious but some of the events are, alas, not. I am indebted to many friends for stubbornly tending the lanterns in the asylum, and particularly to Mike and Tami. I would also like to acknowledge the advice of Uriel Masad in some of the theological aspects of Joe Dekel's dilemmas.

LONDON:
MARCH, 1984

1

They told me Moishe-Ganef was dead. They even showed me the body. There it was, sprawled on the single bed of a London hotel, making a fearful mess of the covers. The head was staved in by a massive blow, delivered to the left temple. It was a hideous sight, but there was little doubt, this man did look like Moishe-Ganef. There was a mole on his chin that had been there since childhood, and even a trace of that gargoyle grin he had adopted in army days. On the other hand, the light was bad, it may well not have been Moishe-Ganef at all, for all I knew, but a double, skin grafted with care by whoever you fancy, in Oshkosh, Nebraska or Irkutsk. These are strange times. We had come a long way from the streets of Jerusalem, the old carefree days of callow mischief in a country basking in its dream. The brave new world in its ancient setting. Hear O Israel, and the whole kitbag.

"Well?" said the tiddly little crumb who had brought me to this pass, all panic and eyebrow quiver.

"Well what?" I asked. At least one joy in the misery, to watch his tiddly eyebrows quiver.

"Is it him? Can you make an identification?"

"It's a good likeness," I said. "He used to look like himself fairly often, before he began playing secret agent."

"But you're not certain?" He was obviously presenting his best *sotto voce*, to avoid raising the alarm. If you sneak a reluctant witness into a hotel room at midnight, to view a corpse, you would tend to be hot on discretion.

"I am certain about the Lord Blessed Be He," I said, "but about nothing else."

A bold manifesto, given the state both of my psyche and of the Israeli nation. Pulverised by war, ineptitude and its own shattered self-image, serious doubts might be raised by the most faithful as to whether there is a Guiding Hand. Nor was the twittering pilchard playing his torch by my side much of an advertisement for the Chosen People.

"Why me?" I whispered, caught in the conspiratorial mode. "Why haven't you summoned the good old British bobbies? They have the best Scotland Yard outside Scotland. I know, I have watched them on TV for years. *The Sweeney*," I listed them, *"CI5, The Professionals. Z Cars. Shoestring.* You miss all these things, being posted here. In Israel you are fed them nightly."

"Please be serious, for God's sake," he pleaded, "we have a dead man in this room."

Are not our policemen brilliant? This one was typical home grown. Most probably Military Police at eighteen, Investigation Branch, a natural Arabic speaker. Assigned to hide in dustbins, outside Arab high schools, or the editorial offices of *Al-Fajr*. Shown some aptitude perhaps for foreign languages, demobilised into the Security Services. The spook type, too runtish, or so he seemed, to be your garrotte and karate hit man. Spends his free time, no doubt, in one of those Israeli shebeens in North London, haunts for spooks, burglars and heroin smugglers, the soured cream of our human export. Tiddly Crumb, I read you loud and clear, but how did you get pinned on my backside?

I was on holiday of course, taking a well-earned breather from the embattled Homeland, but someone must have been keeping tabs. It would be no problem, but why the bother? I am no longer a player in the National games. In the scramble for Causes, I am non-aligned. I have resigned from the club. Jews, Arabs, Palestinians, moderates, zealots, let them all kill each other. The only organisation I am a member of is the Jerusalem Cinematheque. I ply my trade as a TV critic, with an occasional humoresque for good measure. Fat old ladies doing Jane Fonda's workout on the beach, that is about my forte. I live in the Holy Land because I can afford the rent. Don't come the stiff-necked patriot with me. And if you insist, motherfucker, then I tell you I have paid my dues. 'Sixty-seven, 'sixty-nine, 'seventy-three, the litany of wars, cataclysms and disasters, it makes you ill just to conjure the numbers.

Nevertheless, the ghosts of the past crept after me, knocking on my poor English hosts' door: Camden Town, urb of Albion, twenty-three fifteen hours, Saturday. The rigours of the Sabbath over, James Cagney commencing on Channel Four. The prospect of bliss. But no. Thunk thunk thunk, the old-fashioned door knocker. The Crumb, enter frame bottom, with "Embassy", "Security" and "Property of the State of Israel" written all over his repugnant dial.

"Yosef Dekel?" he had said, in our ancestral Hebrew language, "I apologise for bothering you, but we need your help on a very urgent matter."

The royal We, forsooth! "I am sorry," I quoth, "but I am slow of speech, and of a slow tongue. And anyway, the Children of Israel have already been saved, I have been constantly told, from bondage."

"We know your politics," he said, still in the Windsor idiom, "and this is not a recruiting drive. It is a personal matter. You had a close friend, I believe, one Moshe Sherman? He is the cause of my visit."

Oi. Spare us this. Not Moishe-Ganef – Moishe-Thief! The chicken risen from its own ashes. A Pandora's box I prefer to keep sealed, locking away private memories along with the public detritus of our popular nightmares: victory orations, funeral dirges, the salute of rifles over coffins, the PLO, UAR, WIZO, Messrs Peres, Begin, Sharon, Levy, the scandalous boredom of our national television, the defence tax, the Peace For Galilee tax, the shame of winning the Eurovision song contest . . . Each one of us an Atlas, carrying the world, without benefit of foreskin even. One more feather, the last straw of Moishe-Ganef, could tip the whole shebang over. From his first day at kindergarten, the man had been nothing but trouble. Now he lay in a Russell Square hotel room, with his head like a squashed watermelon, if it was he, that is, in the waving circle of The Crumb's pocket torch.

"We will leave now," said The Crumb, consulting his luminous watch. It was waterproof too, I'll bet, in case he might be detailed to shadow an Enemy of the State from the bed of the Serpentine. He ushered me out, carefully, noiselessly unlocking, locking the hotel-room door, drawing me to the fire escape. Three cats, who thought they had a clear night lined up with the house garbage, protested, but I shushed them, with the born expertise of any tenant of a Jerusalem dwelling. "Take me home, James," I said, sitting back in his Fiat, as he tried to gun the motor quietly. "Or are there any more bodies on view tonight?" I saw him taking me on a grand tour of friends' carcasses, and even, for good measure, relations. You thought London was your bolthole, Joe Dekel. Take a peek into your personal catacomb. For a gross moment I saw my Anat's face, contorted in death, perhaps strangled, her raven hair spattered with congealed blood and mud. Imagination has always been my curse. My shield from conformity, yes, but also my daily, nightly terror. I was coming to believe I had really seen Moishe, just a moment ago, smashed, like a cast-off marrow. One has seen The Dead in their natural habitat: deserts, rocks, disembowelled sandbags. But in the Edenvale Bed and Breakfast in Russell Square? Everything should have its limit.

"If you bear with me," said The Crumb – he had dropped his imitation of Prince Charles with nasal catarrh – "there is one more visit. My superior here. He is also someone you know, but very much alive, thank God."

Do not take the Lord's name in vain, I thought at him, before we know with whom we are dealing. There were a dozen questions I could have thrown at this lackey, this shitty errand boy of an even shittier system I try to excrete every morning, but alas, excrement is within you, you manufacture more, constantly: the Enemy Within. Get behind me, Satan ... My mind merged with the shrill grind of the Fiat.

He took me to a private address, in a mansion block in a crescent behind Lancaster Gate. The kind of posh area, close by Hyde Park, where Saudis and other Gulf Arabs congregate, prostrating themselves on the green. No wonder Arabs often look so dour and woebegone, if they hate the desert so. A queer area for an Israeli to settle, unless he is on masquerade ...

The name on the bell The Crumb pressed was Bronson. I was now taking care to notice such things. I had told my English hosts to contact a journalist we knew, if I did not return by morning. In every Israeli Jew lurks a certified paranoid. In most, he has leapt on to the surface. To The Crumb I had merely said: "If I am not back by five a.m., Yassir Arafat will be informed." He grunted. He must have read my file, but refused to appreciate my oeuvre.

The night's shocks were obviously not yet over. This "Bronson", opening his door cautiously as we climbed the stairway up to the third floor, was indeed familiar. Baruch BenTovim, alias Guttenson, alias Gingi Tussik-Punim: "Ginger Arse-Face", as we had called him in the army, because he was both freckled and covered with acne. Now he still resembled a snowman with German measles, but he was balding, too, which shows you what happens if you follow a career in Intelligence to its pay-off. He and Moishe had served with me in the Israel Defence Forces, a period of one's life some dote on, but not I. More worms escaping from the can. Amnesia, where is thy sting?

Tonight was not going to be among the top ten of my life, not even the top twenty. The ginger simpleton sprang forward and purloined my hand before I had the chance to hide it. His grip was strong. I could see him working out with a Bullworker at dawn, freckled pectorals flexed in the bathroom mirror.

"Joe Dekel!" he exclaimed with that kibbutz bonhomie he had laid over his citified background. It used to be *de rigueur* for social climbing, but in the Begin Age it has become a no-no. The Nationalists hate the kibbutz marginally less than the Fatah, and on a par with the *Gulag Archipelago*. The Gingi must have done something useful for his new masters, though, to rate the cushy London station. "How have you been? We haven't met for ages! I'm so sorry it's under these circumstances."

"You've grown fat," I told him. He should not think the Bullworker absolved him from the perils of smugness.

"Do you think so?" he sounded surprised. "I thought that

department was adequate. But of course it's been a long time. You look A-OK. The grey in your hair suits you. I see you're no longer with the Faithful."

"You are mistaken." He was referring to the absence of my little knitted hattie, the skullcap of the religious stalwart. I am damned if I am going to call it a "*yarmulka*". I was not going to explain to the likes of him why I wear it at home but whip it off when abroad. At home at least they know my face and my views, and the chauvinists give me a wide berth. Abroad I loathe people assuming by the hattie that I am a nationalistic zealot. Jews who come up to me in the street and say: "Don't be downhearted. I think your Menahem Begin is wonderful." What can I say? You are not in luck, Reb Yid, I am Israel's only religious anarchist . . . "It must have blown off on the way," I said, just to annoy the Gingi. "The police will pick it up and know everything."

He sighed, his eyes saying Joe, Joe, when will you ever be serious. He had by now ushered us into a sparsely furnished living room, with bare walls, a sofabed, two straight-backed chairs, a plush grey carpet and a low table with a brass Arab tray and coffeepot upon it. Urging me to the sofa by his side, The Crumb dutifully perched on a high chair, the Gingi poured coffee into three small white cups.

"This is a sad business, isn't it? I am really sorry we dragged you into this, but there is a reason. Of course, you could have refused."

Schmuck, you know me for a curious bastard. And you know Moishe was a childhood friend, despite all that passed later. Don't give me this hint, hint, nudge, you are still one of us at heart. "You are not going to leave him lying there, I suppose," I said, "for the beasts of the field."

He glanced at his watch. "The police should be finding him about now," he said, "I shall be informed in the morning." He sipped, closing his eyes at the marvel of his own brew. It was nothing to write home about. "The fact is," he said, "we have not seen Moishe for going on three years. We meaning The Intelligence Family as a whole. It was a great surprise to us to find he'd been seen in London. Frankly we were keeping an eye. And now this. We had to make a quick decision. Check connections, given his recent history. You understand, of course."

"No."

"Running a quick check," he continued blithely, "lo and behold, who do we find slumming in London but Joe Dekel, companion of our Moishe's misspent youth, partner of his masturbation contests. Of course, I said to myself, it's probably a coincidence. Annual Joe Dekel holiday time. You fly off every year when your army reserve duty's due. It's a familiar scene. They tend to shuffle you to the back of the pack and the Nation is spared another embarrassment."

"I would go to jail as a war resister," I explained, "but the food is better over here."

"Had he been in touch with you?" he asked directly, peeping over the rim of the coffee cup.

"Moishe? He has been crossed off my social list. I merely followed his seamier exploits in the *Police News*."

"He was going to sue the State, you know, for wrongful arrest. He wrote a whole epic for the Ombudsman. Then, pfatt, he goes right off the map again, disappearing into thin air. The Director General was most upset. This was in November 'eighty. Since then not a whiff, till London, three days ago. And before we can make contact - this."

"He always was an unreasonable chap," I agreed.

"Now I've brought you in on a hunch." He leaned forward. "All right, I know you hate our guts these days, but this could be beyond politics. When you pass through The Family, you become a relation, even if you come to hate the parents. Blood is blood. Even you can't deny that, skullcap or no skullcap."

"It's two in the morning, Gingi," I said, "what the fuck do you want of me? Why all this identification charade? Do you know your own man or don't you?"

"Of course," he said, "there are dental records, which are supposed to be infallible. And fingerprints. But these are hi-tech days. Do you remember the Oswald hooh-hah? They exhumed the body and pronounced the teeth kosher. But were they fooled none the less? We have sawbones who can give you the face of a monkey, or change you into Sophia Loren. There have been cases of double-bluff: a face redone as itself, with minute flaws. I can tell you, it's a minefield out there."

"So, remove the body and examine it."

"Not everything in life is simple. Intelligence is not what it used to be. There are constraints, rules of engagement. I am a small cog in the wheel. He was never close to me as he was to you. I want a friend's hunch, an instinct. Was it Moishe Sherman lying in that hotel room? What do you truly think, Joe?"

2

What do you truly think, Joe?

Because you believe in God, in your own private manner, which seems to make sense to no one else, should you believe in ghosts?

The ghosts of a lost Jerusalem, and Moishe Sherman in short trousers ... The city of Little Israel of the 'fifties, divided higgeldy-piggeldy by a concrete wall, but united by a shared mystery. We used to run down to the end of the Jaffa Road, pressing up against the coarse-grained barrier, peeping through the tiny square holes here and there at the Other City beyond - Arab Jerusalem, the Unknown Land, the Hashemite Kingdom of Jordan. Even in those smalltown days Moishe-Ganef was a thief, already a veteran of that nickname. The legend goes he'd stolen his own pram and nappies off the racks of the Hamashbir store. Certainly as children in Yellin Street all the rest of us had to guard our toys. Plastic panzers, a wooden steam roller, the magic rabbit's foot, the salvaged condom, all were booty for sticky-fingered Moishe. His subsequent career was no surprise. In a world of change, he was constant. But at least then you could be sure he was Moishe-Ganef, not an ersatz imitation. Everyone at school thought he was destined for reform school. The kids all shunned him, except me. I remember we shared a dream of becoming famous train and bank bandits. Strange that he has more or less found that niche in history, whereas I can't even fool the taxman.

It was, in fact, due to our pact of grand larceny that Moishe scaled down his petty thieving and scraped his way with me into high school. Or so I believed then. It may of course have been a delayed puberty, or the waning of his anal fixation. Freud is Anat's forte, not mine. But he never lost his interest in the criminal world, progressing from detective magazines to professional journals some geek cousin of his sent from America. *Law Enforcement*, or something similar. His mother, who brought him up on her own, his poor pa having died early, was dead scared he was going to become a policeman, but I knew that was not his angle. (Odd that he eventually combined the two - his mother's fear and our boyhood fantasies.) We grew apart through high school, mainly due to my discovery of God and His bizarre demands on me. I shall dwell no further on this. It is a private matter. If you hoped for a sermon, tough shit, comrades. The safety curtain comes down here. At any rate, what with me agonising about my soul, and Moishe trying to learn safe cracking by mail order, our adolescence passed in turmoil. And, of course, girls had entered the arena by then and decorum demands a further veil ...

Nevertheless, having been drafted in the same army intake, we drifted together again. Fate sent us to a technical course concerning "communications". Hush-hush elements were involved. Civilians stalked among us grinning strangely, like cats that had struck a secret milk field. All the army recruits talked in whispers. High antennae seemed turned towards Cairo. "Moishe," I said to him once, late at night in our tent, residual static crackling between our ears, "why be pawns in this lousy Intelligence Corps game, when we might become bishops or knights?" I was always the leader between us, or so I was led to believe.

"Sure," he agreed, "this is strictly a mug's game. Let's go for the whole pot." He always wanted to go for the whole pot. Perhaps that's why he lies in a Russell Square bedroom, with his brains dashed all over the floor.

The long and short of it is, we applied for "KAMAN" Course, the Intelligence Officers' Training. Oh man! Over the years I thought I had put that madness behind me, but one is not rid of one's follies so neatly. "KAMAN" Course, winter of 1966! The climate was a bitch, the commanding officer a sow, the whole affair a complete turkey. I can't understand what possessed me to undertake it, I must have been a complete moron. The moronity was compounded by the fact that the course committed us to three years in the Regular Army to follow our two and a half years' conscription. A career as an armed forces spook! My brain must have been blancmange. Years later I asked Anat to explain myself to me, but she was no help at all. "You wanted to serve your country," she said. Imagine - the woman I live and love with saying that! The enemy is all around us. It was true, of course, that those were days of innocence. Little Israel in its rosy cradle. The Six Day War was yet to come, the Occupation, the Yom Kippur horror, Menahem Begin, Arik Sharon, Lebanon. And I was barely nineteen, fuck it all! The case for the defence rests ...

We tore our arses thoroughly, that foul winter, crawling through mud and thornfields. "The whole pot, eh?" I shouted at Moishe, while some lunatic sprayed live bullets above us. "You can't make an omelette without breaking the eggs," he yelled back. We were the eggs, you see. Ginger Arse-Face was a waif we picked up on the way. We felt the need to patronise someone. He was a Jerusalem kid as well, but from the posh Rehavia district. The gilded lily of the cesspool. His father was a toilet-roll manufacturer, and we never failed to hold that against him. We became a trio, and then a quartet, of Jerusalem boys in our platoon. We called ourselves the Four Sons (Of Whom the Torah Spake), after the Passover Haggadah - One Wise, one Wicked, one Simple and One Who Does Not Know How to Ask. Oddly enough I was elected the fourth, with Gingi Arse-Face as the third. The Wicked was Moishe, whose reputation preceded him, and who was the squad's chief blanket stealer. The Wise was Meisinger, rampantly miscast, though destined to go too far ...

Meisinger ... shit! A phantom yet to appear? There is an inevitability in our woes. A bent, ravenlike figure, with a beak of a nose, he was at once platoon geek and genius. Top of the class, the Commanding Officer's darling, the jewel in the "KAMAN" Course crown. He had an infallible memory:

maps, briefings, codes, references were photographed on his retina. He knew the Beersheba phonebook by heart: nights in the desert, when the Negev air froze us, and the angst of three years' Regular to come chilled us to the bone, we would pick up the transmitter and, routed through the Command, call the numbers he would conjure at will. "Mrs Kadurie?" we would say. 'We are so glad to find you in. You have won our prize ICM bicycle. There is no need to pick it up. We deliver."

Terror makes shameless farts of us all.

"So what do you think, Joe?" Gingi-Arse-Face, breaking in on my meditations. The loo-paper maker's son who made good. Another miracle of the Hebrew renaissance.

I sighed and contemplated the thick dregs of his coffee. "I think I'm tired," I said, "and past my bedtime. I've missed James Cagney in a Raoul Walsh picture, and the commercials for holiday chalets. I feel sick that someone seems to have killed my old friend, and whatever else I feel about it I don't want to discuss with you. I think you can phone me and meet me in the day somewhere. The Patisserie Valerie will do. It's obvious your doggie here knows where to find me. I think I'll just get up and go."

"OK," he said. "I know how you feel. Menashe will drive you home." He inclined his head to The Crumb, who stood up, ready and willing. He was clearly Downstairs to Gingi's Upstairs. Both of them made me want to vomit. Why involve me in their rotten shenanigans? Could Gingi not have indentified the Ganef himself? What stew were they spooning me into?

"Do you ever see Meisinger?" I asked as I turned to go, hoping to catch him off guard. But he betrayed no surprise except a raising of eyebrows, as he returned the three drained cups to the brass tray. "Ah, Messinger! Now that's a schemer for you! He's far beyond you or I . . ." He arranged the cups in a neat triangle. His mother had taught him to abhor disorder. In the Course his blankets and kit were so tidily folded the instructors couldn't resist kicking them over. "Don't imagine I know everything that goes on," he said apologetically. "I am just in charge of station security. You know how things are in The Family. What you don't know doesn't lose you sleep. Now and again I have to pick up a body from the natives and ship it home for burial. But it has to go through channels. This one is specially difficult. Don't think it's a holiday for me. You should have stayed with us, Joe. We need people like you. Especially now, when the going is heavy." I had a feeling he wanted to say more, but desisted, The Crumb's ears flapping alongside. Poor Gingi, still looking for a shoulder to cry on. His mother was a harsh taskmistress. I know, Gingi, you are a Labour man. It's hard lines kissing the arse of fanatics who belong to another party. You are the type of agent who goes down on his knees daily to thank God you are not in Lebanon - kowtowing to murderers, manufacturing widows, choking with refugee blood and pee. Hurray for the "clean" anti-terror war outside, Len Deighton country or Le Carré. Maximum a stick of gelignite up a PLO rep's arse, or scraping your friend off a Russell Square carpet. Praise the Lord, who hath not made me that much of an idiot. I nodded at him and went to the door.

"I haven't the foggiest idea whether it was Moishe or not," I said, and followed The Crumb down the stairs.

It had been a cold London mid March. The snooker had not yet begun. The Crumb navigated the deserted back streets of Bayswater like an army commando driver breaching the gullies of the Southern Sinai mountains. You could see he had not yet learned to trust two-wheel drive. I leaned back, cramped and weary beside him, watching the Edgware Road go by like the gorge of Umm Shomar. There were so many questions I had failed to ask the Gingi, so many flaws in the drama. How come my file was so close at hand the instant they found the Ganef's body? Why should anyone be assumed to have an interest in planting a fake Moishe anyway? Why was I allowing myself to be used, again, to be led up and down the garden path and fire-escape stairs in London? Was there still a little Joe, a ghost of loyalties past, inside me, standing up to salute the flag? Broken chains of obedience, trailing behind, the rusted tin cans of old civic nuptials? Brain damage sustained in youth, alas, may not easily be repaired . . .

He left me at my doorstep in Mornington Terrace and slipped a scrap of paper into my hand. "You can find us at this number," he said quietly, "ask for Menashe or Baruch." He drove off before I could think of a suitable riposte, such as "Kiss my arse" or "Fuck your mother". Once I could have demolished a runt like him at a moment's notice, any hour of the day, a.m. or p.m. No longer. As I turned to fumble with my keys at the door I learned the answer to one of the questions I had been too tired or befuddled to ask myself, viz: where are the Brits in all this? Where are the Sweeney, Bodie and Doyle, Inspector Barlow and Fabian of the Yard? All those guardians of civilisation I cherish among my video-cassette collection. Echoes of a potentially ordered society, I don't care if it is just in my mind. I crave stability, and I have it not. A lone tear might be shed for me now. But before my key screeked in the lock they had me by the arms and were bundling me into their car. There were two of them, a very elegant team, everything I might have wished for. One was a short and slobbish Cockney, looking very unfit, with a protruding belly. He was silent, apart from heavy breathing. He appeared to have a lung condition. The other was tall, thin and grey haired, with a tiny fleck of a moustache and an Ulster accent. At least that was what I guessed it to be. He sounded like Ian Paisley on downers. He said: "Mr Joseph Dekel? CID Special Branch. Would you come with us, please, sir? There is a small case of a death I would like to discuss with you."

They had a blue Jaguar. Very swish. I was going up in the world.

3

They took me via Euston and Gower Street, turning in to Soho Square. "This is Soho Square," I remarked, pointlessly, just to keep up the friendly atmosphere. "Very good," said the Ulsterman, nodding sagely, while the other propelled me out of the car. Summertime having not yet arrived, there was not even a glimmer of morning. I was relieved I was not entering an actual police station. That might have brought me down to earth rudely. A strange numbness had overtaken me, a dreamlike apathy. Let the waggon roll. At a certain hour my poor hosts were going to struggle awake to find me absent, and telephone the fourth estate. What they would then do I hadn't the slightest inkling. Nor, without a doubt, would they.

Taking me past a dim lobby, down a flight of stairs, the Professionals left me to stew alone a while in a small neon-lit room with white walls, a bare table and two chairs. I passed the time trying to remember my Israeli Vehicle Registration Number. When they returned twenty minutes later the Cockney slob was carrying a third chair, which he put down in a corner and sat on. The Ulsterman was carrying a pile of nine or ten files, secured together by two thick rubber bands. He offered me a king-size Dunhill, and lit it, launching a smooth barrage of chit-chat.

"Cigarettes have gone up incredibly in Israel, have they not? Five hundred shekels for a pack of Marlboro. Two dollars, at last week's rate of exchange. I don't know how you people live down there. How do you keep life and soul together when money loses its value? Four hundred and eighteen percent inflation, my God! Here if it nudges ten we run for the hills." He began flicking through the files rapidly, his eyes massaging the pages with pleasure. Cockney slob sat by the doorway with folded arms, like a turnkey at Newgate jail. Applying every ounce of his willpower, it seemed, to refrain from picking his nose.

"I hear all the action in the Left in Jerusalem has shifted to the Artist's House Café. They tell me the T-n Café is played out," the Ulsterman continued, "No one there but Likud wallahs, with a sprinkling of Meir Kahana's zealots. Not that there's many of the old crowd left anyway. With Zalman in Paris and Raif in Los Angeles, The Shogun contemplating emigration to Europe, Sirkin defecting to parliamentary politics and Guber growing mushrooms in Rosh Pinna, there can't be much fun around. Even the Vanguard Movement seems in the doldrums. I'm not surprised you came over to London. It must be getting lonely out there."

He was becoming more beautiful by the minute. Before long, I might propose marriage. I might have urged him to remind me of my shirtsize, which had slipped my mind. He was the type who made friends with you, so you might say, when they took you in later and began beating your brains with clubs in the dark: Hold, villeins! I know a man here – call Inspector MacFriendly! I am Inspector MacFriendly, the man with the club would retort, kneeing you in the groin.

"Who do you favour for the coming elections?" the geyser was unexhausted. "My money is on Shamir. He is a cautious man and not as dumb as he seems. I have a file on him as thick as your arm. It goes back forty-odd years, you know. My training officer arrested him in 'forty-six. We sent him to a prison camp in Egypt. But he escaped in an oil tanker headed for Addis Ababa. Today he's Prime Minister of Israel. Sometimes it makes you wonder." He closed the file he was flipping through and put his palm on it decisively. "So, Mr Dekel. And what can you tell me about the Edenvale Hotel?"

Careful, Joe. This is a major minefield. What's at stake here is more than your hide – it's your visa. One slip and your only escape from the madhouse is cut off at Heathrow Airport. Pity about the wasted trip, Mr Dekel. Your next flight out is in three hours sharp. Don't bother to call again. *Schvantz.*

"I don't have anything to conceal from you," I said. I told him the whole story. Fuck Gingi Arse-Face and all his cohorts. I was not going to be their scapegoat. The A-Team must have been on our tails all the way, Tiddly Crumb, Lancaster Gate and all. Never underestimate the British copper. I am not Israel's foremost TV critic for nothing.

He heard me out quietly, and then the questions. A deluge of curt one-liners. At what angle had I been examining the body? For precisely how many minutes or seconds? At what angle had The Crumb's torch been held? How much could I see of the hotel room? Which side of the face was the major injury? How much blood was on the pillow? He seemed obsessed with the aesthetics of the corpse. My painful childhood was so much farfel to him. Moishe's past, which I had hinted vaguely at, seemed to be old news. He let that strand dangle, and returned to the contorted dead kisser in Russell Square. Going over the timing, again and again, checking my watch against his own. God, it was only four ten in the morning. I thought a week had passed since James Cagney.

At the end of the round he had definitely scored. I was on the ropes, limp as a dishrag. Fantasies swarmed through my mind. Was all this a set-up? Perhaps they hadn't even found the body? I was confessing my knowledge to a crime that might not even have been discovered . . . Little tiddly crumbs, clones of Menashe, might have removed the corpse after my exit, leaving a bloody pillow and a puzzled Ulsterman determined to squeeze the pips from Joe Dekel . . .

"Come with me," he said, suddenly, standing up and hefting his files. Cockney slob rose and unlocked the door. I was ushered out into a corridor. Pressing the button of a lift they stood on either side of me, the Ulsterman humming dourly. I think it was the tune to Psalm 23, but Protestantism is not quite my forte. The Lord Is My Shepherd, I Shall Not Want. All I wanted was a hot chocolate and bed.

Inside the lift the Ulsterman pressed B3. His humming

had abruptly ceased. We were not, evidently, making for green pastures which restoreth the soul. Exiting under a maze of overhead piping, I was led through two white swing doors. We paused at a third door, which slid open, emitting a substantial chill. It was cold even for a London March. The walls were tiled, like a seedy bath house. Two white-coated young men, excessively cheerful, led us to a slab-like table. The more cheerful of the two pulled back a sheet with the flourish of a headwaiter at Maxim's revealing the *potage du jour*.

"Well?" said the erudite Ulsterman, flashing me a quizzical eye.

The man was dead, no smidgeon of doubt there, and his head had been certainly mangled. He had the same horrible injury I had seen on the bed at the Edenvale Hotel, Russell Square. But it was on the right, not the left temple.

And it certainly was not Moishe-Ganef.

4

I got back to Camden Town about five p.m. Sunday. My poor hosts were suitably frantic. They had been in hourly contact with my journalistic safety valve and were poised to file a missing person's. My hack acquaintance had in turn canvassed a CID contact, who would be roused if I was not heard of by seven. Sometimes it is pleasant to have friends. It never ceases to amaze me. My host is a lecturer in Sociology and my hostess gives legal advice to the poor. They have a degree of altruism which back home is found only among the truly sainted or among those serving some abstract ideal, usually of a neo-fascist nature. I, personally, have never entered a claim. Wrestling with God's strange habits is enough for me. My friends, though devout atheists, put up bravely with my barbaric practices. They make me spaghetti with kosher mince, which they hate, and separate the meat and milk dishes. On Saturdays they perform as Shabbes goys, Sabbath-gentiles, switching the TV on and off for me and flicking channels at my request. "Channel Four," I say. Or "BBC 2." And they happily oblige.

Apologising profusely, promising to tell all later, I fell into bed and went under. Almost immediately, it seemed, I was attacked by a dream, of unparalleled clarity: I dreamt I was ensconced in heaven, in a lush three-bedroom apartment. Axminster carpets, Harrods' armchairs, Laura Ashley wallpaper and a video-cassette recorder in every room. I responded to a knock at the door and Moishe-Ganef stood before me. I knew it was him by his high school rollneck sweater and the lazy way he sagged in his jeans. He was headless, the sweater ending in thin air. Behind him the deep deep blue of the sky, criss-crossed by feather clouds. "Hallo, Moishe," I said, "what can I do for you?" I was annoyed at his invading my privacy. "You got to hide me, Joe," he said, hoarsely, his voice coming out of the breach of his neck. "The Authorities are after me. You are my last chance." "You want me to hide you from God?" I understood him. "Yes," he said. "All right," I said, "get in the closet."

He had hardly been in there for a split second before the sirens began wailing outside. I looked out of the window. Hordes of angels were piling out of winged commandcars. Taking my FN off the wall rack I began to pot them carefully. They went down like ninepins, plummeting with thin wails through jagged black holes in the clouds. A megaphone voice cried: "Come out, Dekel! You'll never make it - we have you surrounded!" From the back of the crowd I could see they were wheeling up a battery of Katyusha rockets. I turned back to the closet and opened it, somehow sure Moishe's head would have reappeared by now. But he was slumped there, just arms, legs and torso, in among my clothes and Anat's. His blood spreading over my shirts and her dresses, dribbling into our shoes ...

I awoke with a start, to the welcome clatter of dinner being prepared below. Daylight had scarpered, and I lay back trying to reconcile the events of the past twenty-four hours with reality. I was, after all, in England, not in the Beersheba Command bunker ... frisson of the bad old days, with air conditioning, and the chill of the Soho Square slab: the dead man who was not Moishe ... an absolute stranger, though with the remains of a Middle Eastern appearance ... an Arab face, actually, not unhandsome, before the blows to the temple. Somewhere in his mid twenties, Mr Ulster had said, as he put me through my paces again. Hours of grind, ploughing the same fallow ground back and forth with a rusty blade ... Checking and rechecking my story till it came out of my eyes, nose, ears ... "Let's just go over that wee bit again ..." He was like one of those ferrets I understand certain Englishmen of the working classes put down their trousers. You hang on for hours, praying the beast will not disqualify you for the Parents' Association. Finally spared, the Protestant teeth withdrawn, cast out with an uncertain future. The world of spookdom. What a mess. The mug's game par excellence. Intrigue, conspiracy and paranoia, and in the end it often amounts to bumpkins. Plots curdling in a sealed cauldron. Delusions of grandeur rotting the brain. If spies manipulated and controlled events as well as they claim to we wouldn't have had the French Revolution, the Russian, the Chinese, the Cuban. Iran, now there's a cracker for you. Nothing but poison ivy. If our spies were so hot we wouldn't be bogged down in Lebanon, or blown up at Jerusalem ice-cream stalls. Or is that too, the paranoid surmises, a deliberate, planned situation? There is no true escape from the coils of a proper conspiracy theory. No wonder God told me: you fucking idiot, get thee out of this insane country into an England which I will show thee – for a sum of a few measly hundred bucks – where no one you would wish to pass the time of day with gives a monkey's fart what the government, the Minister of Defence or C-in-C Intelligence thinks. And where the Four Sons (Of Whom the Torah Spake) are just a fading memory ...

I should be so lucky. Vivid recall: the last time that we met, all four of us ... The day of the Document Trauma of Beersheba: mid-May, 1968. A genuine turning point, perhaps the dividing line between the old Joe and the new. A peak in the slow process of a realisation of the ghoulish and the Absurd. May, '68. Some milestone. In the outside world, students rioted. In Paris, they sacked the Stock Exchange. In the Homeland, business as usual: preparations for a fourth round against Egypt, running battles with Palestinian irregulars in the rolling brown hills of the occupied West Bank. Classic guerrilla encounters by Hebron and Nablus. Classic counter-insurgency tactics. Surrounding villages, rounding up suspects, running spies, paying off informers. All the classic methods that lost the British Cyprus and Kenya, the French, Algeria, and so on. I was not directly involved in all that (I vos only following orders ...), but nevertheless, already the rise of a certain moral panic, liberal guilt and existential cold feet. "This is going to be a permanent occupation," I had told Meisinger. "That's right," he said, "isn't it great?" His eyes gleamed for the birth of the Greater Israel. Mine were watering for the death of the Small. Not, you understand, that I claim incredible prescience. Just a normal case of cold feet. Now, after sixteen years of it all, my feet are frozen, I walk about on ice blocks, everywhere.

Mid-May, then. We met in the Beersheba Bunker of the Southern Army Command. Our first reunion since the 1966 "KAMAN" Course, the four of us now well into the run-up (more of a crawl-down) towards our pledge of Regular Service. I was a Lieutenant at the Beersheba Command, shuffling Intelligence files. Gingi was helping secure the Sinai base of Bir Gafgafa for the Nation. Moishe was undergoing some outside training which kept him permanently in mufti, and Meisinger was also on a hush-hush course, already destined for Higher Things. The occasion was the formal introductory visit of the new Head of Internal Security (SHABAK) to the Southern Command Intelligence Family. SHABAK Head's identity is one of the country's most guarded known secrets. He has three hard-bitten female secretaries, the famous "aunties", who cover him in shifts round the clock. Male chauvinists say they run the show. I couldn't care less, it's all the same to me. At any rate, the Section prepared a luncheon do in the Command bunker. Tomato and cheese sandwiches and "Tempo" orange and cola, with individual straws, the works. People stood around jawing and us Four Sons formed a spearhead unit and began rapping. The latest news and spook chit-chat – did you hear about, etcetera: the bizarre disappearance of two Officer Trainees who turned up last week in Cairo ... the stash of skeletons at Bir el Hamma ... the KGB guest at the Academy ... Strictly routine. After eighteen months in Intelligence nothing surprises you except your own lack of surprise. Then Moishe produced, from his grab bag, a half bottle of Bells whisky. We poured it into a cola bottle and passed it round between ourselves. Moishe in particular took heavy doses, and soon began to loosen his mouth. He put his arm round my shoulders and told Gingi and Meisinger stories of our childhood they had heard before, how he stole his own nappies and how we dreamed together of becoming great criminal brains. Now it's all coming true, he slobbered proudly, I've been training the past half year. A professional safe cracker from Jaffa, on an eight-year sentence, has been teaching me the whole trade. Do you want me to show you? he offered, bragging: I can do the bunker safe here in no time.

You're on, we said. Let's see if you have any character. We faded to the emergency stairs. Everyone was in the map room getting stoned on "Tempo" so the bunker safe was unattended. I know this sounds bizarre, but we were, after all, in the family sanctum as it were. The Intelligence Family trusts its own. This is the main reason our Moishe later caused them such emotional anguish . . . He opened the safe. It was child's play to him. Just a fairly common strong box. A matter of course stash, usually, of papers in transit, classified Secret and up, which any secretary here was cleared to handle. Moishe cackled, saying See, even pissed to the gills I did it under two minutes. OK, we said, now swing it shut and Arrivederci Roma. But Moishe-Ganef was Moishe-Ganef. The man born with flypaper fingers. He grabbed a sheaf of papers and began flicking through them, muttering: "Boring. Boring. Boring. Hallo, what's this?"

He shoved the rest back in and spread his find on the table. Loose sheets in a red leather folder. It was marked "Ultimate", a classification even I didn't know existed. The folder itself had been locked, but Moishe had picked the lock nonchalantly with a paper clip. The papers within were a top copy, no carbon or even Xerox photostats. They were marked at the top of each page: "Inner Group Only. Strategic Base Positions & Options."

Meisinger and Moishe were the closest to it, with Gingi and me looking over their shoulders. Meisinger's eyes no doubt going click-click-click, photographing every comma. The chapter headings were enough to make me run screaming, with kitbag, for the Sierra Madre. "COUNTER-ACTING US NUCLEAR SUBVERSION." "THE BIOLOGICAL DETERRENT - GENES." "PROTECTION OF THE IRAN ALLIANCE." (Well, that one was an open secret.) "FLEXIBLE ALLIANCE OPTIONS." Meisinger lapped up that one. But it was the fifth which was the absolute lulu: "POST NUCLEAR-EXCHANGE STRATEGY: THE CASE FOR URGENT APPLICATION."

That was enough. I lunged between the two of them, swept the pages up and snapped them shut in the folder. "Are you people certified? Get this fucking thing back there! None of us have seen one comma!" For a moment I thought they would poke my eyes out. But then Meisinger returned to base firmly. He nodded to Moishe, who replaced the folder, shut the safe carefully and wiped its handle and dial with the edge of his shirt. Too late we realised we might have left fingerprints all over the vile thing inside. But there were sounds on the stairs. We skedaddled groggily and rejoined the celebration of shadows ...

Sometimes it returns to me in dreams. A hidden destiny in a bright red folder. Our wise Guardians, ready for anything: the Jewish State after a nuclear holocaust. I can see the religious conundrums: is a man with two heads Jewish? Can a man with two pricks marry two women? And where would God be in all this? Auschwitz was one thing, this, quite another. Even I would begin to have doubts, and I have let Him get away with murder ... My whole army "career" became a sudden farce. I realised I was heading for a mental condition which would be clinical were it not endorsed by the State. All the post-'67 twinges crystallised into a decision. From that day on I prepared the repudiation of my signed three-year contract. I threw tantrums. I cast doubts on my loyalty. I said I could not condone oppression. They laughed, but eventually I had my way. I convinced the psychiatrist I was incapable of following legal orders. Drummed out with mental ignominy. Contemptuous eyes stripped my shoulder bars, my shirt buttons, my flies as I gathered my release papers. I signed the Official Secrets Act three further times, in ink, blood and adrenal fluid. Thus I failed to become a Regular Army Intelligence Officer, and became instead just another bum.

Ginger Arse-Face remained, the eternal sucker. Meisinger rose, ascending Jacob's ladder. Within a year he was lost in the clouds. You couldn't even locate him by radar. And Moishe-Ganef began his long-cherished career as an official burglar.

5

I slept through Monday morning and awoke alone in the house in time to catch the one o'clock news. There had been a terrorist attack in the streets of Jerusalem, during the peak morning shopping hour. Three young Arab men had walked into a jeans shop and come out of the changing booths not in the latest gear *à la mode* but with Kalashnikovs and grenades. Local shopkeepers had fired back with their own arsenals. Over forty people had been injured. One gunman had been shot dead, the others captured. After the events, the report added, some passers-by ran amok, beating up Arabs on nearby building sites. Calm now reigned in the city. A likely story. I immediately telephoned Anat in Israel. She was not at home but I managed to catch her at her desk in the office. Anat works for the Municipality, arranging arts exhibitions. She has to massage the egos of sculptors who believe futurism is modern and engage Arab labourers to transport across town the ectoplasms of their illusions. Or to mould into the semblance of a schedule the shattered psyches of Bokharan potters. A major show of local daubers had prevented her from joining in my present raid on Albion, necessitated by the sudden arrival of my wretched Reserves summons like a dead mouse plopping through our letterbox. I detest being without Anat, but loathe the Reserves even more. "It's as you would expect," she said, calm as ever, "gunfight at the OK Corral. All the citizens of Dodge City turn out with six-shooters blazing. No one can tell who shot who."

"It was Tombstone, the OK Corral," I corrected her. But again, our ludicrous national destiny. Our forefathers dreamed of a Tolstoyan idyll. We have to clean up the cow shit. "Why don't you come out on the next plane?" I said. "We'll go for political asylum." But we both knew I was due back in eleven days, I had a booking for a family Passover. This God idea has its drawbacks. And all this run-around just to avoid driving up and down the Tel Aviv beach, dressed in khaki, peeling my eyes for terrorists. Sometimes the extent of my betrayal astounds me. Other times, not.

I ventured out into the London drizzle, but it was not the same as before. Before the weekend of Moishe-Ganef, Gingi and the BBC news. My beloved haven defiled, Camden Town and Euston echoing to far-off war cries. Times like these I really need Anat by me, to settle my psychic balance. To say "keep right on", "turn left", "stop", "take cover", "paddle like hell for the shore". My female sanity meter, clicking wildly when the needle goes into the red. Myself, I click permanently. A walking dial of disaster. I do not understand what makes her able to navigate the deadly reefs and shallows out there, but navigate she does, sailing her sloop trimly in the storms and tidal waves. Nothing human appears to shock her, nor anything that is downright swinish.

I returned to the scene of the crime, I'm not sure why. Agatha Christie said it is *de rigueur*. As a devout anglophile I cannot defy the house gods. Hercule Poirot. Lord Peter Wimsey. Gideon Fell. Sir Henry Merrivale. Perhaps I didn't like the idea of Gingi Arse-Face laughing, or I couldn't bear to wait for the Ulsterman to enlist my aid again in his inquiries. At any rate, my feet, my brain, my quivering antennae, would not let me rest *in pacem*. I walked down Gower Street, past the university, turning left into Montague Place. To my right the imposing black-pillared back of my beloved British Museum. Is there not a Hitchcock film which ends with a chase on the roof here? The villain falling to his doom? Russell Square, in comparison, before Moishe hit it, was about as thrilling as reheated falafel. Even now it sulked in the dismal aura of a thousand and one bed and breakfasts. I manoeuvred my way round the Park side of the

Square, trying to look inconspicuous. The grey drizzle was steady, I had my commando cap on, my bomber jacket's collar turned up. I was doing fine. I had considered donning my sunshades, but in that light I might as well put on blinkers.

Very little moved in the Square. A businessman type, with his umbrella serving as a propeller. A young couple, weighed down by rucksacks and their own private angst. A dog that looked as if it had seen No Vacancy on every building in the terrace. The Edenvale Hotel looked as if everyone in it had died of the black plague last century. I was not sure I even remembered correctly the floor, let alone the number of the room I'd been brought to. Dekel, I said, This is an own goal. There is no point in going further. Even coming this far might have got you in the viewfinder of some watcher who might have otherwise missed you. Every sniffle, every squelch of your soggy shoes might be echoing in the ear of some bored operative round the corner in a plumber's van. Not to speak of being broadcast on the armed forces' network. *Ici Londres! Ici Londres!* Damn it.

I left the Square, retracing my steps through Montague Place towards the West End. I had hardly reached Tottenham Court Road before I was sure someone was definitely on my tail. It was not a shattering deduction to make. Elementary tests confirmed it. I stopped, turned, hurried on, slowed, stopped, and the figure a hundred yards behind me did likewise. He was visible through the drizzle as a navy blue greatcoat, bare headed, with his hands in his pockets. When I looked straight at him he just stood and looked nonchalant, as if searching the sky for Zeppelins. He was either a rank amateur or intended deliberately to show his hand and put the wind up me. A flash of insight informed me, by the size of his build, that this was the Tiddly Crumb in person.

I led him on my leash, across the road to Goodge Street, round the Middlesex clap clinic, down by the Greek restaurants and across Oxford Street. He closed distance to remain within sight of me, but still too far to be identified. Lazily I ambled into Soho, pausing at kebab shops and film showcase windows. I tried shaking him off through the

Berwick Street market but still the bastard persevered. No amateur after all. I finally led him into the cul-de-sac of Carlisle Street and cornered him by the social welfare office. I hid round the corner, putting my finger to my lips to shush the two loafers lounging there. The grey sky was becoming duller and darker, United Kingdom spring visibility. He almost bumped into me rounding the corner, and I grabbed him by the lapels. "Hi there, comrade!" I said, merrily, taking a good gander.

It was not The Crumb at all, more's the pity, but another face which was familiar. They are all after me, ghosts of my history, shadows of failed exorcisms . . .

"Hallo, Joe," he said, "it's been a long time, hasn't it? But you have survived. I'm so pleased."

6

He was a Palestinian. His name was Zaki Khatib. He was about my age. We were both alumnii of the same defunct finishing school of the dissident Jerusalem Left: the T-n Café. Kop at the counter, Carmela the waitress, the ringmasters of the show. A mere space of five metres by two and a half, we all slumped there, right through the early 'seventies, biting the bullet of the occupation next door to us. You might have lobbed one grenade inside and finished off the entire anti-Zionist Left in the country. If you wished to bother. And if you didn't mind liquidating Shtik, the police spy, who was in there on a special mission. He was trying to convince the comrades that blather was useless, and the time had come for serious action. His success came with the formation of the Red Struggle Fraction, which contacted the Popular Front for the Liberation of Palestine, with explosive events in mind. Today most of them are still in jail, except Shtik, who wanders Jerusalem, moaning and whining and claiming to have been maligned. The sceptics remained behind the bar of the café, eventually to be winkled out by sheer boredom. The *déjà vu* of years of routine contemplating the Decline and Fall.

Zaki, when I first knew him, was a deviationist Nationalist attached to the Marxist-Leninist (Fourth International) grouplet. For three years he drank endless glasses of mint tea and devoured the morning and evening Hebrew newspapers while passions raged all around him over the Lessons of

October and Stalin's Falsification of History. I don't think his heart was in the joint struggle of the Jewish and Arab working classes, manifested in the attempted sale of the group journal, *Unity*, at factory gates and in Arab villages. The few discussions he did join indicated loyalties that were simpler and more dangerous. He was too shrewd a cookie, however, to become involved in Shtik's fiasco. Nevertheless, he vanished, shortly after the '73 War, leaving behind vague rumours. He had received a grant to study abroad, some said, winking, from guess who, say no more . . . Others reported Zaki sightings years later, tending a bar in Hamburg, Brussels, Amsterdam. Another refugee is born. Kop! Another glass of mint tea!

"Let us talk, Joe," he said, "there are one or two things we might toss about to mutual advantage."

"Fine," I said, "but no secret pow-wows. Let's go somewhere good and public." I took him to the Patisserie Valerie in Old Compton Street, the closest thing to a real café in London. Everyone crowds in along communal tables and kibitzes on their neighbours' problems. It is usually fairly packed with semi-vagrants, genteel punks, film directors and ex-bohemians. Strange-looking women sit there for hours, nursing a hot chocolate. Today was par for the course. I squeezed my Arab shadow into the most crowded table available. We ended up between a crew-cut lady with four sweaters and a bald man with a Karl Marx beard, sucking sugar lumps, lost in his private world. Zaki did not look happy, but I am damned if I will go in for private assignations. Years later you are hauled in on a traffic charge and they show you a telephoto snap of yourself, shimmering in haze, on a park bench, with the year's most wanted terrorist.

"Well," I said, trying a cinematic joke, "so they call me Concentration Camp Erhard!"

He looked blank. Evidently a philistine. Ernest Lubitsch meant nothing to him. I caught Teresa the waitress' eye, and the two of us compromised on coffees. The cakestand looked promising. I took my pick. He hesitated above an éclair. "Do you do this for a living," I asked, spearing a passion cake, "playing the Quicksilver Shadow?" We had begun speaking in Hebrew so we might as well continue. My Arabic has become rusty.

"One usually leaves these things to professionals," he plumped for gluttony, "but who can find trustworthy servants nowadays?"

I looked at him sharply. He appeared to be quite prosperous, clean-shaven, fleck of grey in the hair. Good suit under the navy greatcoat. The Naif Hawatmeh moustache which had signalled his heresy had been completely excised. He looked like the heir presumptive to a minor kebab empire. As long as it is not me on the skewer.

"I want to make something clear," I said, "even before the first cake. Whatever's going on, leave me out of it. I am a private citizen with a girlfriend, a job, an apartment and a video-cassette collection. Whatever game you are in, I don't give a shit. This is an official Joe Dekel bulletin. Issued in Hebrew, English and Arabic. Notarised by the Lord Blessed Be He."

He put his head to one side and ploughed quietly through his chocolate éclair. "Poor Joe," he said, "always the funnyman. Always the one abstention. How you would love the Western bourgeois life. And yet you live down there, in the snake pit."

"I adore snakes," I said, "I love to hear them slither. It gives me that ducky feeling."

"No," he said, "you are a patriot. You passionately care for your country."

"Nonsense," I retorted. "You have been reading the preamble to my latest tax return."

The man with the Marx beard glanced at us benignly, a sugar cube held in his teeth. Satisfied it was not his brain but we who were talking in a foreign language, he resumed his inward contemplation.

Zaki sighed. Our coffees arrived. He gazed into his as if the popping bubbles might form the date of the salvation of Palestine.

"Were you waiting at the Edenvale Hotel," I asked, "just in case I came along? Or would you have lit out after anyone? My brother-in-law Elisha, for example, or Menahem Begin?"

"Oh, no," he said, "I was following you earlier. But I was keeping out of sight. When I saw your strange act outside the hotel, I decided to take the chance and reveal myself. I would have approached you eventually if you hadn't ambushed me. I just wanted to be a little more sure."

"Sure of what, as if I wanted to know?"

"Sure that you don't know much more than we do. Sure that you might be part of our solution, not only part of our problem. Of course, there can never be total certainty there."

"I don't like this 'we' business. Let's stick for the moment to Zaki Khatib. Have you seen any of our old pals lately? Zalman, or Raif, who is in Los Angeles? I know, because a cute Ulsterman who hums Protestant tunes bellowed it in my ear."

"That would be Chief Inspector McIntosh," said Zaki, "Now he is a real number. You know he speaks fluent Hebrew and Arabic, both maghrebi and of the mashraq. His Farsi, though, is very basic. Iraqi spies, Libyan hit squads, Israelis, us poor stateless bastards, we are all in his little kingdom. After all, London is a clearing house for so much of the Arab East's growing pains. A minor punishment, one might say, for Sykes-Picot and Allenby." Gravely he contemplated another éclair. This place might be a death-trap for him. "Do you remember Pickled-Herring Naim?" he said, apropos of nothing apparent. "You used to play a lot of chess with him, in T-n, didn't you? He's an engineer now, in Libya."

"I hear the climate there is very fine," I responded, "as long as you stay a hundred yards from the coast."

He sighed, lost in his own thoughts. "What do they all expect from us?" he said, dripping with melancholy. "We are just ordinary people. All we really want to do is lie about on the beach, drinking arak and swapping stories. We are not a nation of fanatic puritans, like Gaddafi or that madman Khomeini."

"I will mention this to the Prime Minister," I said, "the next time we share a plate of humus." I was becoming increasingly worried about the direction of this conversation. Any further diversions and we might end up marooned on the Galapagos Islands.

"Let us talk about Moishe-Ganef," I said, trying to cut through the flim-flam.

"I would like another coffee," he said. The man with the Marx beard beamed at him. *"Perfetto!"* he exclaimed, forming a ring with his pudgy thumb and forefinger. *"Bonas kafes,"* he added, in a pleasant basso. *"En las gattos. Muy satisfato."*

"What does he want from us?" asked Zaki, as we both nodded solemnly. "It may be Esperanto," I whispered. Or any other vehicle of cross-cultural opacity. The man resumed sucking sugar. "Fsst! Fsst!" went his tongue and teeth, through the rest of our conversation.

We despatched Teresa back to the hot stove to slave over our second portions. "Yes, Moishe-Ganef," he said, sadly, "I understand he was a childhood friend of yours."

"My life is an open library book," I said, "that no one bothers to return."

"Well," he said, "you know the public part of the story: his arrest, the secret trial, imprisonment ..."

"Moishe-Ganef," I recapitulated, "was a Mossad agent specialising in overseas burglaries. He stole a large sum of money, while on official duty, and did a bunk to good old Rio. Like Eichmann, they snatched him and brought him back, though they spared him the glass cage. He got ten years and did about six. Last heard of he was out, sueing the government for kidnapping and false imprisonment. That much I can tell you in perfect legality. It was an article in *Maariv*. The rest I can't speak of. I have not yet negotiated the world record and cassette rights."

"And now he turns up here, apparently dead, and everyone is shitting bricks. Why?" He took a suitable pause, which was filled with the sibilant eruptions of our table companion. The girl with the four sweaters to my left looked up briefly, then returned to her rapt perusal of *Automobile Mechanic*. "I'll tell you, Joe. We have reason to believe that Moishe-Ganef is alive. We know about the charade in the hotel and we think it was staged deliberately. We think you were a chance passer-by in this. The real target was your ginger ex-comrade. It is clear there are very high stakes involved. Serious people are concerned. Your old friend was up to his tricks again: he stole something, I can't tell you what it was, but it has raised a fair storm. We have reason to believe it has not been found, and so the man is still alive, in hiding, and has his loot in a place of safety. You were dragged in because it's thought he might contact you. Who else is there he can trust? We know his parents are dead, he was an only child, and he has betrayed his bosses. He is the classic agent with nowhere to go. Such people become sentimental. People know you, Joe. You can be scared into silence, but you cannot be easily turned or bought. You have this private God thing and your stubborn arrogance and your instinct to survive. Moishe Sherman knows this, and so do we. We respect you, we respect what you stand for. But you can't sit on the fence for ever. You have become involved. This won't go away now. Until Moishe dead is finally confirmed or Moishe alive is drawn into the open."

It was quite a good speech, not witty, but candid. The longest utterance I had heard from Zaki since the espresso machine in the T-n Café exploded back in '71. And God has created smart Palestinians. Once we Jews stunned the world with our mental prowess, but now that we have a State like everyone else we have become like a mongol with haemorrhoids. There is no doubt – exile broadens the mind. Just wait till *they* get their own passport ...

"Who is we," I asked, finally calling the play, "the Belzer Hassidim? The Rockefeller Foundation? Since this crap-game began everyone's been addressing me as if they were a national entity of their own."

But he had obviously gone as far as he intended, and sat back silent, finishing his second coffee. A bubble of reticence had closed about the two of us, sealing us off from the crowd. Even Marxoid baldie had lost his sound track. His sugar cubes suffered stoically. The waitress floated wordlessly past, the punters, struck dumb, gestured wildly. The only voice that broke through this geodesic dome was of the *Automobile Mechanic* girl. Thrusting all her four sweaters towards us, her crew cut and earrings completing the three prongs of an armoured ambush, she announced, in clear Tel Aviv Hebrew: "You don't impress me at all, the both of you, with your so-called spy talk. I've heard it all before. But if you ask me," she zeroed in on your Joe, "you ought to listen to what this man is saying. It's time the Palestinians had a homeland. You should pull your finger out and give them a hand."

I was so flabbergasted I missed my cue. I should have said: "Lady, that would be most unsanitary." Instead we conspirators rose, hastily, and I tipped a few ten pees on the table. Paying rapidly at the counter we straggled out, into the full blast of the drizzle.

"I might be in touch with you," Zaki said, hiding his hands in his coat pockets again. "If you are contacted, be very careful. Store information in a safe place. I don't think the Gingi is as dumb as he looks. Goodbye for now, and God be with you." He turned away and hurried off towards Wardour Street, leaving me becalmed on the kerb.

People who know me should bear witness to my general *savoir faire*. Most times I am imperturbable. I am absolved though, at certain moments. Two years ago I allowed myself to crack, twice, once in June, again in September. The launching of the Lebanon War and the Sabra and Chatilla massacre. Not since then to this day had I had the irredeemable sense of being sucked into quicksand. He wants to lie about on the beach drinking arak. I have my own pastoral longings. All I want from life is to sit back in my armchair with my veins plugged into the TV set. I am an easy addict to satisfy, anything sends me soaring: British cop shows, American soaps, *Dallas, Popeye,* the nine o'clock news. The interminable serials on Jordan television. The seventh re-run of *Ironside*. My specially mounted aerial can often pick up Syria, sometimes Lebanon, and on rare days, Egypt. I look forward to the utopia of satellite broadcasting, when I shall barricade myself in, sealing the doors and windows, with only a flap perhaps for Anat to crawl through, to bring me solace, sex and groceries. In summer, my feet in a basin of ice water. In winter, hot peppermint foot-lotion. Dictating my reviews to the outside world by telephone, telex or computer modem.

I tried it all, being pro, and anti, and this was my adopted stand. But now it all lay oozing in the gutter of London's Old

Compton Street. I tried to soothe my battered soul with sleaze, trying out, in the line of professional duty, the pornographic video booths. A thin lady baring her vagina through electronic interference. This was not my day. I stocked up instead with delights from the Italian deli. Weighed down by mortadella and dolcellate I caught the bus back to Camden Town. I half expected my poor hosts' house to have been done over, ransacked in the best tradition. Clothes strewn on the floor. Drawers upturned. Carpets ripped, floorboards torn up. Instead my friends were there, welcoming me safely, having prepared a quiche. There was no point in passing on my terminal jitters. I ate the quiche and watched the BBC news. They had a full report on the morning's rampage in the streets of my Jerusalem. I could make out on the screen the King George Street railings, the junction of the Jaffa Road. Blooded wounded were rushed into an ambulance. Every person in frame was hysterical. An outraged man with a hattie who had tried to attack Arabs was being strangled by a policeman. Many people were wearing jackets and coats, spring had obviously not yet come. Again, there is no escape from anguish. I went to bed and missed Paul Newman.

A dreamless night over, I awoke on Tuesday and resumed my London rambles. Revisiting familiar haunts: the British Museum manuscript room seemed full of agents, pretending to admire Kant's handwriting. Strange reflections glimmered in the shop windows of Lasky's electronics store. Even the Berwick Street market was chock-a-block with spies, half heartedly fingering lemons. I tried less crowded streets, but a Viennese zither kept echoing in my brain. Round every corner I expected to see a chiaroscuro Orson Welles emerging. Moishe-Ganef, inflated by the fleshpots. Brother, can you spare a dime. In a moment of weakness I even considered phoning the number The Crumb had handed me. "Give me Gingi Arse-Face," I'd say, and when he came on: "Is that you, Gingi? Fuck your mother!"

I refrained, but the next evening he phoned me, smack in the middle of *Coronation Street*. Rita and Fred were in the midst of discussing Mavis's tangled romances.

"Hallo, Joe," he said, "Baruch here. I hear you've been

seeing Palestinians."

"I see them every night," I said, "I count refugees crossing over the Allenby Bridge. I find it much more effective than sheep or Valium. You should try it some time."

"Meeting in cafés," he said, "on street corners. Dangerous moves, my son."

I had heard of cold fury, but had never felt it before. Apathy or panic is my forte. What was this Arse-Face trying to do to me? Was the girl at the Valerie one of his? Was he expecting me to discuss Zaki and be immortalised on some magnetic medium? Vzz-vzz, the recorder whirring, Joe Dekel in the flytrap. Later on: Your Honour, the State rests its case ... And the outcome of Mavis's romantic dilemma will remain a complete mystery ...

"What do you want?" I said. "I am extremely busy. This is my working hour."

"The police have identified the body they found," he said, "it seems to be a Turk called Siskuglu. He was a minor runner in the heroin trade. Don't you find that rather intriguing?"

"Pardon me, while I insert a needle," I said, "I'd better do it now, if you predict a shortage."

He laughed, the bastard. "Plenty more where he came from. But we are still missing one of ours."

"I'll look in my socks tonight," I said, "if I find him you'll be the last to know."

"Well, have a good flight back anyway, Joe," he said, "and don't forget who your true friends are."

"I've already forgotten."

He cackled again. "See you at 'Peace Now' demonstrations."

7

The situation was becoming a little hairy. I spent the night reflecting on it, watching the stars glow on my bedroom ceiling. My hosts had stuck small luminous dots up there, thinking that was both amusing and restful. After a while, I got into real problems looking for the Big Dipper. Nothing made sense, except as a scenario dreamed up by mental patients. I now had two dead bodies at the Hotel Edenvale, one Turkish pusher, one ghost from the past. That added up to one Joe Dekel, going round the bend. Due to return in four days' time to the frontline, the land of curdled milk and sour honey. Why was I not born a Swiss citizen? They have a nuclear bunker under every house. With the rest of the world dead they will emerge to take over, bloated by Toblerone.

I crawled into Thursday like an aardvark that had inhaled ant-killer. There was all-day snooker on BBC 2. While the little balls clicked softly on the green I half waited for another call from the Gingi, rehearsing bloodcurdling expletives. But not a peep. Thursday night I gave up on the stars. Friday is a no-go day for me. In the afternoon, wherever I am, I perform my werewolf act: donning my hattie and clutching my *siddur* (prayer book), I disappear into the nearest synagogue. Stubbornly pursuing the atavistic rituals that are the despair of my friends. You wish to know why I do this? Fuck your grandmother. Saturday morning, the saga continues, petering off through the afternoon. I was now left with only Saturday night between my ignorance and my Sunday flight home.

This would not do at all. I had to make some move, or spend the rest of my life seriously considering plastic surgery. I took the Central Line tube to Lancaster Gate. I had not caught the name of the street I had visited but I remembered the contour of the Crescent. Groups of people in white Arab dress floated by on the pavements. From behind a veil a female voice raised demands, not, I think, for Marks and Spencer's knickers. The motors of limousines ticked over. From the upper windows of the house I identified came the sounds of a party. Disco, loud, the clink of bottles, babble babble and guffaws. I was glad someone was having a good time. I hoped it wasn't Gingi Arse-Face.

My urban topography proved sound. There was the doorbell marked "Bronson". I took a note of adjacent names I had not registered: Pryce-James, Letelier, Maaluf. Two names were scribbled in Arabic only - Usman, I think, and Halim. More than ever it seemed odd that Gingi had touched base here. But maybe, being a Jerusalem boy, he just wanted to feel at home.

Getting in might be an annoying problem. Surprise was the essence of my plan. Not that I had a plan of any clarity, except that surprise would have to be its essence. Though for all I know I had trailed a crowd of shadows all the way from Camden Town.

I stood there like a schmuck for a couple of minutes, until my brain re-engaged. I pressed the upper bell, marked "Maaluf", and my ear to the intercom grille. A woman's voice answered, a long drawn out "Yeees?" with the tell-tale disco thump behind it. "It's the man with the whisky." I dredged up in Arabic. Immediately the buzzer sounded.

Up the stairs, to the second floor, finding the right flat, without a doubt - 3C, as I remembered, but no name on the jamb or door. The light I had pressed at the ground floor flicked off. A door was opened two floors up. The beat poured out, and the woman's voice, in Arabic, calling: "Where are you, sweetie?"

The light came on. I flattened myself to the wall and cursed my smartass stroke of genius. Hell hath no fury like a

Middle-East party scorned of the hope of whisky. Not that there should be any lack of fluids, I imagined, up there in the higher regions.

A male voice called out. The woman retreated. The closing door muffled the music. I stayed spreadeagled in the yellow light, until it mercifully clicked off again. I turned back to 3C. There was light showing at the bottom of the door.

The Psychiatrist Is In, then. Deciding to go for gold, I rapped on the door. No answer. That was hardly surprising, with the party beat above. I knocked again, very loudly. *Nada* from within. I tried the doorknob. *Schvantz.* The door opened. I stepped inside the lighted hallway.

No sign of Gingi. The furniture was there, the sofabed, the carpet, the hard chairs. In a recessed small bedroom, a single bed, made. An empty closet, no clothes, books, or bags. I went into the kitchen. A matching story. A few clean plates, pots, mugs, glasses. Nothing in the fridge, which was merrily whirring, freezing two cubic feet of stale air. Typical of Gingi, the Jerusalem wetback. Waste not, want not. It's genetic. At the very least he could have left me a cheese sandwich. Or even a tin of sardines.

This was not my idea of a Saturday night. And the good times blasting out above. Again I stood, more a schmuck than ever. Then the phone in the hallway rang.

I picked it up.

"ICM Bicycles," I said. It was a habit of our youth. The company used to give a free bicycle to the first person whom they would ring up at random and whose first words would be their product.

"Bad luck," drawled a voice which froze my veins into icicles. "If you had said 'That's Good, That's Osem Soup' you would have won our trip to Borneo."

For a moment I thought that *déjà vu* was Moishe. But then the penny dropped and spun.

"Meisinger," I said, "the Wizard of Oz! Still chasing the end of the rainbow?"

"You should have followed the yellow brick road yourself, Joe," he said. He always had a voice like the taxman. "But you were ever the cowardly lion."

"Better than the tin man without a heart," I said, "or was it the scarecrow with no brain?"

"Get out of there, Dorothy," he riposted, "you are not in Kansas any more."

"Kansas or Dallas, what's the difference?" I countered. "Can't you hear? It's J.R.'s birthday up there."

"No, that episode was broadcast two years ago," he said, "twelfth November, '82. On our national station, that is. Jordan broadcast it six weeks earlier."

The fucker loved to show off his memory for trivia. He used to think it would impress the girls. But they ran a mile from that fishy stare, fixed on a private Shangri La. I said nothing. It was a telephone stand-off. We seemed to have milked our exchange of repartee into the driest dugs.

"Get out of there, Joe," he repeated, more brusquely. "Take your plane tomorrow and go home, yankee. Plug in your television and sit back. If anyone contacts you, just forget it. If you see strange things, close your eyes. If you're asked to say anything, stay dumb."

"Being one monkey is quite enough for me," I said, "being three seems a little schizoid."

"It's Passover soon, Joe, everyone reclines. Enjoy the festival of our freedom. You're a devout person. Think of your sins. Don't brood so much on those of others."

"Is this the Lord Blessed Be He speaking?" I just wanted to make sure.

"Near enough for you, Icarus. Don't come too close and burn your wings."

"Is Moishe-Ganef alive or dead? Why is Gingi Arse-Face Bronson?"

"Joe, you're such a nice guy really."

Everyone approves of me. Gingi, Zaki, now Meisinger. There must be something badly wrong.

"Why is this night different from all other nights?" I asked.

"Because on this night you eat bitter herbs. Joe, I'd love to chat with you, but I'm afraid I have got to go. Melodrama aside, look at reality. You are not going to change a thing. I can hardly make matters turn out as I want them, so what chance have you got, *schmendrik*? You have a lovely girlfriend, and a colour TV set, and a video-cassette recorder. So enjoy life. It doesn't last that long anyway. Leave us tradesmen to deal with the laundry. Have a good flight, *shmegegeh,* and love to Anat. Don't look back. Remember Lot's wife."

He hung up on me. I looked up to see a woman standing in the flat doorway. She was in evening dress and dark and raven haired and sozzled right out of her mind. She was pointing a lethal-looking cocktail at me and finishing me off with her eyes.

"That was Hebrew, wasn't it?" she asked, in Arabic. "It was you who rang the main door before?"

I had to admit both crimes. My rusty Arabic could not withstand a rigorous night inspection.

"I thought you were a burglar," she said, unperturbed, "but everything has been taken away. You must be a friend of that man, Bronson."

"Large, ginger fellow," I asked, hesitantly, "with the face of a football?"

"A ginger-faced Israeli, yes, obviously, from his accent. Very quiet, polite man. In some ways it is a pity."

"He left? Did he take all the things with him?"

She screwed up her face, looking puzzled. "A car came and took away the boxes and bags," she said, "this morning, after the funeral people. The Jewish people, with the beards and costumes. They put him in a black van."

My grasp of Our Enemies' language was slipping. "Funeral?" I said. 'What do you mean?"

"Your poor friend," she said, "wrapped up in a shroud. Died in the night, they said. The heart. Poor Mr Ginger Bronson. They took everything away. We thought, my husband and I, should we cancel our party? Even for a polite Israeli? We are Palestinians, you see. My family are from Hebron. Do you want to join us upstairs?"

Voices echoed from above. The music had stopped. Then someone changed the tape or record. The chords of a full Arab string and wind orchestra swept down like a tidal wave. Then the singer. It was Fairuz, the Lebanese Nightingale. A song of Lost Palestine: Jerusalem, City of Prayer. In Israel it was a banned record. A siren call for six months hard, it curled through the hall, eddied into the living room, chasing the vestigial vibrations of Gingi into his abandoned bedroom. "No thank you," I said, "I have to go now. Perhaps some other time."

"*Tfadal,*" she said. "Anytime. Just press the bell marked Maaluf."

I shuffled past her, staggering down the stairs. She leaned over the banister after me.

"And you don't even have to pretend about the whisky!" she shouted, as I spiralled, out into the street, dampened by the inevitable rain now, the looming solid terraces of an England indifferent to the charades of transients.

MEISINGER! YOU FUCKING BASTARD! I shook my fist at the sky.

But the sky over London is good for nothing. Drizzle and fog hid the face of God.

I rejoined my hosts and watched the snooker finals. But they had lost their power to soothe me. The sounds of war had come even closer. The spent shells were coming out of my ears. My nostrils retained the reek of cordite, the cooking-gas smell of corpses. My memory safe had been blasted open. All my traumas stood revealed. Undone! Undone! My defences down, my city open to mine enemies!

Basking again in familiar terrors ... No aircraft needed to transport me ...

JERUSALEM, and Environs

8

Nevertheless, Jerusalem, the impact that never fails. The sharp contours of sun on stone, the hard brownness of the hills. The massive walls of the Old City, spires and cupolas forested with television aerials, tourists perambulating the battlements for a dollar a throw, gazing across the valley at Gethsemane and the Intercontinental Hotel. Concrete blocks of the new infiltrating the old, art galleries set in Roman marketplaces, junkshops in Byzantine sewers. A hundred rival convictions rising from the ground, striking you in the face like a dead porcupine. Every return a winner, hitting the jackpot of your deepest traumas and fears. The shock of constant change which is no change at all, endless episodes in the horror serial. The shekel has fallen twenty percent since I left, and that was barely three weeks ago. A cup of coffee now costs what a two-bedroom flat went for in 1953. The date for general elections had been agreed: fifteen weeks ahead - July 23rd. A decisive battle looming for what is left of the kingdom, the Promised Land of dreams and nightmares. The opposition Labour Party promises profound change, a return to the Good Old Days. The ruling Likud promises more of the same, a consumer paradise in the Greater Land of Israel. Ex-generals are vying to outflank each other on the party political battlefield. Meanwhile, the police have arrested two groups of Jewish zealots for indiscriminate attacks upon Arabs. One group fired on a bus in the Occupied West Bank. Another planted grenades at

Moslem and Christian targets, and had been stockpiling explosives in order to blow up the two great mosques of Islam. They called themselves the Sons of Judah, and lived in an abandoned ruin of an Arab village at the western edge of the city. They did not eat meat and always faced the sun, even if that meant walking backwards. In Jerusalem, unfortunately, they were not conspicuous. The police had a hard time finding them. And there were other acts of terror, Jewish and Arab, whose perpetrators were still at large …

Jerusalem, the anvil of history. Never a dull moment. Blood and fire from the very beginning: Joshua, Nebuchadnezzar, Titus. Godfrey of Bouillon, Salah e-Din. And in our time, the feuding cousins. Arabs killing Jews at the Western Wall, Jews destroying the Moghrabi Quarter … Nor is one's flesh and blood exempted: witness my father acting as a scout for the Irgun, circa 1946, while performing his innocent duties as Surveyor for the Water Department. Patiently listing the daily movements of the British patrols so that later the "boys" would fire at them from ambush, or limpet mine their armoured cars. You would not tell it of him now, in a less heroic era, as he reclines on cushions at the head of the family Passover table, holding the plate of *"matsah shmura"* aloft as he leads the main invocation:

"'THIS IS THE BREAD OF AFFLICTION WHICH OUR FOREFATHERS ATE IN THE LAND OF EGYPT. LET ALL WHO ARE HUNGRY COME FORTH AND EAT. LET ALL WHO ARE IN NEED COME AND CELEBRATE PASSOVER. THIS YEAR WE ARE HERE, NEXT YEAR IN THE LAND OF ISRAEL. THIS YEAR WE ARE SLAVES, NEXT YEAR - FREE MEN.'"

But he did not follow the underground leader, Menahem Begin, into post-Independence politics, and opposed the "Herut" Party Begin founded to carry on the "revisionist" battle. My father was of those who believed the Irgun had fulfilled its purpose the day the State had been declared, and should not wage a political war against the majority Labour government. Mistrust and loathing of Begin from that point on has been our only common ground, apart from basic religion, though he never understood mine, shaking his head and saying sadly: "You can't wipe away daily sins, my son, with a *yarmulka* and some prayers." He never understood I was not concerned with my sins, but with my private inquiries. "You know what happened to Sodom and Gomorrah," eventually became his favourite statement. It used to refer to the girlfriends of my youth, and later to my non-marriage with Anat, but still later it was wielded more and more as a catch-phrase to take in the State of the nation. The corruption of ministers, noveau-riche ostentation, the growing crime and violence in society. "I don't know why you're surprised at what we do to the Arabs," he told me recently, "look what we do to each other." As usual, he had got it the wrong way round, but I had long ceased to argue. He did not despise the leftist path I took after the army, but considered it hopelessly naïve. He was a German Jew, who had escaped Hitler early, and hated all brands of Socialism. "Hitler, Stalin, Bevan, Ben-Gurion," he said, "they are just varying degrees of the blindness." He claimed to believe in unfettered competition, although he was a failure in business. Oddly enough, he loathed Americans too, for their lack of culture and vacuity. "In twenty years, they will cease to be human," he declared with his usual conviction. The only people he had a soft spot for were German Jews, and they had proved the greatest flop of all. Now he subsisted, ironically, on German reparations, living, like so many of his generation, collapsed into himself, besieged. My old man. My mother kept him going, with strudel and applecakes, a listening ear and oceans of Russian tea.

"'SLAVES WERE WE TO PHARAOH IN EGYPT. AND GOD TOOK US FROM THERE WITH A STRONG HAND AND WITH AN OUTSTRETCHED ARM ... WITH GREAT TERROR, AND WITH SIGNS AND WONDERS ...

"'BLOOD, FIRE, AND PILLARS OF SMOKE ... THESE ARE THE TEN PLAGUES WHICH THE LORD BLESSED BE HE BROUGHT UPON EGYPT: BLOOD. FROGS. LICE. BEASTS. BLIGHT. BOILS. HAIL. LOCUSTS. DARKNESS. SLAYING OF THE FIRST BORN ...'"

Anat's knee nudges my thigh under the table. She has never liked the Passover Haggadah. "This bloodthirsty book that has screwed up generations. It will be the end of us yet." What am I doing living with a woman who does not believe in God? Perhaps it is pure lust. The lure of the raven hair and the hazel eyes. Or perhaps that the available religious women fill me with sheer terror. Opposite me at table is my sister Nehama, who is married to a fanatic West Bank settler of the "Gush Emunim" movement - the "Block of the Faithful" - who believe God has told them that Arabs are sheer scum. My brother-in-law Elisha: bushy beard and saggy eyes, a real sad sack exterior concealing the inner constitution of Attila the Hun. The heart trembles at the sight of their two little kiddies, Muki and Shuki, all bright-eyed and bushy-tailed. God, wait until puberty, then the shit will really hit the fan. "What else can I do with this, Papa?" "Nothing, Mukileh, come out of the toilet." Utter catastrophe. As a contrast, beside them, my elder sister, Sarah, who is a systems analyst and gives a fuck for nobody.

"The Haggadah celebrates a liberation from oppression," I have reminded Anat, "not a Mafia protection contract. When we were the Egyptians, and someone else was in Goshen, it was to us God handed out the drubbing." I gave her chapter and verse, but she was stubborn as a mule as usual. "This is just your wishful thinking," she said. "Everyone reads into the writings whatever they want. You have your God, Elisha has his. Is God a left-wing humanist, like you, or, as the Gush would have us believe, a proper right-wing bastard?"

"Lightning will strike you," I answered testily, moving for safety to the edge of the bed. Can one truly know another person? Twelve years and we're still slugging it out. She in her corner, I in mine, an endless boxing match with unspoken rules. She had grown up, like me, in a semi-religious home, but with no lingering afterglow. When we first began living together she had one proviso: "You will not recite, when you get up every morning: 'Blessed art thou, our Lord King of the World, who hath not made me a woman.'" I kept the bargain. I struck it from my repertoire. And the "gentile" and "slave" clauses too. We put too much stock in what God has not made us, and not enough in some long looks in the mirror to see what handiwork He has in fact wrought . . .

"'BLOOD, FIRE AND PILLARS OF SMOKE . . .'" There has certainly been too much of that lately . . . 1948, '56, '67 . . . The dead, spread like spoiled meatloaves across the crests and dips of sand dunes . . . Anat has true cause for alarm. And my own baptism of terrible signs and wonders: Mid-June, 1967. The newly occupied West Bank. A subject population, fleeing from the oppressor – myself, Joe Dekel, in person. Men, women and children, with pots and pans on their heads, blankets, knotted bundles of household bric-à-brac. It had never occurred to me that *I* might be feared, people might shit themselves at the sight of my face. My gym teacher would have collapsed at the thought. But of course it was my uniform that made them quake. And the steel khaki ordnance with which I approached them. Nietzche might well have written: "Goest thou to a subject people? Do not forget thy tank." But . . .

"'IN EACH GENERATION, EVERY JEW MUST SEE HIMSELF AS IF HE PERSONALLY CAME OUT OF EGYPT.'"

"This is not my idea of the Jewish destiny," I remember saying to Meisinger, of all people, one night. We were in the officers' quarters of a Jordanian barracks, captured in the war the week before. The commandant's three-roomed den had a bath and bidet. The junior officers had a dorm and washbasin. The soldiers' quarters were cattle pens. Meisinger was testing the bidet and I caught him literally with his pants down. He had turned up, in mufti, at two in the morning, looking smug as ever, with a briefcase containing lists of local residents who were to be picked up for questioning. Obviously he had already been officially seconded from army Intelligence to SHABAK, or some other, equally shadowy branch of the "civilian" Family.

"You surprise me, Joe," he said, "a big boy like you being childish. What do you expect, tea parties and kaffeeklatshes?"

"I don't expect kids to run screaming from me. I am not yet the wicked witch of the west."

"Have you looked in the mirror lately?" he asked,

spritzing water on his nuts. "War is hell. We do what we have to do. It's the law of the jungle, baby."

"Dragging people from their homes at night," I said, "blindfolding them, unleashing sadistic interrogators on them with fists and clubs?"

"We're a new nation," he said, contorting himself into a ball, trying to look up his arsehole. "We kick and scratch to survive. If we play fair, we'll be torn limb from limb."

"What about them?' I asked, gesturing out into the dead Samarian night. The fearful silence of crickets, the growl overhill of a night commandcar patrol. "Infiltrating cowsheds, blowing up houses? Won't they have to kick and scratch too?"

"They'll never be a nation," he said, uncoiling, "and if they are, it's tough shit. You know there's no room for both of us in town. Take your pick, Joe - Self or Other."

If this is my Self, I want an id transplant. "'WHEN ISRAEL CAME FORTH FROM EGYPT ...'" But then it had been the Egyptians who had the tanks; we, the little bundles of bric-à-brac ... As in '73, when they caught us napping, and almost had us in the bag. The Yom Kippur War, another National Trauma, the day our great rulers ate humble pie. No sign of Meisinger then, with his clever planning, his lists of everyone and his computer brain. Maybe all his energies were taken up with the case of Moishe-Ganef, who had been snatched from Rio to be put on secret trial four months before the war. A case that only came up, in the T-n café, many months later, in the form of misty rumour ... "Do you remember your old friend, Sherman ...? Well, you won't believe this story ..." Not that it would have registered anyway, lost in the mass of several thousand casualties ... The era of the awful graveyard jokes: I know a friend who has stopped smoking ... he's gone to sniff flowers from below ... I gave a hand to the security effort ... I let my fingers walk before me ... And Joe Dekel, spewed out of The Family, stuck on shit detail on the Jordan River, quaking for an attack that never came on that particular front ...

"'BLESSED ART THOU, GOD, KING OF THE WORLD, WHO HATH REDEEMED US AND OUR FOREFATHERS FROM EGYPT, AND BROUGHT US

TO THIS NIGHT ON WHICH WE EAT MATSAH AND BITTER HERBS . . .

"'*SHULKHAN OREKH* - DINNER IS SERVED"'

The following day, after the Seder night, I pursued my atavisms. In the evening a quiet time at home with Anat. I had already briefed her on the course of events in London, the accumulation of ghosts. She said: "If they want to get you they'll get you anywhere. Just relax and let me take off your angst." It is no easy task, it is attached so tightly. We made love, but the tightness remained. Now we sat, gathering in the night silence that oozed through the apartment window. Silence, except for the tippy-tap of holiday shoes, the creak of unoiled pram wheels as the orthodox residents of our quarter visit their relatives within the prescribed sphere. Anat, sunk in a García Márquez novel. She does her own travelling inwards. Often I find it difficult to work out if she is with me or deep in the jungles of Macondo. Myself, meanwhile, continuing to catch up with the enormous press backlog. Bad enough to have to read this shit day by day. Three weeks' pile up is a health hazard. The limbs become heavy, the brain soft, the eyes tremble to a blur. You gasp, like a fish out of water. Chronic persistence has been known to be fatal: "PRESIDENT HERZOG TOLD QUEEN ELIZABETH: THE ARABS ARE TO BLAME FOR EVERYTHING." "FROM JUNE: WEEKLY FLIGHTS TO MOZAMBIQUE." "GRENADE ATTACK ON POLICE AGENT." "THROWN FROM THIRD FLOOR IN DRUNKEN ARGUMENT." "DOLLARS HIDDEN IN DENTIST'S SURGERY." "SHARON: MINISTERS PLOTTING AGAINST ME." Somehow the entire mechanics of the collapse of the government had passed me by while I was out there, playing Philip Marlowe, tripping over dead bodies and being flummoxed to hell.

"NAVON AND PERES ATE FISH AND SUNFLOWER SEEDS AND DECIDED NOT TO FIGHT FOR THE LEADERSHIP." Still, the glimmer of Moishe's death mask, Gingi Arse-Face's unseen shroud . . . Why had I not lingered, at Lancaster Gate, to press the Arab lady on her story? It might have been possible, if I had only had time, to check the hearse, to track down the funeral arrangers, to try to separate the lies and half-lies ... As Lord Hercule Peter Wimsey Marlowe I was a complete herring.

I may have left London behind. But I had come to the centre, the nub of the whole damn stew. If there was any answer, it lay within reach of me.

Overnight, I made the wrong decision.

9

The problem was this: Anat apart, who, I surmised, cared for my safety, it was my enemies, Meisinger chiefly, who were telling me to fuck off and stay neutral. Which was, damn it all, my natural inclination. The man I had a degree of sympathy for, Arab Zaki, was urging me to get involved. An idea to which every one of my cells was opposed. A proposition of earth-shaking folly.

Having decided to tempt fate nevertheless, I proceeded with great care, by belly crawl. Passing the holiday week mooning about the City with Anat, pretending to be at peace with the world. Here it is difficult to see Moishe-Ganef, Gingi Arse-Face and dead Turkish heroin pushers as anything out of the normal. The bizarre, the demented, the lost, the damned, are so commonplace in Jerusalem. I need only look out of my window to see decent couples, dressed for the Sabbath of the Polish ghetto of 1853, ambling past, followed by what appears to be a congregation of midgets but is actually their own offspring, clad in black coats and homburgs, platzing in the Mediterranean sun. The orthodox quarters of town are like a continuous fashion show of resplendent headgear and beards, some literally sweeping the sidewalk, as an aged survivor hobbles by, jacknifed, perhaps to be the closer to holy soil. Elsewhere, the converging pilgrims of every metaphysical hue you can think of: Jewish Americans, pursuing their own ethnic version of John Wayne. Fundamentalist Christians, pledged to convert the heathen by the example of pure living and yoghourt. Groups of guided tourists, wondering why the Old City is so often shut down and bolted. Political turmoil, general strikes, sabotage, flash by them as so much local colour. And when the Arab City is itself functioning, an entire further level of madness: the occupied, the frustrated, the eternal merchants, the elderly pederasts, the plotters in corners. The Islamic zealots, reproaching local youths for smoking on Ramadan. And everywhere the non-denominational fanatics, wholefood yogis, barefoot preachers, leather fetishists, secret lesbians, apostate Leninists.

At Passover, particularly, the Jews go spare, the orthodox rushing to the Wailing Wall, the secular to the Arab shops and stalls selling bread which has been banished from the Jewish parts of town. In constantly flowing streams they meet, the devout, rigorous and disapproving, the lapsed, high on leaven, their eyeballs popping at the exquisite texture of the large soft Arab bagels. At least, I imagine the texture thus; as an abstainer, I avoid temptation, while Anat, proving her twisted love for me, yearns in silent solidarity. Perhaps she rushes off and indulges in secret, I do not know or ask. But she does not, as the People of Israel do wantonly, stockpile loaves in the freezer before the High Holiday to last for eight days. To cap it all, the Christian Easter then hits the fan, and all hell truly breaks loose. Hordes of pilgrims, Belgian tourists, black-clad women from Greece with little folding chairs, the Holy Sepulchre, Calvary, claims of Resurrection ... dangerous vibes indeed.

On the closing evening of the Passover I emerged from my cubbyhole into the ebbing twilight. Clouds hid the sky so one could not tell when the first stars might appear, heralding the festival's end. Knots of people clustered furtively in doorways with the air of punters on a Saturday night in Soho waiting for "Lucille - Third Floor". They were waiting for the pitta bakeries to commence work, churning out the first legitimate bread. Up the road, by the deserted Mahaneh Yehuda market, another group was in altercation with three orthodox vigilantes by the open shutters of a *burekas* shop. The orthodox, young men in their twenties, all flowing garments, sidecurls and fresh beards, were adamant that there were fifteen minutes to go before the Passover met its doom. Anyone ingesting the crisp, leavened, filled pastries in the next quarter of an hour would be putting his soul in jeopardy. The *burekas* fans, countering, waved timetables clipped from the religious press to prove that bread was now legal. One even pointed wildly to the sky, which was completely opaque, and said: "See, there are three stars already!" As I lingered awhile, in the instinctive hope of violence, someone tapped me on the shoulder and I turned to find a familiar face grinning at me.

"Hallo, Nahum," I said, "what are you doing here? You came at me from the blind rear."

"The best defence is offence, Joe," he said. "Don't tell me you're in line for the staff of life too. When did you get back?"

"Just before Passover."

And I thought suddenly: this man might be the answer to my grudging desire for enlightenment. In Jerusalem, one learns to navigate by circumstance and synchronicity. Nahum Lauterman was the West Bank and Gaza Strip correspondent of the rag I wrote my TV reviews for. It is a labour with some smidgeon of honour, as far as our meal ticket is concerned. While most other newspapers are cheering on the government for killing Arabs or castigating it for not killing enough, our journal sometimes sits back on its haunches, looks pained and says: "Well, really . . ." I do it an injustice. Since the Lebanon War, it has become quite feisty. Editorials have continually suggested the government might do well to resign, or hang itself *in toto*. The mental and moral health of the Prime Minister has been often impugned. The phrase "War Crimes" has been sighted. I played my meagre part, covering the news programmes, but mainly I stuck to insulting *Dallas*. Nahum Lauterman, on the other hand, has been playing Cassandra for the past thirteen years. Beware the Ides of March! he wrote weekly. And sure enough, Caesars fell like ninepins. First he was a thorn in the side of Golda Meir, who called him "that PLO fifth columnist". Then, when the Nationalists of Begin came to power, the insults became really serious. It was Lauterman who first exposed mass landgrabbing from Arabs on the West Bank, the terrorisation of the Gaza Strip under General Sharon, corruption in Military Administrations, the first stirrings of a settler underground. He also wrote informative articles about the internal politics of the Palestinian Arabs under occupation, their true allegiances and associations, which no one seemed to take much notice of except the Meisingers and Gingis. And of course, his typewriter hammered anguish and fury at the Lebanon War, the growing West Bank repression, the Jewish terror, the Sabra and Chatilla massacre. He was a small, plump, jovial fellow of about my age, and we often spent time jawing together. He knew where all the bodies were buried; which skeleton belonged to which closet.

"I have a story to tell you, Nahum," I said, "but *entre nous* – strictly off the record."

"It's already in print," he said, cheerily. "I'll give you the name of an excellent lawyer."

We agreed to meet at my flat the next morning, with a fresh supply of *burekas*. Anat would be out educating the masses. The neighbours comatose from excess of religion. And if Meisinger's minions wanted to hear our conversation they would hear it if we met on the moon. For this reason I opened with a government health warning, perhaps also because I had some doubts whether confiding in a journalist, even a close friend, was not like jumping off a bridge with a stone.

"This is a spook story," I said, "and we may well be broadcasting to the entire House of Israel."

"That's nothing new to me," he said, "I have them often rooting in my dustbins. Delaying my mail, breathing down the phone. But," apart from the *burekas*, we had a plate of chestnuts between us, and my nutcracker, "is it a story that I want to know?"

"Probably not. Meisinger is involved."

He made the sign of the cross.

"Is it true he's now deputy Mossad head?"

"No, he is going for the Joint Committee Chairmanship. Fresh from his recent triumphs in Lebanon, his pyramid of skulls." He cracked a nut, whose shell flew out, seriously endangering my hi-fi.

"What the hell," he said, "sock it to me, baby."

I told him the tale of Moishe-Ganef.

10

"This is not a story, this is shit," he said, "sell it to the *Labour Youth Monthly*."

The street was very quiet. My neighbours were mice. But from not so far, Easter bells tolled. My nice beige tiled floor was covered with nutshells. My bust of Beethoven was crowned with one, like a little ragged *yarmulka*.

"I tell you it like it is," I said. "Embroidery I leave to my mother."

"Joe," he said, "do you trust me? Do you really trust me?"

"Yes," I said.

"Then you're a fool," he retorted, "a fucking fool. I have a wife and two kids, as you know. I eat, I feed my family. Every year we patrol a bit abroad. I will endanger them for no one. Do you accept that?"

"Yes."

"Then listen to me: don't fuck with the Intelligence Family, Joe. You don't need me to tell you that. The principle of politics in the age of the snoop: no secrets, no hidden clauses. All cards on the table. Like me or strike me. Joe, we are an endangered species. In Argentina, people like you and me disappeared every day. Bodies found embedded in concrete at the bottom of the Rio de la Plata. People tortured and disposed of in secret cellars, no date, no plot, no gravestone. A plier in the balls and *buenas noches*. We haven't reached that here yet but I can tell you there are people working on it. Why bring the day forward? Just hang on, enjoy the ride while you're still a paying passenger, before it gets to be cattle-truck time."

"I'm not expecting the overthrow of the State," I said, "I'm just asking for a little advice."

"Meisinger told you the score, didn't he? State zillion, Joe Dekel zero. What the fuck is Moishe-Ganef to you? He was just as slime as the rest of them. And the Gingi? One Arse-Face less. Plenty more where he came from. Inflation in schmucks overtakes the shekel. And the value of life? *Nada.* Two years ago the State killed seventeen thousand people in Lebanon. If you can explain why you'll get the Nobel prize. Less than one thousand were PLO combatants. And there are plenty more where they came from ... Cities bombed, a capital blasted, refugee camps razed. And our army is still sitting there. Who cares, Joe? Wars are ten a penny. There are twenty going on around the globe. Iran and Iraq are killing each other's populations off by a couple of hundred thousand a year. Khomeini has sworn to conquer Jerusalem. We supply his army with arms. We also supply vital parts for American missiles that are part of the US strategic armoury. Wake up, Joe. Meisinger was right. We are crumbs. We can achieve nothing. The Family usually balk at killing their own. But for you they might have a special offer. Let the killers kill each other in peace. That might be our only solution."

"Mene Mene Tekel Upharsin," I said.

"You took the words right out of my mouth."

I did not want to mention at this point in the trauma, a nagging ingredient of my anxiety: the Document of the Beersheba bunker, glimpsed, in our brittle prehistory, by the Unmagnificent Four. Two down now, two to go - Meisinger and yours truly? Was it an update on that Document that Moishe stole from his bosses? Or an item even more bloodcurdling, runes of a truly hi-tech age? If so, what the hell could he do with it? Papers like that can be discredited. Intelligence fog can shred them. Journalists speculate on such flim-flam daily. Still, was there something there that day that I missed, that Moishe, Gingi and Meisinger seized on, to spark off a lingering feud?

This was not a concern I could unload on Lauterman,

even if I had wished to do so. But he broke the pregnant pause that had ensued. "I'll throw you a bone," he said, "something unconnected, but who knows, in our day and age? How about this, if you have ants in your underwear: your friend Zaki Khatib has a brother. He used to live in the Balata refugee camp just outside Nablus. It's possible he runs errands for the Popular Front, but at any rate he has been left at large. I think he helps run a café, Sha'abani's, which is owned by a very old man, a Maoist, who is a real character. He was imprisoned by the Turks, then the British, then by the Jordanians. By the time we came along he was in his seventies. We were kind, he just got a few weeks' detention. If nothing else he can give you your money's worth on the history of Palestinian nationalism. Go and talk to them, if you can't sit still here. It's safer to poke about there than in spookland. After all, Matti Peled and Avneri go to meet Arafat in Tunis and nobody gives a monkey's. Maximum you'll sit in a military jail cell for two days, while the guards use your ribs for a xylophone."

"Do they play classical?" I asked innocently, "I can't stand those ghastly sephardi jingles."

"You might get religious interrogators these days," he said, "who will do you to 'Sabbath the Bride'."

"Isn't a Jewish State wonderful?"

"I have always found it so."

I threw him out, swept up the chestnut shells and went out to see Anat. She was not at her office at the Municipality but I found her in a gallery downtown. She was supervising the hanging of the selected works of a painter, the pugnacious dwarf Rumachansky. He was sitting on the highest stool he could find, dangling his legs spasmodically and grooving on vertigo. His clipped stubbly beard and short hair were dyed ginger, to emulate his hero, Vincent Van. His paintings were imitative too, great whorls and gobs of yellow and blue depicting synagogues, wheatfields, Hanukkah candles, Jerusalem characters and his wife Zelda. Any residual similarities ceased there. After all, Vincent Van was a genius and Rumachansky a sheer schmuck.

"I'll strangle that man one day," she confided to me, in the adjoining health-food joint, over an orange soup. I refused to touch anything in the place, for fear of being permanently damaged. "What would they call it? Midgetocide? They would have to invent a new legal term."

"You might only have to serve half time," I said. It was not one of my best.

"There is some order of display in his mind," she says, "that he keeps changing. Then he denies he has changed it. 'My greatest asset,' he says, 'is my iron consistency.'"

"Just hold him in the air and shake him," I said, "I find it always works with dwarves."

She sat spooning her orange soup while I plucked up courage to tell her I was going north to Nablus to look for a member of the Popular Front for the Liberation of Palestine.

"Think I'll go to Nablus," I said, nonchalantly, "Zaki Khatib seems to have a brother in the refugee camp there."

"You're going with that, of course," she said, pointing to my hattie, "I'm sure they will go a bundle over you."

The woman had, as is her wont, unerringly found my Achilles' heel. I could not afford to go among the dispossessed accoutred like the fascist Gush Emunim, the settlers who were stealing what remained of their land, shooting at them and in general treating them as semi-human turds. The least I could expect would be a faceful of spittle. The worst, a fistful of knives in the back. But I recovered:

"The West Bank is gentile country for me. My rules allow me to remove the hattie."

She paused, gathering her forces. "You're going to take a gun, of course."

So many Achilles' heels sprouting. I hope these tumours are not malignant.

"I will take the Luger pistol, without shells. That should buy me time in a crisis."

The assault did not falter. The third wave – Intelligence Corps assessments: "If, as you say, Meisinger has you under surveillance, you'll barely get past Shueifat. Remember the last time we drove through northwards? It was like Stalag Seventeen."

"No," I said, "they'll want to know what I'm up to. On the

contrary, I should get through them like butter."

"You overestimate the co-ordination of forces," she said, still lobbing grenades, "you know it's official anarchy out there. The civilian administration versus the military government. SHABAK against army. Texas."

"Well, I think I should go," I said, activating my minefield, "you don't want me a nervous wreck from frustration, stumbling about the house like a zombie. I might break your mother's birthday vase, or even, God save us, the TV or the video-cassette recorder."

"I don't mind you being a nervous wreck," she said, "as long as you are alive. I have this strange reluctance to attend your funeral. I need someone around the house to clean the toilet, and you won't believe this, but I am rather fond of you."

Much as I dislike sexist comment, there is a woman for you. Just when you think you have deployed the best, most rational arguments, they dart out and use the blackjack. I had thought the most she would dredge up would be a prior booking to use the car for the next three months.

"I am fond of me too," I said, emphatically, "look at me. Do I look Japanese? I intend to live to a ripe old age, and die surrounded by relatives, all seething because I haven't left them a shekel of my vast wealth, dividends, guided missile investments, profits from video-games."

"You are a mule, Joe Dekel," she said softly. "*Vaya con dios,* and don't fall flat on your face too often."

11

I loaded up "Alexander", my open beach buggy, with sandwiches, a thermos of coffee, a number of cans of Löwenbrau and my Luger pistol without shells. Not for the first time I wished I had a less conspicuous vehicle, for example, a tank. It was a beautiful, pin-sharp blue-sky Jerusalem day as I puttered past the Old City walls. Paying homage, as is my wont, to Suleiman the Magnificent, who gave us these wondrous contours. The quarried stone, the turrets, domes, pediments and arches. Turning north, along the old Nablus Road, past Zahira and the American Colony. The winding black thread of asphalt, past mossy stone fences, terraces and olive trees, set in brown earth and gravel. Patches of yellow, purples and whites of the springtime crop of wildflowers. On a day like this you'd think all's right with the world, life can be a soft mountain breeze.

Boy, would you be wrong.

Trouble starts just before Rammallah, with the obligatory burning tyres. Four of them slung across the wide potholed road, spewing black oily smoke. Not a person in sight, though young men with stones are almost certainly not far away. Further into the town the street life is sparse. A small boy, holding forth a basket of fruit. An old man on a chair, with a stick, waiting for the end of foreign rule. The fine stone houses behind their fences and lush gardens seem deserted. Perhaps this is the Jewish dream. On the road, however, cars packed to capacity flashed by, their "R", "J" or "N" number plates marking their origins as Rammallah, Jenin or Nablus. As many as sixteen black eyes from each threw me daggers, which stuck, quivering, in my guilty conscience. Lone tourists are rare, and most Jewish wayfarers here are en route for the West Bank settlements: citadels, on hills, of double barbed wire and watchtowers, behind which bearded men from Glasgow or headscarved women from Scarsdale inform foreign television reporters: "We came here to live a life of freedom."

Having passed through the town without being stoned, I headed into the heart of the matter. An ancient noticeboard, put up in 1967, warns travellers of the road restrictions: You are entering an Area of Military Administration. You will obey orders of Military Personnel. Do Not Stop, Slow Down or Diverge from the Main Routes. Photography Forbidden and Access restricted to Military Bases and Refugee Camps. You are within the Jurisdiction of Emergency Defence Regulations (Amended) 1965. The sign is faded from lack of attention. This is no longer considered frontier land. For the Nationalists it is the heart of Israel, its Arab inhabitants – strangers. And yet, still Danger, Do Not Stop, Do Not Diverge From Main Routes.

The road now curves, curling by villages nestling on the slopes of lush hills. Cultivated fields, terraces, olive groves, flocks of sheep, kaffiye'd shepherds. Again one can be lulled by the calm that belies the forces of the storm. The heart of Israel. The heart of Palestine. The coronary of the world? Is it for this, the domination of these sheep, these very furrows, that so that many thousands have died in the dunes of Egypt, the mountains of Golan and of Lebanon, the dank bedsheets of the Edenvale Hotel?

Further up the road there were roadblocks. One can never tell if more than usual. Jeeps and commandcars, with the wretched of the earth, done up to the ears in guns and pouches. Their fatigues stamped in five places "Property of the Israel Defence Forces". At the first I forgot to whip on my hattie, but they waved me through anyway. At the second I donned the *yarmulka* and got stopped, and dirty thumbprints all over my ID card. A lieutenant with the face of one of those nine-year-old children who are destined to die of old age at ten went and checked it over a jeep radio and came back and looked at me with bored loathing. "Whither are you bound, this fine day?" he queried. "I have a cousin at Keren Shomron," I lied. I was sure his check had shown me to be a prime specimen of the bleeding hearts of the nation. But he just said: "Don't do anything rash," and waved me on, dipping his rifle. His colleagues just stood there, looking as if they had been sentenced to death in 1863.

Shortly afterwards I began to notice a car following on my trail. It was a cream-coloured Mercedes, keeping a distance of about two hundred metres. I tried slowing. It slowed. I tried stopping. It stopped. It was definitely in tow. We continued thus until the Nablus turn off, which was not a long while. This entire flashpoint of the third world war to come can be crossed by car in under two hours. When Yassir Arafat met Mao Tse-Tung, Mao was said to have told him: "What's the problem? Can't you over-run these Israelis? I hear they are only thirty millions."

As one approaches Nablus one gets the whiff of real troubles ahead. Knots of young men sit on crates by the roadside, looking expectant and mean. Vendors stand behind watermelon stalls, looking wary and ready for any activity, whether it involves watermelons or not. The road had bent so I could not see for the moment if my tail was still attached to my rear. Luckily I did not have to venture into Nablus town itself, a labyrinth of Palestinian nationalism. Grenades are often lobbed at passing vehicles. Jews are not in the top twenty. Unluckily, I was due to turn down into the Balata refugee camp, which was said to be a hundred times fiercer and, to boot, impossible to exit once entered except by the road leading in. From the highway an immense swathe of tightly packed stone huts, low dirty white concrete boxes and indeterminate dwellings, stretches as far as the eye can see. There do not appear to be any streets. Five thousand television aerials spring from the mêlée like spikes set to impale the Almighty if he dares step barefoot in this vale. And dust, dust, dust, dust hovers over it all.

Total astonishment showed on the faces of people who watched me turn down into the camp. Perhaps they had not seen a beach buggy before. A man in a white short-sleeved shirt and baggy trousers ran after me, shouting "No! No! No!" "Yes! Yes! Yes!" I hurled back at him, accelerating mildly. Within thirty seconds I was completely engulfed in the ambience of the camp. Grit, odours of sweat, fear and excrement, the babble of multitudes, the press of their bodies. It was as if I had been warped into another universe by a twist of the steering wheel. Everything I found familiar and handleable was lost behind me. I was alone in the whirlpool. Children ran after the car, yelling, some grinning, some stern as my old sergeant-major. Young girls moved aside, melting into doorways. Men with laden carts stood still, making me swerve. The camp was a seething pot of confusion, markets, homes, shops, stalls on top of each other. Or rather side by side, because there was virtually no building more than one storey high.

I braked to a halt as an enormous wooden waggon filled with brushwood loomed in the road's centre. A man, dressed much as the fellow who had cast his negatives at me, but with tighter trousers, and brilliantined, sleeked-down hair, ambled up to me and rested his arms, thoughtfully, on my windscreen.

"Israeli?" he said in Hebrew.

"What can one do?" I said. "The Lord just picks us out of a hat."

He took a glance to make sure I was bareheaded, as if that counted for anything. "I like this car," he continued in Hebrew. "It is an Austin beach buggy, is it not? About 1965."

"Absolutely," I said. "Do you collect them?"

He made a gesture that could mean, I'm considering it. Strangely enough, no one else joined him at my car flank. Four or five young men, though, seemed to have drifted to cut me off, front and back, at about five metres. Other people just went on about their business, squeezing between me and the walls.

"I'm looking for Sha'abani's Café," I said, "can you direct me to it?'

His face said, I'm considering that too, as he flicked his eye over my dashboard. I now bitterly regretted toting along my useless pistol, which was as much defence to me as a flywhisk, empty, and as a hara-kiri knife, loaded. I took out a can of Löwenbrau and gave it to him. He popped it open and drank a little, returning it. I took a sip. It had achieved the temperature of fairly fresh piss.

"What business do you have there?" he then asked bluntly. "You know it's illegal for you to be here."

"What's the law," I said carelessly, "when you're in need of a good cup of coffee?"

"Is there no good coffee in Israel?" he said. "You know you Jews are mostly Arabs too."

I could see I was going no further unless I cleared a way with this man. He might have been the local shtinker, or government agent, but with the youths around this might not be the case. "I am looking for Sami Khatib." I said. "I saw his brother Zaki, in London. We used to be old friends, in Jerusalem. I came to pass on his regards."

"And who are you?"

"My name is Joe Dekel," I said. "I write about television programmes for newspapers and magazines. I don't give a fuck for politics but I do care about old friends."

His face said, This is a likely story. Then it said, Well, what the hell. His forearms released the car. "You'll find Sha'abani down the road, one-fifty metres, turn left. Nassr will take you there." He lifted a hand. One of the young men climbed on my flank. "*Yallah*," he said, "let's travel." The loaded waggon was turned aside into an alley, giving me just enough room to pass.

We proceeded, like a Presidential motorcade, acted out in some remote Latin barrio, the blare of Arab music, from either side of me, swelling from transistor radios.

12

"So you write about television," said the old man. "Everyone here watches *Dallas*. Also we liked very much *The Brothers*. And the *Forsyte Saga*."

"The *Forsyte Saga* was excellent," I agreed. "were you in favour of Soames or Irene?"

"The man was very honourable," he said, "but the woman had a mind of her own. We Palestinians believe that is important. We need the strength of every one of our people."

We were speaking English, as the old man could or would not speak Hebrew with me and had brushed my halting Arabic aside. Perhaps he wanted to engage me on neutral mental ground. Or it may have been nostalgia for the mandate. We were facing each other across a low folding table, with two white cups and a battered coffeepot and tray holding down an almost white tablecloth. Around us the same young men lounged, locked apparently in a slurping contest. At an adjoining table a game of checkers seemed to have been going on since Stalingrad. Grains of dust from the camp were lit by diffuse sunlight oozing through slatted shutters. It was like a Joseph von Sternberg movie, with no hope, alas, of Marlene Dietrich.

"We also watch the Arab films you broadcast," continued the old man, "that you steal without paying copyrights. I know, because I have a grandson who owns a cinema in Cairo. The Imperialism is like that," he nodded, "there is nothing it can let alone."

"When there's peace," I said, "they'll pay copyrights, and then they won't be able to afford to show them."

"Ah, peace," he said, mispronouncing the "p" as "b" as many Arabs do. He took a slow slurp of his coffee. By his elbow dishes of titbits began to materialise, olives, tomatoes, hot pitta, *zahtar*. My Löwenbraus had been put in the fridge. No one seemed in any hurry. The old man was quite remarkable. By Nahum's count he must be pushing ninety. But he didn't look a day over eighty. His face was a map of the Levant in this century, crisscrossed with forced border changes, ravaged by deep occupations. His eyes were withdrawn but undried, the still waters of his people. His mouth, though, was shrunken, fixed in an eternal pursing of shrewd and unyielding inquiry. I am Palestine, it seemed to be saying, What have you done for me this week?

"I was born in 1894," he said. "Your great-grandfather might remember it. There was a war between Italy and Abyssinia. The Italians lost. It was a great scandal. The Imperialists were outraged. Your great-grandfather was probably praying then in the synagogue in Poland. Or maybe he had even heard of Dreyfus. When I was two years old Theodor Herzl published *The Jewish State*. When I was sixteen I was in a Turkish jail. They had very bad jails. Many prisoners died. I was helping with an Arab newspaper calling for a free Arab nation. In 1915 the British made us promises. Two years later they also promised the Jews. They were much cleverer than the Turks. But they have also gone home. In the end everybody goes home. But we, the Palestinians, stay."

He looked at me as if expecting a challenge, but I remained silent and sipped my coffee. I too can play What's My Century, while waiting for the sea to dry.

"You Jews say you have come home here," he said, "after two thousand years. But a homeland you grow in, you do not steal. We will see who will last out to the end."

We will probably both go together, Grandpa, locked in an eternal embrace. Rigor mortis *über alles*. But I just said: "There is always enough room, if people will respect each other."

"You are from 'Peace Now'?" he said, lowering his head a

little, giving me the look which said Time for your ID, comrade – animal, vegetable or mineral.

"I agree with them most of the time," I said, "but I'm not keen on the communal singing." His gaze did not flinch, so I had to elaborate. "I think we should always look to the future, not to some glorious past."

"It is from the past that the future is constructed," he said, pushing the pitta plate towards me. The pittas were fresh. Even here, in this shit-hole, the niceties were observed. "That is the Jews' problem. Your own past lies in so many different nations. In Poland, in Rumania, in Russia, even America. And also in Iraq, Morocco. Your early Zionists knew this was a problem, that you had to be involved with a land. But a land is passed on, from father to son. It does not come out of a book. Of course, Imperialism was not interested in your Borochov, your A.D. Gordon, your Tolstoyan, Herzenian, utopian ideals. Imperialism wanted a war machine, which, of course, it now has."

"These olives are very good," I said.

"Of course," he said, "they are ours."

He was a very certain old man. And he would not let me go. Circumstances had handed him a *bona fide* Israeli bleeding heart, and he was going to scratch at the lining.

"Our past," he said, "is burning away under your feet. Burning like slow embers. Wherever you are sitting, our past is there. You cannot avoid the discomfort. Even if you think to kill us all, the embers are there to scald your buttocks. It will just need the smallest spark to start the fire again. Of course today you have America, the great fire brigade. With their big hoses, their F-16s, their Minutemen, their missiles ... But that too will pass. They tried to bombard Lebanon with battleships. What do you expect of such people?"

"Nothing much. But they make exciting movies."

"Hollywood! That is all they are good for. Their President is a film also. They do not understand death, because in a film the actor dies and is alive again in the next one. Two hundred casualties and they go home. They are a paper tiger. What they think, they can buy everyone with money. But we are not selling. Two hundred casualties! We have two hundred thousand! We smell death with every breakfast. We wake up and it is in our noses. You Jews, who were burnt in the ovens, you should know the strength that comes out of your own dead. We respect your fighters. But you do not respect ours. That is how we will defeat you. You think if you inflict pain, destruction, we will give up. But we are only strengthened."

Bully for you, old buzzard. You must have already outlived eight generations. But when are we getting to the price of eggs, London Zaki and the shade of Moishe-Ganef? As Nahum had promised, this was very educational, but not doing much for my private angst. Not to speak of the problem of the cream Mercedes, parked probably somewhere within eye and earshot, crammed no doubt with Meisinger clones.

A curtain parted, at the back of the café. But it was only one of the youths bringing out my Löwenbraus after their half hour in the freezer. Still, I did seem to catch some furtive movement, a slink back with the fall of the curtain. A strong smell of Peter Lorre, probably in my mind.

We contemplated our ghosts in silence a while, interrupted by the plop of beer-can tabs. Broken only by the cries of the market, the clatter of barrows and a hundred and three transistor radios. Other than that it was oppressively close. Dust chased down the Löwenbrau. Then a man came in from the street. He was a muscular, body-builder type, dressed in a flamboyant Hawaiian-style shirt. His hair was a little grey at the temples and his face was like the prow of a battleship adorned with that common Naif Hawatmeh moustache. I could guess his identity with no introduction but he gave me one anyway, after sitting down and pressing the old man's hand.

"I am Sami Khatib," he said in Hebrew. He pressed my hand too, treating it as if it were the neck of Menahem Begin. "You met my brother Zaki, I understand. How is he? Does he look good?" After trashing mine, his hand flashed to his shirt pocket, extracting a pencil and notepad. He tore out a page and began to scribble, talking at me with his eyes down.

"As well as can be expected," I babbled, "considering the climate out there. It can ruin the complexion. But he looks OK. A hundred percent. Very suave."

"You knew him in Jerusalem," he stated, still scribbling. "I think we met once, at a New Left meeting. I remember you asked for a show of proletarian hands in the room. Everyone was very scathing."

"Just a routine provocation . . ." I said, but he handed me the note abruptly. It said:

"ZAKI SENDS HIS REGARDS. HE HAS THIS MESSAGE FOR YOU: YOUR GINGI SENT AN ENVELOPE BEFORE HIS EXIT TO A FRENCH EX-PRIEST IN TIBERIAS. HE LIVES AT THE ECUMENICAL HOSPICE THERE. HIS NAME IS FATHER PARRY. DO NOT SAY ANYTHING. YOU ARE CANDID CAMERA AND MICROPHONE CHAMPION, 1984."

I goggled at the page. He snatched it from me. I snatched it back and motioned for his pencil. I wrote: "IS THE GINGI REALLY DEAD?"

He lifted his head, in the levantine positive, dismissing the dispatched freckled soul with a light opening of his palms.

"My brother is a fine man," he said, "good in business. The family will be very proud."

He ate the note. I had never seen anyone do such a thing before. Panic entered my nostrils, then sank to my groin.

"You will drink another coffee," said the old man.

There was definitely a furtive movement behind the inner curtain. I got up and pulled it aside. There was a small boy there, brewing new coffee on an old primus.

"Life is precious," said the old man, still in English, "but it is not measured only by your self. Your family, your class, your people, they will live after you have gone."

Sami Khatib sat back, his palms on the table, his eyes watching me from afar. It was difficult to tell upon which battlefield he seemed to be taking this pause to reload. The young men slurped their dregs. The checkers clattered. I made the only move possible. I glanced demonstrably at my watch.

"I have to get back now," I said.

Was the old man smiling? Had the cat swallowed the cream? Joe Dekel, budgerigar of the month. Wipe those feathers off your mouth, *ya effendi.*

"Thank you very much for the hospitality," I said, "we should meet in better times."

"*Inshallah,*" said the old man. Were his eyes laughing like a drain?

The youths helped me evict from "Alexander" two primary schools' load of the curious. By luck, or by design, they had left the buggy intact. I gunned the motor. They chorused "*SHALOM*". The brilliantined buggy freak who had pointed me hither stood with folded arms in the road. I nodded at him. He nodded back. A path opened in the human mélange.

Whatever you can imagine, the truth can surpass it. In the Middle East, there are no limits. The children ran after the car, yelling, waving empty cans, rolling metal tyreframes. Five hundred adult eyes wished me perdition. Gobs of spit spattered the dust. The Balata refugee camp had its message spelled out to me: Joe Dekel, Fuck Off. I exited as I entered, ignorant, my brain a dry pea in its pod. What new manipulations were now at play? What was the half-time score? Which was Zaki's "Family" – ours or theirs? How did Sami Khatib time his entrance so neatly? What did Tiberias and French ex-priests have to do with all this, not to speak of the Arab copyrights scam . . .? Everyone seems to know what I am up to except my own poor self. Just as everyone seemed to know there was a stiff at the Hotel Edenvale except its own wretched management . . . The skeins of coincidence stretching too far – Nahum Lauterman, where art thou? The voice of thy baffled brother crieth from the earth . . . What price the Mark of Cain now?

As I turned back on to the Nablus Road I saw the cream Mercedes. It was parked a way up towards the town. At the crossroads an army half track had pulled up. Bored soldiers sat slumped inside. Outside a jeep with four border police guards basked in the summer sun. They climbed down and ambled in my path. I slowed the buggy and halted. Their officer, a Major, came forward jauntily. He was a middle-aged man with an immaculate uniform and shave and a Kirk Douglas dimple.

"Yosef Dekel?" he said, bright and cheerful.

"It is I," I replied, somewhat less so.

"You are under arrest," he said, virtually ecstatic. "You have been a very naughty boy."

13

"The main problem in jail," said the cheerful Major, "is getting fucked up the arse. Some people, of course, enjoy it. Are you one of that merry band, Dekel?"

It was barely Thursday afternoon and my second arrest in one month. My first time, though, in Nablus prison. I could have passed up the honour. The looming bulk of a transformed Teggart fortress, a great grey block of misery and Lysol, a fetid human zoo. The barbed wire, the watchtowers, the military police jailors, with their white belts and Brasso. Sweaty hands and arms pushed through the bars, pressed forward by overcrowding. No wonder the pedestrian flow outside was so sparse. Everybody was in here. Men with mops, endlessly chasing scuff and spittle, like an academy of chars. The inmates looked much like barbers caught fiddling the till. The guards, like the damned. I remembered with fondness my first arrest, December 1970. A sit-down climax to a "Black Panther" demo. Twenty of us good children of the Jerusalem bourgeoisie joining the five insurrectionists of the poorer classes in a detention cell at the Russian Compound. We sang "We Shall Draw Water From The Fountains of Salvation", and Sa'adia B—, who is now a Member of Parliament, delivered a medley of Prison Six songs. The Arab prisoners in the next cell banged on the wall, demanding to be allowed their sleep.

Not now however, *plus ça change ...*

The cheerful Major was named Kazaz. I had never met the man, but he was no stranger to me. I had been running from his like all my life. The real fear in my belly was Anat. If I lingered the night there'd be ructions. I am allowed my adventures as long as I keep the eleventh commandment: Thou Shalt Not Be an Idiot.

"I am not prejudiced," I answered the Kirk Douglas dimple, "but I am very choosy."

"You are confident," he said, "because you are Good-Boy-Jerusalem, an ashkenazi on safari. You thought you had it made, then we blacks came along, so now you run to the Arabs for help."

It was a neat analysis. Some people spend four years figuring that out at a university. But in places like this great mental leaps are possible. It was evidently the Major's own office. I had no clear idea what his role was in the building, I had certainly not passed normal process. Frogmarched by minions directly through the gate to this bare room, with a table, three chairs, a filing cabinet and an MP waxwork guarding the door. A row of paper-tacked pin-ups adorning the walls: Begin, Shamir, Sharon, "Raful" and Rabbi Kook The Younger, doyen of Gush Emunim, who had recently died at ninety. His portrait had a black funeral frame. The others, not yet. All in good time.

"You know," the Major said, "people think I am a nice guy. But actually I am quite cruel. Not out of sadism or anything like that. I am just doing my job. You write for the newspapers, the most dirt you'll get is typewriter ink on your fingers. Me, I have to drink in prisoners' vomit, excrement of Arabs, blood. And I'll bet you my salary is not half of yours. Tell me there's justice in the world."

"There's justice in the world." I told him.

"Ah, you mean the justice of God!" he nodded sagely. I had earlier re-donned my hattie. "What I really can't fathom is a good Jew like you turning against your own people. Communists, atheists, that's something else. They get it out of books. But you know the One Book that matters, and still you are a piece of shit."

"A turd by any other name would smell as foul," I said, but he did not follow me. He got up and looked out of the small grilled window, sadly surveying his princedom. The asphalt crest of a turret rose up against the true blue sky. Then he turned back and did something very odd: sitting down at the table he smacked his forehead twice hard against the wooden surface. It seemed an extreme way to smooth out wrinkles. He leaned back, spreading his arms in supplication.

"Why is it you intellectuals are so fucking ignorant?" he implored. "Why can't you see the real world out there? I have people in here who have done things that would make your intestines uncurl. They murdered a taxi-driver and scooped out his brains and fed it to their fucking chickens! I won't speak of what they do to genitals - you are a religious man. Why can't you fucking milksops understand we are dealing with savages here? The things they did when they ruled South Lebanon - raping girls and scooping out their eyes and sewing cockroaches inside! Oh, you are so stupid!" He refrained with obvious difficulty from smoothing his wrinkles again. "The Arabs are a cruel race. Violence is their hidden language. Learn to speak it and you have their respect. They have contempt for weeping willies. I know, my family came from Iraq. For decades we lived side by side with them. Then one day in 1941 - poomph!" he threw his hands up, "they slit my great-uncle and great-aunt's throats in the city market! Poomph! They raped pregnant girls and threw the embryos in the garbage! You wouldn't know! Your family came from ashkenaziland, where you all had it made."

"That's true," I said, "my father came from Germany. They were so good to us. They made us into detergents."

"You see! The only place a Jew is safe is here. But you have to fight tooth and nail. Three years ago Assad of Syria butchered fifty thousand of his own people. Sunni Moslems, in Hamma. Even they rebelled against the tyrant. Did he serve them with a court order, I ask you? No, he sent in tanks and air force, with poison gas. They left nothing but a hole in the ground. But of course he had no journalists there. If they had shown up they would have been porridge. We try to straighten out anarchy on our borders and poomph! The New York *Herald Tribune*!"

"I write about television for H-z," I said, "like: has J.R.

gone too far this week? Does Sue Ellen have a run in her stocking?"

"Television, newspapers, they are all the same," he said, "we know you are paid Fatah agents. You'd be surprised at the names on our lists . . . I have been shown some invoices . . . but you know all about that. Why else are you here, eh? Tell me that, know-all, clever dickie, why the fuck are you here?"

"I haven't a clue," I said, calm as I could, "is it a word with three syllables?"

"You are a piece of shit, Dekel," he said, having come full circle. "I've had enough of this. Yochai!" The waxwork came to life, stalking forward to stand over my chair. The Major turned back to me, "I am going to keep you here," he said, "because of your beautiful eyes. It's love at first sight, *ya habibi*. I have some great quarters lined up for you. Five-star luxus. One day you'll be grateful to me for showing you life as it really is."

"Can I make a phone call?" I asked, thinking, here are Anat's nerves down the toilet.

"Anything you want," he said, "long distance. Satellite. You want the Space Shuttle? You're welcome. But not today, unfortunately. The lines are down. Malfunction. The Walk in Space is tomorrow. Put him in Thirty-five six," he gestured to the waxwork, who took me stickily by the arm.

"One word," he added, as I was got to the door, "forewarned is forearmed, they say. The Arabs here do it without cream. If they really like you, they might use saliva." I caught a glimpse of him throwing himself back in his chair, exhausted, as I was marched out to the corridor, his voice echoing plaintively as the gap grew between us: "Oh Why Is Not Love Eternal?"

I was put in a cell with three other prisoners. A termite might have found it spacious. The three Arabs, who were all fairly young, in their twenties, looked suspiciously at my hattie. I told them: "My name is Joe Dekel. I am involved with God, but I am not with the fucking fascists." Oh, the horrors of our present politics. What was wrong with the Diaspora? Pretty soon we will all have to wear little labels, or lights winking on and off.

"You are from 'Manam'?" asked the youngest of the prisoners, perking up and looking hopeful. They made room for me to sit on one of the two bottom bunks which about filled the cell's width. Our knees could not avoid touching. The eldest produced a cigarette and a very battered matchbox.

"'Manam'?" I said, puzzled, taking a drag and nodding thankfully.

"Orthodox Persons Against the War," said the younger, "they are a new group, but they have had some demonstrations."

"Ah, yes, I have heard of them," I said, "but I'm afraid I am not an activist. I am here because it seems Major Kazaz has fallen in love with my beautiful eyes."

"Yes, Kazaz, our 'Education Officer'. He is a racist. He enjoys torturing. But you should be OK as a Jew. They once had some 'Peace Now' demonstrators in here, but they only kicked them about a bit in the yard. They had come to protest against a new Gush settlement just on the hill outside town. We shouted our support: 'Arabs and Jews together'." Absolutely, in the hoosegow. We shall end up in common graves, as in *Exodus*.

"I had gone to see the brother of a friend, in Balata," I said, "a Palestinian comrade, now in London. It was strictly a personal matter. He had asked me to see his family . When I came out of the camp this Kazaz grabbed me." I did not like telling even white lies to these people, but of course they might be Kazaz's stoolies. I might have been planted in this cell to talk. Prison subterfuge ploughs a narrow furrow. As if to confirm my suspicions they began pumping me, one by one, about life on the outside. Who was I, what did I do, which party was I going to vote for in the coming elections. Would I explain the split in the National Religious Party. What was the nature of German Jewish cooking? I responded with queries about Arab cuisine, the real village stuff, not restaurant fodder. We unravelled the toilet roll, and wrote down several recipes with a pencil stub on the coarse paper. I had been cleaned out, my thermos flask, sandwiches, presumably in Kazaz's cabinet. The thought of my empty pistol, which had completely slipped my mind, suddenly hit my gonads. I hadn't even checked it coming out of the camp. Now that would be a pretty pickle. There was so much to worry about I became paralytic, despite the company, drifting with the flow of my fears.

Supper was slops in the main prison mess hall, somewhat like David Lean's version of *Oliver Twist,* except that no one, having downed the swill, would be mad enough to rise and say Please sir, can I have some more. At night, on a lower bunk the Arabs cleared for me, I fell into a deep-freeze sleep. I seemed to find myself back in the prison mess hall, but now it was jam-packed with all my relatives, my high school mates, my comrades in army basic training. They all sat lined along the steel benches fixed to the floor by the equally fixed steel tables. One table was reserved for the regulars of my synagogue, who had their prayer shawls pulled over their heads. At the head of this table my poor old father slumped on a pile of Passover cushions. Slop had been delayed, and everyone except my father was banging their tin bowls. My father's lips moved, in the familiar litany: "You know what happened to Sodom and Gomorrah." Sitting opposite me at my table were the bodybuilder, Sami Khatib, and old Sha'abani. They were whispering together, in prison ventriloquy; I could not catch a word they were saying. There was a sudden roll of drums, and a gong was struck. At the corner of the hall curtains parted. A parade of chefs, dirty white smocks and chef's caps, wheeled on to the mess hall podium. Dividing in a Busby Berkeley "V" they then joined and minced down steps towards us. Each line was carrying a long six-foot plate with a large silver cover. They placed both plates on my father's table, as the congregation nodded, swayed, genuflected. The chefs whipped the covers off. There were Moishe-Ganef and the Gingi, *garni* with Jaffa oranges.

I was shaken awake by a rude clanging, a bare lightbulb coming on, and swearing. "Is the Jew in here?" I heard in Arabic. I thought, this is it, the Black Hundreds. Hands pulled me upright. A voice said in Hebrew: "You don't look like an Arabush, do you?"

My cellmates remained silent on their bunks. In that space there wasn't much else they could do. "Come with me, snowdrop," said the Hebrew voice. I found myself outside the cell.

It was dark. I saw the sky. There was a faint glimmer of dawn considering its options. Two uniformed men were frogmarching me along the steely blue cell catwalk. As we flickered past lamps I observed they were regular, not military policemen. They looked very harassed, stubble-faced, as if this was not their idea of a good time.

"What's going on here?" I asked, a lame effort, but the best I could dredge up at the moment.

"Just don't make trouble," said the misery on my left, "God knows there's enough crap already."

Yes, and it's time He did something about it. I was ushered into the Major's office. Only this time it was not as uncluttered as before. It was positively a conference centre. The Major sat in a corner, like the class dunce, looking extremely sulky. Another two MP officers, both Lieutenant-Colonels, sat in another corner, tight lipped and wary. At the Major's table a mean-faced civilian who looked as though he chewed tyres for bubble gum sat before an array of gadgetry. He had a short-wave radio and an odd electronic box and a portable suitcase computer. I could not identify the make, but swallowed my disappointment. The computer was connected to a modem attached to the short wave's receiver. On other chairs about the room seven other people slumped, police, army and more mean mufti. Almost everyone was smoking. The place was like a gas chamber. The entrance of three more seemed to give the room the tension of the imminent release of Zyklon B.

I was placed in a chair. The tyre-chewing civilian nodded at me and turned to Major Kazaz.

"Is this the Jew," he asked, "or is there another one, hidden maybe in the john?"

"I don't know," said Major Kazaz, "I never saw this man in my life."

The civilian glanced at the two MP officers, who shrugged, denying Joe Dekel too. If I were of the Nazarene faith I might have had hopes for posterity. As things are, no.

The mean man looked weary, as if he were about to spit out a Michelin radial. "Bring in the guard," he said. My two policemen stepped out and hauled in my favourite waxwork.

"Your name is Yochai Smoocha?" The waxwork nodded, melting in the desert blast. "Entertain me," the civilian invited him, "with a rendition of your favourite story."

"I've told you all I know," said the wretched exhibit, "this man was brought in, I was detailed to deal with him. The orders were to bypass normal process. I just followed my commander's orders."

The civilian whimpered, and a sigh of sadness echoed throughout the room. Major Kazaz was impassive, drawing on his cigarette, expelling smoke from his nose. Blue wreathes curled about the ceiling. A fly buzzed away from the lightbulb.

An army colonel, who obviously despised everyone, put his hand forth on the table. "Why don't we put this prick in with the Fatahs for a while," he grated, "I have a trowel in my car, for the remains."

The MP officers stirred resentfully. The mean civilian looked woebegone. He pressed his palm down for calm. "We'll have to sort this out later," he said, sniffing at the MPs, "if I ran a prison the way you do . . ." he sighed. "It's lucky they're not all out on the streets." He turned and laid heavy eyes on me. "I don't know who you are, sir, or what the fuck you are doing here. There is no record of your arrest or a charge sheet. Do you mind enlightening us, at least a little?"

I gave him my name, rank and number. He fiddled with his computer. A series of beeps and trills ensued. Then he looked at me with studied apathy.

"One arrest for disturbing the peace, 1970," he intoned, "traffic citations, eleven counts. Non-affirmation of army Regular contract. Peacenik, soft. The usual petitions. Voted twice Labour, once for Uri Avneri, once for the New Communist List. You are just another schmuck, Dekel, what are you doing here?"

I began telling him the story I had told my cellmates. He didn't give a fuck for it either. "I have nothing against you," he said, "it's a free country. If you stick your hand in fire, it'll burn. We'll take you back to Jerusalem. You may be called as a witness. Your co-operation will be appreciated." He turned to the others. "Let's wrap up here. Take Kirk Douglas and let's hit the road."

The policemen came forward and handcuffed the Major. He leered at me as they hustled him out. His wrinkles had disappeared, he seemed smooth as formica. His MP commanders looked glum.

"Pardon me," I interjected as the jamboree broke up, "just what is that man being charged with?"

"Terrorism," said the civilian, "underground activities. Killing Arabs without a licence. There'll be a whole batch of them, before breakfast. The stables are being cleaned. Read all about it in the afternoon papers. Hear all the liberals crow. But will you thank us for it, eh, Dekel? Will you have a good word for the chain gang?" He zipped up his computer, while another man in mufti shouldered the short-wave radio. "We're just the pump in the cellar," he said, "keeping your air clean. I don't expect anything from you except one smidgeon: just don't get under my feet. I like to wear hobnailed boots when I'm working, and I'm slightly deaf, so I don't hear scrunched bones. *Yallah*," he summed up, "let's go to Jerusalem. Al-Kuds, the Holy City."

14

The afternoon papers revealed the following:

For the last three years, since bomb attacks were carried out on three West Bank Arab mayors, the police and SHABAK had put deep-cover agents into the right-wing settler movement. During the rule of Menahem Begin, rumour had it, those investigators were impeded, but Prime Minister Shamir, himself an ex-spook, had reapproved the operation. The crunch came when the investigators found a major raid was in the offing. In retaliation for an Arab terrorist hijack of a bus near Ashkelon, the Gush underground planned a massive bomb attack on six Arab buses in Jerusalem. Each bus would be mined with three separate devices, front, centre and rear. The buses would be packed, mostly with Easter pilgrims, and few, if any, might survive. The powers that be could not allow this action, and the final round-up was ordered. The bombers were allowed to plant their bombs and then arrested red-handed, while police units swooped on other cell members and back-up groups elsewhere. Apart from my Major Kazaz, two other West Bank military government officers were held. The rest were known Gush Emunim activists, ultra-religious settlers, both from the West Bank and the Golan Heights. Thus had the Word of God finally been taken by some as a command for mass murder.

The Ayatollah Khomeini was no longer alone. Our future loomed, with beards and hatties. I went out to my synagogue, but prayed alone. Everyone else there was in his shell too. An air of shame pervaded the streets of my orthodox but non-nationalist neighbourhood. I returned home and sat alone with Anat, the television blank in the corner.

There had been, mercifully, no full-scale ructions when I had been slipped, like an out-of-season tax demand, through the door at seven-thirty in the morning. Anat did not scold, lock me in the closet, or do the sullen silence, dusting the shelves, cleaning the floor. Instead she put a coffee in my hand and said quietly: "Are you applying for Emergency Crisis Status?"

"I am giving it serious thought," I replied.

"My nerves are not what they used to be," she said, "I want advance notice next time."

The nerves of none of us are what they used to be. We are all shipwrecks of old glories. Or so we would like to see ourselves and our past, ocean liners where there were perhaps only canoes ... Delusions of grandeur, Bible fantasies of the special confidants of the Lord. Joe Dekel as much as the rest of them, believing the world owes me an explanation. But I had made no progress at all in *l'affaire* Moishe-Ganef and my country was once again imploding, gorging on its own tumours. There is a name for the syndrome: "Lebanonisation". And it is not a new story ...

June 5, 1982, marked the point of no return. Then as now, the hawk of a rabid madness hovered over the country, but Anat and I, like all the other liberal suckers, basked in the sunshine, believing the latest spasm had passed. One could chart, in hindsight, the inevitable run-up – the slow but inexorable fuse: from the appointment of General Sharon, Action Man of '73, as the new Defence Minister, through the rising unrest and repression on the West Bank, the "private" bombing of the Arab Mayors. The solo attack by a mad American upon the Mosque of Omar, the settler riots over the withdrawal from Sinai in keeping with the peace treaty with Egypt. Not to speak of the destruction by bulldozers of the abandoned settler town, Yamit, so as to show, as the Iron General stated, that "no Arab army can destroy a Jewish city. Only we ourselves can do it." But we were blasé. This was grist to the mill. We trusted the wily Yanks to hold Action Man back despite his threats to the PLO in Lebanon. We had, after all, had a ceasefire with the Palestinian forces since the summer shelling of '81 ... It was doubly a shock then, when I was taking my Sabbath pre-synagogue nap, the Friday newspaper pyramided over my face, Anat happily scissoring out of a glossy weekly an item on an exhibition of blind painters she had mounted in Herzliya, to have a colleague, Schitz, bang on my door and shout: "Joe! We are invading Lebanon!"

Nightmare alley, and the entrance to a long tunnel ... the sense of being at "carpet level" ... barely daring to peek above the chair legs, hiding under the bed with tinned meat and orange squash, sitting out the siege of one's brains ... the radio, switched to non-stop "Homeland" ditties, interrupted by cryptic bulletins: "Operation Peace for Galilee nears completion ... a matter of forty-eight hours, say spokesmen ..." "After forty kilometres, fighting will cease ..." "Lebanese welcome troops as liberators ..." "Great success after first week of campaign ..." "No intention to fight Syria, says Begin ..." "Clashes with Syria not serious ..." "Operation virtually completed ..." "No intention to even approach Beirut, say sources ..." "Our correspondent with the troops in Beirut says ..." "Escalating battles on Beirut-Damascus Highway ..." "Seventh ceasefire will hold, unless broken ..."

One learned that one's psyche can become unstuck, like an onion, layer after layer. And, of course, the tears. Even tank goggles are no help. For the first three days I dared not leave the house. Anat, beyond the call of duty, bought groceries, which were usually my department. She reported back on the mood in the street, no enthusiasm, much gloom and confusion. It was an odd war. Even those who were for it were against it. Doublethink had rented our minds with the Occupation. Now it had procured a mortgage. Where were the voices of dissent, of "Peace Now"? They were all muffled in their tanks, up there. My Reserves officer called, with the one gleam of good news. He said: "Joe, you stay at home. You are such a wet blanket for the unit. Just march in place for the duration." I plugged my veins into the TV set, but my drug had become a poison. It was impossible to tell what was really happening. The "fog of battle" had descended. And on the radio the endless homeland melodies, with which I had outgrown short trousers: "Night of Roses", "Go My Love Towards the Bride", "I Had a Love that was So Fair". My youth, mangled, polluted and garbaged.

Our neutrality, our precarious balance, was shattered. I kept cutting my feet on the shards of it. The floor was awash with blood. I woke up soaked in it. As if to match our brains the temperature soared. By the fifth day of the two-day war it was 34 celsius. By the thirteenth it nudged 37. We thought we were alone in the universe, the last bleeding hearts among the dry. Then there were rumours of dissent, here and there. A small demo at the university. Thirty people with placards, in Tel Aviv. Passers-by jeered and spat on them. "I must do something," I said. "Who's stopping you?" asked Anat. "Major-General Fear," I replied. Wild thoughts entered my mind. I would improvise a noticeboard and walk out alone down the teeming Jaffa Road. "Fuck Off, Warmongers!" I would pronounce, front and back, before being mashed to purée. A little later we ventured into the streets, which were becalmed in an odd slow motion. The population had been thinned out, selectively, men aged up to about fifty were absent. It was strange to pass another male of my age, and exchange a sort of furtive knowledge. They didn't take you. You neither. Think I'll mosey off home now. During the '73 War, if you appeared young, male, out of uniform and uncrippled, people hissed at you in shops and on buses. Now they looked at one with an unconcealed longing – Oh, if only my own Yankel were spared . . .

We took to long walks at night, when the sun loosened its tyranny, turning to zap China or India. Down, from our flat, through the orthodox quarter, past the time-warped, stetl-like houses. Yellow light on coarse bricks, tiled roofs punching into the full canopy of stars. The air clear and pure, as it wafted from another dimension. Past the folding over of new and old Jerusalem, the division line of pre-'67. The unique turret, like a Renaissance hat, of the Italian hospital. Turn of the century buildings of the Imperialist concessions, the Austrian, the Russian, the French. The

Ethiopian church, that domed marvel of garish blue and black-faced Madonna and child. Skirting by the walls of the Old City. Watermelons were in season. There were stalls and stalls of them, lined up along the Nablus Road. The Arab vendors sat on stools, clicking worry beads. A goat wandered about bemused. Foreign youths with rucksacks tottered anxiously towards Abu Ali's hostel. Even they could not escape infection with the spirochaete of fear. We returned flatwards, up the deserted centre of town, through the semi-orthodox market neighbourhood. Stone steps leading down narrow connecting alleyways. The vermin-like cats flashing round corners. Ugly, gaunt wild scavengers, they peeked out from rubbish skips, baring their teeth, staking their claim like lions of the Serengeti. And from every direction, from every open window, the clarion of the TV news. Bulletins stretched to ninety minutes, two hours, telling one absolutely nothing. The high-pitched whine of our Prime Minister, wheedling, protesting, promising it would soon be all over. Worst of all, the bass booming of our Defence Minister, reverberating off walls, fences. His voice hammered, it gave no quarter, it echoed in one's brains, lungs, stomach. It was Joshua's trumpet call, and we were all Jericho. Our surrender was only a matter of time. It was of course his war. He had conceived it. He ran it, wave by wave. In the second week of the two-day war he rode into Beirut, steel-helmeted, planted in a half track. His appetite was massive. He ate five steaks for breakfast. His maw looked as if it could devour continents. Certainly there was room for us.

Nevertheless the bleeding hearts began to organise. Advertisements appeared in the newspapers. They were headlined "ENOUGH!", signed first by a hundred, then five hundred, then over a thousand people. Women in Jerusalem demonstrated against the war. Men passing by spat, calling them whores. Anat attended and said it was quite educational. I did not doubt that for a moment. As I could not travel on the Sabbath, she had to represent me at the massed demos in Tel Aviv. Vicariously, through her eyes, I lived the protest of the shocked, bewildered liberals. A hundred thousand of them came out of their holes, all asking the same question: Was this the Israel their fathers had founded? I checked my atlas. The answer was Yes.

Eventually we became anaesthetised. We got so we could hardly recognise the coming of daylight, let alone the twilight of idols. The two-day war stretched to five weeks, to seven, to nine, every day becoming fiercer. Beirut was bombed again and again. New army catch-phrases were unveiled: "light precipitation (of fire) on enemy targets" received my first prize. The neighbours came round collecting goodies for the troops at the front. I gave them a hundred-gram tin of Telma humus and felt a hundred-gram betrayal of my principles. I salved my conscience by writing devastating critiques of the television news coverage. But nobody cared. The television was fair game. The liberals considered it an arm of government deception. Government fans believed it was run by the Fatah.

And the lies ... the lies ... Even the Palestinians welcome us as liberators ... Tales of mass civilian deaths are foreign media falsehoods ... they invented the burnt children, the so-called bombed hospitals, the charcoaled corpses of women ... So consistent was the mind blitz we hesitated to register the final icing on the cake of victory: the massacre by the Christian Phalange at the Palestinian Sabra and Chatilla refugee camps under cover of our own paratroopers. Throats cut, the dead mutilated, mangled fodder for the nine o'clock news. Eventually the earth shook, but at the time - what else had we expected?

Certain memories linger: the booming voice of the General ... the civilian buses dropping soldiers at corners ... the faces of the returning, the halo of wonder at being spared the inferno ... the lone billboard youth, who dared what I hadn't, parading alone in the cool midnight air outside Prime Minister Begin's residence. A lone, rambling scrawl disturbing bourgeois Rehavia: "Are the dead our only testimony? Shall we slay and inherit too? Speak to the bereaved mothers, Begin." Weeks later he would be joined by others, forming a constant vigil on the pavement, flourishing the growing casualty figures: 501 ... 506 ... 545 ... Until the PM himself, hero of past struggles, succumbed to a deep melancholy. He did not shave for months, and locked himself in his bedroom, and would come out for no one. His written resignation was carried out of his hide-out, like a smuggled note from She'ol ...

Yes, these are odd times.

One night, in bed, Anat turned to me quietly and said: "I have to tell you, Joe, I have become quite sure there is no God out there."

It sounded a reasonable comment at that pass. "Nevertheless," I said, "I shall continue looking. There might be a cash prize."

Slowly, painstakingly, we rebuilt our neutrality. I dusted the glass shards off my fence. I resumed the purchase of our groceries. I made my peace with the video-cassette collection, immersed myself in *Smiley's People.* Came the time I could even watch the news without twitching. The drug in my veins ran clear. Until my ill-starred escape from Reserves duty, Moishe-Ganef and the Edenvale Hotel. Now with terrorism rife, and the killer hattie, general and private angsts had recombined. Genetic regression, The Fear again, Joe.

What are you going to do about it?

15

Nahum Lauterman! You two-faced chiseller! Let me through, I'll eat his gizzard!

As the Sabbath waned I cast longer glances at the forbidden telephone. When the sky was suitably dark and God could no longer sue me for breach of contract I tried to phone the miscreant at home. Lauterman, did you set me up, shithead? And who put you up to this? But his wife answered, saying he was in Tel Aviv, at a party at his publisher's home. Nahum had written this book, exposing the settler movement, which had been translated into Italian. "He's leaving for Cairo in the morning," she added. "He's going to interview President Mubarak." Isn't that dandy. The man throws me to Kazaz, without a qualm, and shuttles off to Abdin Palace.

She gave me the number of the publisher, Yigal Zayit. I dialled. It was bedlam out there. The music thumping, the bleary voice of Yigal's common-law amour, Aliza. "Teahouse of the August moon," she announced, although it was April 30th. I asked whether Nahum Lauterman was there. She dithered, then put him on.

"You bastard!' I shouted. "What have you done to me?"

"I haven't a clue," he said. His mentis sounded compos, if a little tight.

"I have got to see you," I said.

"Come to Cairo," he offered, "it's forty dollars by Egged bus. You get a two-day visa at the border. Did you imagine us ever being able to say that? It would be the millennium, if we hadn't made the Peace into even more War than before."

He said he would be gone for ten days. My Fear could not wait that long. It was eight-fifteen p.m. "I'm coming up there," I said, "give me the address and don't dare to move."

"Come, come," he agreed, "don't bother to bring anything. The ordnance here is A-OK."

I informed Anat of my movements, as per her requirement of notice. "I'll be back tonight," I promised. "I'll take the late taxi." She nodded warily, from the depths of García Márquez, a slim volume, entitled *In Evil Hour*. Supportive suffering, or just waiting for the last straw? I grabbed my wallet and scarpered. After all, what can happen in Tel Aviv, except an overdose of cocaine?

I joined the service taxi at the corner of Lunz. It filled up rapidly and shot on its way. Past Motsa a religious passenger asked the driver what he thought of the uncovered Jewish underground. "Jews are always underground," the driver said, "whatever you do for them, they think they're being cheated. They are always plotting and scheming. Give them a finger, they'll take the whole hand. Withdraw the finger, they'll scream blue murder and have you done for discrimination."

"No," said another religious passenger, a quiet bearded man in the back corner seat, "they were good fellows, who took the wrong path. They were desperate to defend their families."

"But you must obey the law!" said a fat lady divided from him by a nebisch who had already annoyed the driver by offering him a virtually decomposed banknote fastened by paper tape. "What's this?" asked the driver. "It's the national currency." Everyone guffawed loudly.

"That's true," said the religious passenger, nodding sagely, "the law should be obeyed." His furrowed forehead seemed to indicate it was an act of supreme self-discipline to comply with the prohibition of homicide.

"The Jews are never satisfied," the driver returned to his theme, "pretty soon they'll discover this isn't the promised land after all, and we'll all go and make trouble elsewhere."

"How can you say that?' squawked the fat lady. "What

about the Bible and so on?"

The driver tilted his head blithely, consigning with a nonchalant shrug our entire history out of the window.

The party was in full swing when I arrived at about ten-fifteen. It was a humid Tel Aviv night, but the air conditioning delocalised the proceedings. We might have been anywhere, playing High Society. On second thoughts, only in Our Homeland. Aliza opened the door for me, her brown thatch cocked to one side, her cleavage revealed in all its grandeur. She is a "public relations consultant", and is on the job around the clock. I answered her warm hug with minimum force and was ushered into a room full of people who were famous merely for being themselves. Everybody who was nobody was there. Yosske Z—, the purged head of Television, Zalman D—, his ex-head of programmes. Tikhon, who used to read out the Biblical verse at the close of each day's transmission. Machuko, a drug pedlar who used to daub canvas. Sylcia R—, "the Tits of the nation". Shish Kebab, the right-wing humorist. Several models, lady psychoanalysts, proprietresses of health-food chains. A man whose name I forget, who always bored people's pants off, telling them how he had slashed his wrists over Lebanon. There was generally one sultry beauty draped over his left scar, another over his right. Mine host, Yigal Zayit, lumbered over on seeing me, deserting a film director whose latest social conscience drama had just been hung, drawn and eviscerated in the national press.

"Joe! Now this is an occasion! We've hardly seen you since the turn of the decade!"

"A gypsy woman told me to avoid the '80s," I replied, "she gave me an even chance for the '90s."

"No, you're a Tel Aviv hater," he said, "you can't tear yourself away from the ghetto. Name your grief."

"Johnnie Walker on the rocks," I said. When all is lost there is no substitute.

The vile Tikhon ambled up to me, shaky on his pins, which were encased in motorcylce boots. His grey hair wobbled over a grey face that might have seen the Messiah once and then lost interest. He pointed a finger.

"Do you know what this man wrote about me?" he asked Yigal, rhetorically. "He said I have 'a voice with the awesome authority of a retired customs inspector'."

"Our Joe is a wordsmith and no mistake," said Yigal. "Why don't you write a me a book, Dekel? Something like the old burlesques you used to do. I never understood why you stopped that."

"You cannot burlesque a burlesque," I said, "reality had me on the canvas."

"One day I will kill you," said Tikhon, sadly, "as sure as my name's God Almighty. Brimstone will strike you, when you least expect it."

"That should at least keep me awake."

Yigal handed me my drink. "Book your blood feuds now," he said, "we pass out the weapons at dawn." A luscious brunette tugged Tikhon away, gnawing at his ear. He vanished among his admirers.

"If you're looking for Lauterman," suggested Yigal, "he's in that room, behind the door where the blonde is standing. If you can't get into the room, try getting into the blonde. This is the night anything goes."

I made my way to the door, squeezing past rounded elbows, dazzling white blouses and suits. For some time now the Beautiful People have been garbing themselves in pure albescence. It has got so one has to wear sunglasses indoors at gatherings of liberal souls. I passed by a couch in which the Iron General was being psychoanalysed in his absence: "The urge to gluttony, to consumption of one's enemies, a strong atavistic streak there . . ." The ex-head of TV bemoaned the loss of the times when he decided what people should think. "Did you hear B—'s latest? The man has bought *The Love Boat*. There's no limit to their crassness . . ."

Flanking the blonde, I found myself in the bathroom. Lauterman was indeed in there. He was perched on the rim of the bath, while a tall army captain leaned his back against the tiled wall. They were sharing a pleasingly large joint. Lauterman passed it to me.

"You know Pasha?" he said to me, nodding at the captain. The captain inclined his dark curls. The stuff was extremely strong, causing the bathroom cabinets, bath and towels to reel about my head. "Jounieh Red," explained Nahum, "the latest consignment. Courtesy of the Christian Phalange. You know what they call it up there? Sabra and Chatilla. A small dose liquidates you completely."

At some indeterminate stage the captain left. I was left alone in the *salle-de-bain* with Nahum. Should I drown him in the toilet? Garrotte him with Yigal Zayit's towels? I was rapidly reaching a point where this would not be feasible. Instead I said: "Nahum, what's going on?"

"I'm off tomorrow to interview the President of Egypt," he said. "Mister President, what are the prospects for peace after the next war? Your predecessor, Sadat, kissed Menahem Begin and got shot. Who are you planning to kiss?"

"I know, I know," I said impatiently, "and the country shall be calm forty years. You know what I'm after, Sami Khatib, Sha'abani and Major Kazaz."

"Sounds like a new pop group," he said. "Very cool. They will probably sweep the charts."

"What really gets me is the casual way you picked me up. That must have been planned, surely. And like a sucker I bit the apple. I think I'll vomit up the worm."

"All right, Joe," he said, "just one minute." He lifted his hand to stop my flow. Parking the joint on the soap dish he turned on both bath taps, at their full gushing volume. "A trick from the movies," he said in my ear, "but it works, they tell me. Please undress."

"Pardon me?"

"This is not love, comrade. Not even sisterly affection. Things sometimes get into clothes, you know. Creepie crawlies, crabs, Meisinger vermin."

"I shall scream loudly," I warned, "at any attempted invasion of my precious orifices." I stripped to my pants. The bastard even looked in them, like the training camp MO. Then he opened the door and shouted: "Aliza!" She floated up. He passed her my togs. "Keep those safe for ten minutes, angel." She bore them off, immune to surprise at any of her guests' peccadilloes. The lunatic checked my hair, like a chimpanzee mother, and gave the room a quick once over. "We'll have to trust the State keeps no tabs on the Zayit latrine action," he said, "I check my own clothes regularly."

"I'm sure the Department of Health will be ecstatic to hear that," I said, "but what has this to do with Mount Sinai?"

He reclaimed his joint, sat back on the bath rim and took a deep drag, looking very sad and thoughtful. "Joe, I'll tell you: five years ago, despite everything, I had hopes for my kids' future. Today I'm not sure at all. We thought the Egyptian peace was a strategic breakthrough. But it might turn out to be a tactical ripple. Three steps forward and four steps back. Lebanon, and now the settler underground. And we ain't seen nothing yet. This particular group's been an open secret. It's only the poor proles who are shocked. I had most of those people tagged long ago. Your Kazaz is a new one for me, though. It just shows, you live and learn. Every day a fresh surprise."

"You sent me up to Balata as bait," I said, "and all that talk about not getting involved. About not fucking with you know who. I don't like being lied to, and made a puppet, even by an old friend."

He looked genuinely pained. "You told me you were being watched, Joe. You told me we might be under surveillance. What else could I do, except play let's pretend? I tried to steer you away from The Family. The Zaki angle was tempting, I'll admit. I thought the café klatsch might give you a lead. I'm sorry that it misfired."

"You're sorry? What about me, incognito in Kazaz's dungeons?"

He passed me the joint. "Yes, that was bizarre. I'll admit it has me in the dark. This Kazaz must have been a Meisinger stooge, but how does he tie in with the underground? I think you'll find it's just another example of *snafu*, my son, the left hand knoweth not what the right, etcetera. Still, something must have happened at Balata to shake your Kazaz out of the trees. What was it, Joe? What did they tell you, Sha'abani and Sami Khatib?"

All this with running water and dope. The towel racks were doing the shimmy. "Oh, no, sweet pea," I said, "no more freebies. I'll trade you, Nahum, secrets for secrets. Show me yours and I'll show you mine." I reached down and stuck the plug in the bath. It began filling in, wreathing the room with steam. He stirred but I stood guard on the taps. "*Après nous la deluge.*"

"My life in your hands or Yigal Zayit's floors," he said, "you do set tough moral choices." He took the joint and dragged deeply again. "There is a crucial struggle within the Intelligence Family," he said, "it could lead to civil war. Sides are being taken. Positions laagered. Weapons stockpiled in the waggons. I am involved peripherally. The Gingi, I understand, played a more central role, but I do not know the flesh and blood of it. As is the wont of such affairs, the least known, etcetera. But Meisinger is a common enemy. The whole thrust of State policy is at stake. The atmosphere is becoming heavy. Licences to kill might be disbursed in vending machines before this is all over. Sorry about the melodrama. Unavoidable. Your turn now, maestro."

"Sami Khatib passed me a note," I said, "he warned me we were watched and then ate it, without salt. It said the Gingi had sent an envelope to an ex-priest in Tiberias. Some Frenchman called Father Parry. End of earth-shattering revelation."

"For God's sake, Joe! When will those people learn? He wrote all this down right there in the café? You're joking! In our days, the microchip age? Come on, man! Stick a doodah in any room fitting, ceiling or wall and presto – a thousand hours' sound and vision! You can read a grocery list these days from a satellite! What were those arse-holes up to? That man is dead, baby. He was as good as buried the moment that note was written. Fucking shit. The hell with all this." He lunged and turned the taps off. Music thumped again clear through the walls. The buzz of prattle. The chink of glasses. The shrill giggling of nameless whoopie. Somebody banged desperately on the door.

"That ends tonight's transmissions," said Nahum. "You can call Tikhon in for his spiel." He flushed the roach down the toilet, then stopped short: "Oh, shit, your clothes, Joe ..." I threw a bathtowel about me. We exited brusquely, leaving our hapless successor to face the fumes of our mischief, the full head of our steam.

"Gangway! Gangway!" Nahum cried. "Man in search of his clothes!"

There was a burst of clapping. I acknowledged the claque.

A voice crooned: "I like a man with good knees."

"Blasphemy. Mockery of The Name," mumbled Tikhon, from out of a press of thighs. Aliza came forward with my clothing and planted me a lingering kiss. "Man overboard!" shouted Yigal Zayit. Someone hit me on the back with a beanbag.

"I like a man with hair on his chest," said the crooning voice as I enrobed.

I stood outside in the street with Nahum, in the humid coastal air. I felt like a pickled cucumber that had just been stuffed into a can full of brine. Nahum offered to drive me to the Central Station. We drove in silence through the city. Neon lights of pizzerias, blintzes parlours, ice cream shops, open cafés. Calm normality. A life worth dying for? Even more, worth living. "I'll be back from Cairo on the tenth," Nahum said, "we can have another chinwag then."

He dropped me on the corner of the greasy falafel kiosk by which a scrum of hopefuls whose application to become a queue had been turned down by their own psyches waited for the Jerusalem service taxi. Fed up with his surveillance paranoia I poked my head back in his window.

"What about Moishe-Ganef?" I shouted.

He gave me his most painful grin.

"You know what Vice-President Bush said about Central America? 'The opera isn't over until the fat lady sings.'"

He drove off, leaving me to the inevitable jostle with a cross section of my people.

16

The world as a marionette theatre. And all the men and women in it ... etcetera. You thought you could live a normal life, Joe, free from strings? An ordinary subscriber to the human follies? Take a look, Pinnochio, at the back of the stage. You had a peek before, once, at one of the blueprints, The Document that haunts your daydreams. And now the terror of Lauterman's "doodahs", hi-technology in the service of shadows, broadcasting for a thousand hours ...

In *The Conversation*, a film by Francis Coppola, a surveillance expert who believes he is bugged tears his own apartment to shreds. He chops down the plastering, rips up the floorboards, and sits dolefully in the ruins, tooting upon his sax. I have no sax, nor floorboards to rip up, and assaulting the walls could bring the block down. This is a 1950s development, all reinforced cardboard. Nevertheless, I drove Anat mad, rapping with my knuckles for hollow spots, screwing out sockets, lightbulbs. Examining my buttons with a magnifying glass, biting the zips of my trousers. Emptying jars in the fridge, the cupboards, scraping through old tobacco tins. One can't believe the junk one accumulates, the countless nests for electronic vipers.

And the worst problem, being unable to confide Lauterman's confessions to Anat. The one person in the world who knew most of my secrets, and who could, I hope, be trusted to keep them. She even knew of my stash of pornographic magazines, though I kept shifting their location. Now our precarious balance was risked by the revelation of my descent into quicksand. I could imagine her answering the usual polite queries at the Municipality: "How's Joe these days?" "Much as normal. I left him this morning on the living room floor, taking the television apart." By the third day I had progressed to the video-cassette recorder, sweating gobs of salt on the relays. *Sacre du printemps*! How can one tell if any of these units has been doodah'd?

I scanned the press daily for tell-tale signs of the next stage, or Lauterman's prophecies. Never, as I have said, a happy chore: "2000 NEW MEMBERS FOR ARMY ASSOCIATION OF CRIPPLES SINCE THE LEBANON WAR." "HAPPIEST INDEPENDENCE DAY EVER FORECAST." "NO PLAN FOR BEGIN'S EXIT FROM FLAT; HIS SITUATION FINE, RELATIVES SAY." Everywhere the nudging tale of the settler underground, whose names have not yet been published. Their faces in photographs are concealed by black strips, like permanent Viewmaster glasses. The hacks reveal the nub of the plan, not merely the bus bombing, but, again, the blowing up of the two grand mosques on the Temple Mount. A queue had obviously formed for this choice project, for which the Sons of Judah had already been busted. The accused gave interviews in their detention cells, saying the government was soft on the Arabs. Open supporters rallied outside the prison, wishing them strength and courage. A deputy speaker of the parliament called them "the cream of our God-fearing elements". A cabinet minister said the maiming of the Arab Mayors was not a true crime. The victims, as sworn enemies of the State, did not count as indiscriminate targets.

What I like about my compatriots is their charm. It never ceases to amaze me.

Oddly enough this perusal calmed me. I was not alone in my bubble. We were all together, in the disturbed ward, floating off to perdition. The original ship of fools. Captain, crew and passengers zapped with opium. They thought they were on a Caribbean cruise. In fact the iceberg had been struck long ago, and all the lifeboats were in the hockshop.

I reconnected the television and the video and settled down

to consider my options. I reran an episode of *Smiley's People* and studied Alec Guinness. He was trapping Karla, the head of Moscow Centre, by exploiting his only human weakness, his love for an illegitimate daughter in a nuthouse in the Swiss Alps. What conceivable weakness could trap Meisinger, except his obsession with his own anus? There was, apparently, no Meisinger wife, no Meisinger offspring to kidnap. Just a calculating machine, with an ambition that was shadowy and disturbing. Only one shimmery point where he appeared no wiser than I was: Moishe-Ganef, dead or alive, an unknown bounty to be claimed. And Father Parry, Gingi, Lauterman? Who else was involved, and on which side? Should I follow the clues supplied so far, or withdraw? What would Smiley have done?

Anat returned from work, and I tried on her my new Alec Guinness look of owlish sagacity. She suggested an aspirin, and we sat down to a repast of fried schnitzel. "Do you wish to unload?" she inquired, probing. I shook my head, pointing at the walls. She sighed, perhaps she was reaching saturation point, but this would not be resolved now, as Sabbath atavisms again loomed. And, immediately following, the Special Festival of Remembrance and Independence Day ... Sirens in the morning, for the day of melancholy, sirens at night, for rejoicing. Sunday night, Independence Day eve, there would be street crowds, noise, ersatz joy. Monday, Independence Day itself, Anat was booked for an exhibition of dead soldiers' works of art. Future Picassos, Moores, Chagalls, no one would ever know. I refuse to accompany her on these nightmares. Even discussion of same is banned in the home. Independence Day at the Dekel fortress is usually video-cassette day *par excellence.*

This year, however, home being no sanctuary, I joined Anat for a Sunday evening's amble into the fierce mêlèe. She has a yen for studying native habits. I let it all wash over my ears. Fireworks from the roof of the Chief Rabbinate buildings. Loudspeakers on every corner blasting the homeland tunes Lebanon had so warped for me. The masses wielding their little plastic hammers, clicking their squeaky folding flanges on people's bare craniums. Anthropologists will one day win Nobel prizes reviewing this weird secular ritual. The anonymous Italian who invented this horror must have died laughing on his way to the bank. It sounded like a hundred thousand grandmothers, knitting. Was this the dream of the pioneers of Zionism? I would not be surprised.

The cacophony seemed to provide the ideal setting to put Anat in the picture. Let the surveillance experts unscramble this one. I put my mouth to her ear: "Big trouble!" I shouted, "Lauterman is a shtinker. Civil war in The Family, he claims. They all seem to want something from me, but I can't work out what . . ." I ground the instep of a thirteen-year-old who reached his plastic tool out to bop me. Taken nevertheless in ambush by an old crone who slugged me from her wheelchair, clickety-click, in the groin. "Happy holiday! Happy holiday!" she cackled, "till a hundred and twenty!" Anat dragged me out of range, as I bellowed at her the gist of Nahum's bathroom disclosures. Explaining my surveillance paranoia, the involvement I could not seem to avoid. She shouted back at me, but a hitherto dormant loudspeaker opened up above us. "Anemones! Beautiful and Red!" Shoshana Damari yodelled at my eardrum twenty years ago. Let's go, Joe, Anat mouthed at me. We elbowed through, ducking up a side street. The crowd thinning out in the direction of the Bezalel Art School. Normally we might think of taking refuge there, at the café, among our own, ruminating over an eggplant salad about Trotsky's anti-Zionist foresight, or the sexual antics of yesterday's comrades, who was presently fucking with whom. "You know Dalia spends half her time now with Yossi – but don't let Shlomo know I told you . . ."

Not tonight. We walked home again, away from the echoes of good cheer. Battening the hatches, we switched on the late night news. The interval for refreshments was over. I always thought the TV news was personally aimed at me, but this was ridiculous. There was only one item – apart from communal joy bursting at the seams nationwide – report of a grisly murder in Tiberias: ex-priest found shot on the lakeshore. One Lucien Parry, a local resident, who lived at the Ecumenical Hospice. A tourist couple found him, mid-afternoon, shot twice, once through each eye. The police could suggest no motive as yet, but it was known he had contacts with Arab villagers, whom he helped with social problems. Another victim for Remembrance Day, albeit an expendable goy. The announcer faded, and Tikhon's successor's voice welled up, reading the Biblical verse of the day: "... Yet they are thy people and thine inheritance, which thou broughtest out by thy mighty power and by thy stretched out arm."

Return of The Fear, redoubled, with goose pimples. We spent a restless night, Anat and I. She humouring my panic, as I commuted between bed and bathroom. The dead priest, like a blinded muzhik from *Boris Godunov*, gibbering blindly from the toilet seat. Another open-ended death, like Moishe-Ganef and the Gingi "Bronson"? My cup of blood runneth over ... In my delirium, I almost picked up the phone to call the Egyptian Presidential Palace: "Excellency Mubarak? Give me Nahum Lauterman ... Not in? Tell him I said Kiss my ass."

This could not go on. In the morning, a wreck, I contemplated emigration to Russia. "I shall give them the layout of the Security College's drains," I told Anat, "they will give me the Order of Lenin, and a guarded dacha at Petroslovosk."

"Just relax, take an Atarax and stay horizontal," she said, "abstain from the media." And she rushed out, to fulfil her obligation to show dead soldiers' paintings. "Show them their soiled knickers too!" I shouted. "Their napalmed feet! Their skin made into memorial lampshades!"

I was rapidly losing my mind. I was in trouble, and I would not get out of it by sitting watching my toenails grow. I had to commit some act of volition again, however ill advised. Dead muzhik Parry or not. At least I could exhibit a moving target, rather than a sitting duck for my "friends". I informed Anat, when she returned, of my turn of mind.

She did not mention the ghoulfest, but she said: "Enough is enough, Joe. *Basta.*"

"A man's got to do what a man's got to do."

"Well, it's your day to do the laundry."

"I'm going to go," I said.

"I have my life," she said, "I have a way of living in this land. We agreed on the *modus operandi*, remember? The distant look. The calm *sang-froid*."

"Everyone here used to have a dream," I said, "but you can't live on sleeping pills for ever."

We had no need to articulate this dialogue further. It was embedded in our karma. – Joe, for years these people tried to make us in their image. Then we broke loose and declared our Independence. You watch *Dallas* and pursue your atavisms, I enjoy what there is to enjoy of the crazy half of our populace. – (I remember a friend's explanation of our country to our hosts in Camden Town: Israel is composed of fifty percent imbeciles and fifty percent crazy eccentrics. But in order to enjoy the fifty percent who are crazy you have to pass through the fifty percent who are imbeciles.) Anat goes straight to the crazy half, blanking out the other category. I try to ignore both. At my peril. A road assuredly doomed to failure. And now I had a third category after me, not so easy to ignore – the psychopathic guardians of the asylum, my mean civilian's sewer cleaners ...

We sat, my love and I, locked in telepathic combat over cold coffee, pretzel crumbs and empty yoghourt containers, marooned in an apartment stripped metaphorically to its girders by my suspicious eyes.

Finally she said: "You're a stubborn bastard. I'm coming with you, then. Somebody has to keep a grasp on reality out there, and it'll be no fun for me here, biting fingernails, waiting for the other shoe to drop. I can take four-five days off from the office, no bother. The fuckers owe me at least six months' furlough. And there are sites up that way I haven't visited in a while. I can tour while you wrestle your psyche."

Feeling the rise of a new anxiety, nevertheless I beamed with confidence. "I'll pack the sleeping bags," I said, "and the Swiss army knife."

Yes. And don't forget the nuclear warhead.

"You're sure you want to do this?" She tried a last salvo.

"I am sure of nothing," I gave her my patter, "except the Lord Blessed Be He." And even He was acting strange lately. As perhaps He always did ...

Ah, brave Joe Dekel. Hit him in the puss once, he comes

back for more. Hit him twice and he becomes even more reckless. I love such characters in the movies. In the real world they are soon fruitjuice.

Nevertheless – the one lead that we had ... What choice was there, except putrefaction?

Bright and early the next day we saddled up "Alexander" and puttered off north, towards Tiberias.

THE NORTH

17

I hate the North. It used to be Balmsville, the escape route from the South, West and East. Wooded mountains, pine and olive trees, green glens rushing into Southern Lebanon. Aye, Lebanon! There's the rub! The War for the Peace of Galilee ... the inhabitants here the supposed beneficiaries of that whole bloody *schmeer*. Their children no longer running to shelters, risking death by Katyusha rockets. Instead they are dying, in uniform, Up There, bazookaed by Shi'ite zealots ...

Nevertheless, the Kinneret, the soft ripples of Lake Tiberias. The looming mountain range beyond. Fishermen in boats, out in the haze, listening for a trout's heartbeat. The Egged buses carrying Christian pilgrims in the footsteps of their Saviour. Pope Paul VI kissed a stone here once, up on the Mount of Beatitudes. The town itself was founded by Herod Antippas (AD 20), and named after the Roman Emperor Tiberius (Herod was no mean toady). Later, after the fall of Jerusalem, it became the main Jewish centre of learning. Both the Mishna and Talmud Yerushalmi were completed here. My turn to nuzzle a stone. Still later, the town declined, and the fleas and the mud took over. The Crusaders, in the twelfth century, reduced it to rubble. The Turks rebuilt it, and so on. In 1948 the Jews chased the Moslems out, and Tiberias was virtually a border town till '67, with the Syrian army on the east bank of the lake, making the whole populace nervous. Now the mountains opposite are in Israeli hands everyone out here feels safe, except Joe Dekel, poking his nose into other people's business.

We sat on the edge of the lake at Abu Yusuf's and ate roast carp with chips and salad. Carp, of course, is a serious business. One slip with the bones and you're done for. Anat cautiously but happily munching by my side. It is good to have one's loved one happily munching by one's side. Selah. It made me feel that, all evidence to the contrary, the forces of life were still stirring. A marked contrast to our inquiries regarding ex-father Parry, which were as stone dead as the carp, and just as spiky. It is not easy to play detective in the country of the paranoids. Father Parry? Never heard of the hombre! And who are you, gringo?! Tiberias is chock full of the strong silent type, in bus stations, grocery stores, cafés. It's due to their backward movie diet. All Steve McQueen and John Wayne, not to speak of Clint Eastwood and Giulliano Gemma. The French ex-priest seemed to have failed to register in the collective consciousness of this one-horse town. Even the horse had never heard of him, until the body was found. "The missionary? The one they say was done in by the Arabs? Which newspaper are you from?" The only firm tick against his name was in the mind of a Mrs A.F.Treen. She was the major domo at the Ecumenical Hospice, or at least the only person there who was not asleep in the early afternoon when we called. Mad dogs and Scotswomen, or rather two cats, dozing on deckchairs, under palm trees, the azure lake in background. Anat, with her talent for communication, teased the red hot manna from the lady, as she bent stiffly, shaking her head, massacring greenfly by aerosol. Oh yes, the poor man, such a quiet gentleman. He once told her he had served in Africa. She thought it was Ruanda, or the Belgian Congo. Without, no doubt, the aid of Katharine Hepburn. He collected wild flowers, she revealed to Anat, and pressed them between the pages of several old volumes of the *Works of Saint Augustine*. She showed us his room, which had not been rented out yet. Spartan quarters - a bed, two chairs, a teakettle, washbasin and three bookshelves, empty as breadbins at Passover in the house of the Chief Rabbi. "The policeman took the books and clothes and other effects," she told Anat, "Inspector Halabi. Such a nice man." It was unclear whether she was referring at that point to the local filth or the deceased. As to Parry's other possible per or subversions, she was not forthcoming. "He used to go out, with a rucksack, now and then," she said, "but nobody visited him here. This place was his sanctuary." There was a hymn, delicately etched on a framed card above the washbasin:

My God, I thank thee who has made
the earth so bright.
So full of splendour and of joy,
beauty and light.
So many gentle thoughts and deeds,
circling us round.
That in the darkest spot of earth,
some love is found.

"Perhaps we should just boldly march up to this Inspector Halabi," Anat said, laying a tail on a side plate. "Play the straight journalist gambit again. Say we're doing a feature for *Woman* magazine: 'It's all In a Day's Work For Halabi.' Who knows, we might even sneak a look at the dreaded wildflower collection."

"It's an idea," I admitted, "a pretty bad one, but technically it qualifies. Do you think we might get some sort of award," I added, picking fishbones carefully out of my lip, "a plaque from the Association of Private Investigators, such as 'Worst Operatives of the Century'?"

"It's a distinct possibility," she agreed.

We were completely stymied.

We returned in silence to our hostel. It was a small tower overlooking the water, which used to be a mosque, but was rebuilt from its ruin to cater for new nirvanas. We had a tiny room, with a tiny balcony from which we could gaze out in hubris towards the Recovered Golan. There was even the hint of a breeze, the night. If the sky had not been cast over with Valley haze it would have been studded with stars.

"This could be a great country," I commented, "if only we could clear the people away."

"Well," Anat said, "you've made a start with the Arabs. Now you just have to push out the Jews."

And whatever next, I wondered. Vietnamese boat people? Filipino maids? Jules Verne's Selenites?

We adjourned to bed. There was not much choice. The room was five feet wide. The bed, about four. The hostel's unspoken commandment: Thou shalt be intimate. No estranged couples need apply here. The bed was creaky, and sagged in the middle. Inevitably, we met. The neighbouring youth centre reverberated to the doop-doop-doop of modern good times. Sleep was obviously not on offer. But Anat, as is her wont, drifted off. I watched her damp profile, trying to avoid memories. But it occurred to me, apropos of nothing, that she had done part of her army service in this dead end of a town. We had not met then, though our paths must have crossed invisibly in the local Soldiers' Hostel. She had been a clerk there, while I passed to and fro, from the far North to the South of the country, in the service of the proto-Gingis ... A dour and grey place it was, that Hostel, and so dimly lit no wonder we never made contact ... Lysol, choked off screams, and murmurs ... Commando dinghies that passed in the night ... We never talk much of those days now. Our life together is blessed with so many silences. Too many subjects are too painful to contemplate. The erratic present, the ominous future, the past, with its naïve conformities ... Anat's parents never wanted her to go into the army. They wanted her to pretend to be ultra-religious, and take advantage of the orthodox girls' exemption ... Polish gentlefolk of the old school, they feared she might meet and be deflowered by someone like me in the Forces. In the event it was a chunky combat grunt named Amiel, who was an early bird of the New Left movement. It was probably he who initiated her into the dissident ranks, though she might already have been reading Lenin's *What Is To Be Done?* or Isaac Deutscher under the bedclothes ... No, still no dreams manifested here ... Just my love's nose, emitting low whistles ... I finally sunk, drowned in my own perspiration ...

Dreams? We should be so lucky.

18

Sweat, valley heat, mosquitoes. Humphrey Bogart never had it so bad. Even in spring, the hot air hangs around the Beit Shean basin, wondering what to do next. Finally it settles on engulfing the populace with a hundred square miles of schvitzbath. I left Anat soaking in the bed in the morning and ambled off down the road into town. Brooding alone among the loud street vendors, the holiday trippers dribbling ice cream. Dutch tourists, looking for the Rambam's tomb. Rumanians, breathing the air of Freedom. Tel Avivians, slumming among the less fortunate. All, no doubt, Meisingers in disguise, or whoever else has joined the show. Dekel-watchers growing fat on piecework. Who gives a fuck, anyhow? Perhaps it's all in the mind.

My excogitations were interrupted by someone waving and calling from a café terrace. "HEY, JOE!" Advertising my presence all the way to Safad and back. This, alas, was not a figment of my imagination, but my bearded brother-in-law Elisha, the rabid West Bank junker. "Joe!" he warned the shipping again. "What on earth are you doing here, sweetie?"

I joined the oaf. What else could I do? He might have bounded across the street and kissed me. The creature has never accepted what he calls my defection to the Red Evil. He thinks I am engaged in secret work among the heathen, a Trojan horse, bearing light into She'ol. "No, no," Elisha, I always tried to rile him, "to me Karl Marx is the new Isaiah."

His eyes would pop, the glare of Certain Faith trying to pin me in my place like a butterfly.

"Anat had a few days off," I said vaguely, "we thought we'd leave town for a while. A change of air. What brings you so far from the homestead?"

"You will have a coffee," he stated, snapping his fingers for the Arab waiter. He put me in mind of the racist post-'67 occupation joke: God calls the founders of the great faiths to his house and they sit around in armchairs - Abraham, Moses, Jesus, Buddha, Confucius. Suddenly they realise someone is missing. "Where's Mohammed?" asks Buddha. God claps his hand to his forehead. "Of course," he says, "I forgot. Mohammed! Bring six coffees right away!"

"We're starting a new settlement," Elisha said, "Naveh Anva, on the Golan. It's a stunning location. Nehama isn't with me," he added solemnly, "our poor Muki is down with the mumps. I had to come up. I'm a delegate. Why don't you join us for the inauguration? It's Sunday, at twelve noon. Everyone will be there. We've even been promised an air force flypast at the peroration."

Bombing and straffing, I should hope. A wee dose of what they call "friendly fire".

The waiter brought us the coffees. I thanked him. Elisha threw me his most suspicious look. Then he went into his spiel. He never gives up on me, because of my accursed misunderstood hattie.

"You know, you continually misjudge us, you leftists in the arts and media. You always exaggerate, making us out to be morons. You of all people should know better. We are just ordinary Jews worshipping the Lord in our way, the way the Halacha tells us to."

"I know." I don't need this, but he makes my teeth jangle. "Blowing legs off Arabs. Bombs on buses. I looked it up. It's on page nine."

"That's not worthy of you," he gave me the treatment, "you know I'm against all that. They misread the teachings. It's been known to happen. But people get driven by despair. If only the government protected us properly from armed attacks and stone throwing ... Our families not safe at night ... I know you think we shouldn't be there ... Maybe we shouldn't be anywhere in our Homeland ... An observant Jew like you ... I must say I don't understand it. To be Jewish has always seemed to me simple. The Torah, the Land, the People. But we're not simpletons, we know life is more complex: we have a National government that supports us verbally, but is held in check by powerful forces – the Americans, the Russians, the United Nations. We can put no trust in those people. So there are hotheads among us who go too far. It's the circumstances that forced them to it."

"You blame society," I summed up, dryly, sipping my coffee and adjusting my sunglasses. There was a blonde at the sunlit end of the café who was not half bad.

"I'm not naïve," he leaned forward, his beard literally brushing the table, "I accept some of our boys did wrong, but this bus thing, it doesn't ring true at all. Jews as well as Arabs could have been killed, the innocent with the guilty. There are strong indications this was a provocation instigated by the Security Services. They wanted a watertight case, so they manufactured this attempt at a terrible crime. These accused men, I know them, they have wives and families. Do you think they have hearts of stone?"

"What about the PLO terrorists?" I persisted. *Schvantz.* "They have families too, if you've left them any, and that doesn't stop them at all. But don't tell me – it's the tainted Arab blood. I know. Shooting people in the eyes ..."

Tiberias. Thirty-three in the shade. I need none of this, truly. But he just shook his head. Joe, Joe. What can one do with the damned? "If you're still here Sabbath," he said, "I'm at the Hotel Motskin. If you're still one of us, vaguely. You really ought to join us for Sunday morning, for the journey Up There. Even you might see things with fresh eyes."

"I have done with fresh, Elisha," I told him, "I now take my ideologies canned."

This encounter really did for me. I walked the streets, chin on the ground, I have spent my life trying to avoid these drivel-fests. Why then do they seek me out? I returned to the hostel to find a message from Anat: "Gone down to the Quiet Beach." I exposed my ignorance to the somnambulant desk manager. He waved me vacantly in a northern direction.

At least she had left me "Alexander". I struck out north along the lakeside Gdud Barak Road. The heat was becoming truly excessive, matching the general social ambience. The waters though were blue and clear, dotted with people escaping the blast. The Lido Beach, first to loom on the right, appeared very slick and relaxing. The Quiet Beach, a little further on, was bedlam. Extended families were camped below signs proclaiming "Strictly No Bathing!" Radios blared under the skull and crossbones. Shrieks, bellows and splashes of heavy objects attempting to displace water. The thok-thok-thok of massed bat and ball playing drilled holes through my temples. Anat, of course, was in the thick of it, exchanging the catch and throw of an immense red beachball with a shaggy-haired dark-hued youth. He was hairy all over, like a doormat, but he had perfect white teeth. Anat is a sucker for people with perfect white teeth. I am my dentist's hope for a Nobel prize. He has been working on me for twelve years and hopes to publish the results in *The Lancet*. "Joe, meet Menahem!" Anat called cheerily. "Menahem, this is Joe!"

Not Doctor Livingstone, I presume. The lout pressed my hand wetly and shook droplets over me like a big friendly hound. "I'm going back in the water," Anat declared. "You two should get to know each other. Menahem is a police corporal," she added, throwing a towel at him, "he says he works with Inspector Halabi." So saying she leapt lithely into the drink.

"Don't drown," I riposted feebly.

The cop wiped himself with my love's towel and grinned, displaying the pride of his gnashers. How does she find them? Such rapport with humanity never fails to stun me utterly. "Let's get in the shade," the Doormat said earnestly, propelling me towards a parasol. He removed his uniform from a deckchair, making room for me, and sat at my feet on the gravel. Then he offered me a Marlboro and went through the ritual, inhaling half a cigarette in one deep draw.

"A very interesting girl," he commented, "you are a man who knows what's good for him. Anat tells me you're writing a book, about unsolved crimes, true-life murders, that sort of thing . . ." Oh my God. I shook a metaphorical fist at my adored, breaststroking blithely out there. Just wait till Starsky-cum-Hutch hits his office, his computer will soon blow that one. Unless, of course, the microchip has not hit this dump yet. The telegraph was installed only yesterday.

"Uh huh," I responded, turning my sunglasses nonchalantly to the sky.

"You'd think nothing happens in a town like this," he said, "but you would be quite wrong. If you knew what really happens here often you'd lay mines right round your bedroom."

"I use claymores, on the porch," I said, blasé. "It usually takes care of the heavy stuff."

"Yes, sir, a policeman's life can be boring," he said, "but you do get to feel the undertow." He looked out, as if expecting the bathers to be dragged under by killer whales. "We had the famous Albaz here, no kidding. He killed his wife and all his family. That was no picnic, I can tell you. They used fifty buckets to clear the blood. Under the surface, take it from me, people are savage beasts."

He that walketh with wise men shall be wise; but a companion of fools shall be destroyed. Proverbs, 13, verse 20. Doomed, I flowed with Anat's undertow.

"You had a strange incident here on Remembrance Day, didn't you?" Nonchalant, picking my nose. "A priest, wasn't it, shot in the eyes?"

"Excuse me," he said, "I'll be back in a minute." He padded off into the crowd, leaving me floundering. No one listens any more in this country. I sniffed my armpits. Not much worse than usual. I checked my pulse and removed my sunglasses to check the mote in my eye. My gaze fell on the Doormat's cast-off uniform. A stubby shape outlined his shirt pocket.

Is this a trap, Dekel? Do you smell cheese, or oxter pong? Sucker or not, one could not resist it. I drew out a leather ID folder. It was his police card all right. There was the mug shot: the shining molars, the doormat tuft bursting below. But there the story stopped dovetailing. No Corporal, no Menahem, no dice. The card was made out to a Detective-

Inspector Dahab, Amnon. Special Investigations Unit, Jerusalem. Goddamn his big black eyes, snaring Anat, giving me the rural hick gunoil. There was another card with the ID – a rather rare "TB Twenty". A pass to most military installations classified Top Secret and down. I ought to know, I carried one for three years.

Seek, and ye shall be found.

19

The lake, shimmering in the mid-day haze. The hills beyond melting. A silence, apart from the whine of my beach buggy. No one walked on the water.

"Fuck! Fuck! Fuck!" I protested. "And where did you get that red beachball?"

We were driving north, still following the shore, towards Tabgha, site of the Nazarene's most famous miracles: the loaves, the fishes, his guest appearance after rising from the dead. No escape, around here, from mythology. Anat had said: "I want to see the Cave of Job," which was also, for our sins, in the area.

"You're looking at it!" I replied, baring my gums, turning for the umpteenth time to my rearview mirror. "See anything yet? Cream Mercedeses? Pantechnicon trucks? Prison vans?"

"You're becoming hysterical, Joe," she said softly. "Nothing has happened yet."

Nothing?! She falls for a Doormat, who then turns out to be Lestrade of the Yard! "And a fucking TB Twenty! The bastard set that scene up perfectly. He's put pincers on our nerves and we have to pretend he's going to show us the Parry wild-flower collection!"

"He was certainly a smooth operator," said Anat, "and he seemed such a complete idiot."

"It's their stock in trade," I explained, impatiently, "it's all part of modern police training. They go to idiot school, and learn to merge with the crowd. At night they study nuclear physics."

The nerve of the guy. Padding back pretending he had seen a girl he knew in the throng. "You have to be quick around here," flashing his chompers, "or you might as well leave your pecker at home." Oh, if only his mohel had cut deeper! Circumcision, where is thy sting? Promising Anat, refreshed from her stint as a mermaid, to contact us to arrange a peek at Father Parry's file, "for your boyfriend's book. It will be a pleasure. Tomorrow. Tonight is special duty ..." I'll bet it is, spawn of Satan, bag of piss, Meisinger stooge ...

The Cave of Job was closed for renovation. The sun stood right above and hammered down, our heads serving as volunteer anvils. Anat dragged me to the Church of the Multiplication, enthusing over the mosaic floor. Herons, doves, lotuses, geese and mallards. Quack, quack. My pores shed hot salt water.

Taking pity on me, she did not insist on Capernaum. We drove back to our hostel hovel. As a further index of her generosity, she allowed me first go at the shower. I stood naked under a lukewarm drizzle, trying to piece together the potsherds of my psyche. Recapitulating the triumphs to date of Hercule Marlowe Holmes's campaign. Not much to show for anything so far. Three alleged dead bodies, none confirmed beyond doubt, except I suppose for Father Parry. One live hairy spook, with beachball. One journalist, hiding from my wrath in Cairo. One alleged message, or envelope, pressed in *Saint Augustine*? At any rate not in my grasp. One brother-in-law Elisha, rude to Arab waiters, accusing the SHABAK of railroading his pals. And beyond the private mess - the communal salad: the underground, the elections, inflation. The West Bank, Lebanon and Peace for Galilee. This country is like a jigsaw puzzle slapped together from a heap of other jigsaws. A saboteur at the factory mixed up the sets. Soap was getting in my eyes.

Après shower - siesta. We massacred mosquitoes, then hit the streets at twilight. Not feeling up to risking carp again, we took an oriental meal in town. There was no sign of Anat's new boyfriend, though his clones seemed to be on every street corner. We talked restrainedly of shish-kebabs past. Then we walked on the shore and watched the water. It was placid and black and dotted with tiny twinkles. A fishing boat passed surreptitiously. Soft ripples. An age-old calm, hiding age-old deadly passions. Beyond, if one gazed, one could just make out the looming black on black of the Golan, née the Syrian Heights, the Arab Maginot Line, the deadly southern carapace of Damascus . . . I remembered the time, pre-Six-Day-War and glory, when our air force shot a Syrian Mig into the lake, just fifty metres from the east shore, probably about the same time Anat was filling out forms in the Soldiers' Hostel's permanent shadow . . . Rowing silently out there, in the dead of night, on a commando dinghy. Helped silently into shnorkeling gear, aware every moment of the kibitzing Enemy hidden in the bullrushes. Underwater, with infra-red lamps and goggles, amid a mêlée of agents of our friendly Western allies, and some we were not quite so sure of. As I helped a frogman attach a grapple to the fuselage on the lakebed, a burly yoik floated by whom I murkily recognised as the US Press and Cultural Attaché. Bubble-bubble-bubble, we said to each other, as small fish parted the gloom.

Nothing should surprise us here.

"What do you want to do next?" Anat asked. "Tomorrow's Friday, remember?" Again, the cursed Covenant with Abraham. If God had chosen someone else, we might all be having sex still with the ritual priestesses of Ashtoreth. On second thoughts, we might have lost out on the world tour – Babylon, through Spain, Russia, Germany . . . On third thoughts, where's the loss?

"Let's sleep on it," I said. "We might call Doormat's bluff in the morning. Call on Halabi and ask to see your dear 'Menahem'."

But it was not quite to be like that.

Still pondering our weighty metaphysics, we strolled slowly back towards the hostel. The night had advanced far enough for there to be a refreshing breeze, and the moon was clearly visible. Our ex-mosque turret stood black against the sky, not a single window alight. From across the way, again the bass thud of the forever young. We passed by the hostel office at the base of the tower. The desk manager had retired. A small night light cast an amber glow over abandoned racks of postcards, souvenir bric-à-brac, wood-carved figurines. A mini-fisherman, bowed under a coil of nets. More carp for the unwary. We climbed the brick stairway towards our room. Anat stopped at the door. "Careful, Joe," she said, "I have a funny feeling."

What else is new? I fumbled for the key, found it and opened the door. There was someone on the bed, shrouded in moonlight. I intercepted Anat's hand on its way to the light switch and pushed her half out of the door. Macho Joe takes control. I bent carefully over the figure. It was definitely familiar. The shock of hair, the teeth, the tuft of chest wiring. One feature added, though. A jagged hole, drilled centre forehead.

Rest in Peace, Doormat Menahem. Alias Amnon Dahab, TB Twenty. Another corpse for the Joe Dekel collection. Hotel room beds a speciality. What price the Parry wild flowers now? There was something on the floor near the bed. I picked it up, then let it fall with a clatter. Dumb, dumbo Joe. You read a thousand crime novels and learn totally nothing. It was my own stupid gun. The Luger, which I had mislaid since Nablus. Which I had put out of my mind.

Alors, I had just shot myself through the head. Nothing remained but to deliver the carcase.

In fact there was no need. They had followed me up the stairs. I barely glimpsed Anat being whisked from the doorway. I never thought a five-foot room could hold so many gorillas outside a television frame, in a nature documentary produced by the BBC. It was like feeding time at the zoo, after an anthropoid Yom Kippur, with us turkeys as the fast-breaking meal. Some seemed to be in police uniform, some not. There was a lightning storm of flashbulbs.

Downstairs, we were bundled in two separate cars. An eery silence, barring sweaty grunts. I glimpsed the hostel office, still amber and empty, the tiny fisherman still bowed by his burden. One of the cars, into which Anat disappeared, was a cream Mercedes. I was crushed into a police Susita. A local product, it is made of fibreglass. Camels have been known to eat them. Odd the data that shoots through your head when it has been emptied of brains.

Journey's end, Joe? What did you expect to achieve? Self-determination? Human dignity? They're not going to push *me* around? Any advance on any other illusions?

The car motors gunned, we departed in exhaust fumes. No one seemed to witness our passing.

20

Whether Inspector Halabi was a nice man or not was to remain an open question. He was a small tubby orang-utanish fellow with a thinning forehead but long hairy arms. Prodded into his presence, bruised, rattled and handcuffed, I found him standing on the glass top of a cluttered desk dabbing the ceiling with a wet rag. He leapt off, flashing me yellow flecked eyes, settling barely in sight behind the litter. "The mosquitoes," he announced, flicking his eyes upwards, "you spray the room. Blessed Be Their Memories. Most fall to the floor, but some die stuck up there. You have to clean them off with spirits, carefully. We can't have a police inspector's office, can we, with little bloodstains all over the ceiling?"

He was right, but I was unappreciative. "I want to make one thing clear," I said, "whatever's been cooked up here, leave my girlfriend out of it." Macho melodrama again ... Did I say that?

But he merely looked pained, as if someone had left a tin tack on his chair but he didn't want to make an opera out of it. I wondered where they had deposited Anat. I wondered why I had my neck in this noose. I wondered why my father had not gone from Hamburg to Sweden instead of Palestine, back in 1935. "I have the right to phone my lawyer," I blustered, "Yeruham Palgin, Jerusalem six-three-six-seven-two-nine."

He sighed, turning to the two primates who had thrust me

into a hard chair facing him. "Leave us alone now," he said, wearily, "I'll call you in if he bites me." They shuffled out, etching deep grooves in the floor, and he regarded me with his cow's eyes.

"This is a bad business," he said.

"I should think so," I regained some equilibrium, "taking part in a frame-up. As a senior officer you should be ashamed."

"I am always ashamed," he said, sadly. "Twenty years, and I'm still not used to it. My father, bless his memory, had it better, back in the old country. He only had to arrest gentiles, Moslems. Our own people observed the Law. Here, every time I nick a Jew, my heart sinks. I see our heritage cast in the gutter. But what can one do? Police work is in the veins of my family. Here, let me show you something."

He took a leather folder from his back trouser pocket with the air of removing the bothersome tin tack, took out a snapshot and passed it to me. It was of a beaming young man, not unlike Doormat Menahem, in light khaki uniform.

"My eldest son," he said proudly, "nineteen last December. Border Police Sappers."

"A chip off the old block," I confirmed.

He leaned back across the desk to reclaim it. "What shall I do with you?" he despaired, after returning his offspring to his buttocks. Then he ladled out a familiar stew, Major Kazaz's recipe, without the relish - originality is not these people's forte, alas - "Look at yourself - an intellectual, even a religious person . . . Someone who should know good from evil. It's politics, isn't it? There's the rot, for sure. I can't believe you did it for money." He had lost me. I was floating, up there in the clouds. Shaking hands with Mongolfier. "Joe Dekel." "*Un balloniste français.*" Shall we perhaps try the stratosphere?

He opened his desk drawer and placed on the table a cellophane-wrapped parcel. It contained the gun, liberated from me, handed in no doubt while I was kicking my heels in his anteroom, under anthropoid guard. He then took out a file, extracted some photographs and laid them fanwise before me. Happily, they were not of his family. Unhappily, they were of me. Telephoto shots, set in local surroundings, the bus station, the Ecumenical Hostel. They made my passport visage look angelic. I looked as if I were casing the town, in preparation for a nuclear first strike. Guilty As Charged, was stamped metaphorically upon each ten by eight glossy. And, physically, the stamp marks of dates on each: 4th, 5th, 6th of May, ten days before I'd even crawled into this forsaken mousehole.

"These are faked," I said, angrily.

"You don't like them? Try these for size." He added to the display two ballistics close-ups of spent bullets and two more glossies, a close-up and long shot of a corpse on a grass verge. A man with a short beard who had once had eyes. Not a pretty sight at all.

"We now have three bullets," Halabi said quietly, "one for each of the missionary's eyes, one for the policeman's forehead. And here we have a gun. You want to take bets, comrade, that we get a happy marriage? Two professional jobs, precision, no wastage. To just look at you, who would know?"

This was no longer fun. I retorted: "My gun was stolen in Nablus."

"Did you report the theft?" He shook his head slowly, "I won't ask you what you were doing there. Or why you have a gun at all. A Peacenik like you! But isn't it typical? Always blame the Arabs, eh, Dekel? Scratch a 'progressive' and you find just another one of us beastly chauvinists."

"I'm not blaming anyone. I'm just stating a fact." But I was on a shunt to nowhere. He had me trussed up good and proper, for whatever Goddamn reason. Leaning back, pursing his lips, tutting like an old grannie. There was no doubt, I had disappointed this man. As is my wont with persons in authority. Major Kazaz, the SHABAK investigator, KAMAN commanders, Gingi Arse-Face, my brother-in-law Elisha ... My father, bless his soul, never qualified ...

"You know all this is a complete lie," I said.

But Halabi waved his hand dismissively. "Thank God," he said, "it's not my problem. My task is just to sign you over. On the other hand it might have done my team no end of good to practice a little on you. It could have improved their minds. You can't imagine what scum we have to deal with normally. But you are meat for Security, Dekel. I am due to hand you over. I have to tell you, though, they are rough bastards. Some of them practised in Iran, you know, with the Shahinshah Pehlavi, God rest that poor devil's soul. They have the expertise with intellectuals. Why not spare yourself all that and sign a confession right here, in a convivial and friendly atmosphere. How about it, Dekel? Shall I call a stenographer?"

"You can kiss my ass and suck my piles."

His disillusionment was total. He called in his minions. They hauled me off, by my hair. I had my traditional last glance at my scourge, poor Halabi, gazing at the ceiling. Oh, if we could only spray 'em all and just brush their bodies off, with alcohol. They dragged me down a set of corridors, into the basement, and locked me in a single cell. The door was solid concrete, with an eyehole. The cell stank like an abattoir. It was a distinct step downwards from Nablus. No Fatahs here to give me recipes. Merely a cockroach, which I dispatched with the latrine pail. I squatted on the bare floor, wet with liquid I did not want to have to analyse, keeping a wary eye roving for carapaced reinforcements. To think that five days ago I was watching the spires of Oxford on my Alec Guinness cassette. As Lauterman didn't say, you live and don't learn. I thought of Anat and had the cold shudders, never mind the stifling heat. I told myself this was not Chile, or Russia. But the dead cockroach laughed. Prison, the universal equaliser. Kings and *schmendricks* squashed alike. Coming full circle to the source of my troubles, I thought of Moishe-Ganef, his six years inside. Four in solitary confinement. Trial in-camera, secret verdict, sentence unpublished. And I, and his few other friends, said nothing, left him lying on the battlefield. A few morose words, in the T-n Café: "What possessed him to defy those people?" Secret Service and secret fate. Requiescat, Bye Bye, Charlie. Areas of our National Life we shun. Three million deaf, blind, stum monkeys. Now it seems Moishe had his sweet revenge, on one of us at least. This Was My Life, I, Moishe Sherman. Over to Joe Dekel and out. And all for what? What web, and what face on the spider at its hub? Another cockroach emerged from the wall. I crushed it. This would soon be a catacomb.

21

But Moishe had survived his martyrdom, his six fetid years. Emerging, amazingly, slick as ever, waving lawyer's writs and denunciations. I did not see him in the flesh, but there was that ferret face in smudged newspaper ink on the back page of the evening toilet roll: the gargoyle grin, the bulging Moishe eyes, the outstretched fingers anticipating a handout. His eyes were always the headlamps of Innocence, the hurt reproach of an accuser. A reborn Ganef facing the big bad world, demanding rehabilitation: I only did what was expected of me – and they slung me in the hoosegow . . . the State used my thievery, then turned and bit me for some piffling private snatch on the side . . . Poor Moishe, unable to disentangle corporate demands from his compulsions. 1979 was the year of his release, a bad year for sour grapes, the year of the aftermath of the Camp David treaty. We were all glued to the box, watching our Ambassador taking the oath in Cairo. And Egyptian diplomats going spare over the delights of the Tel Aviv esplanade. All this courtesy of Menahem Begin! Some thought the millennium was here. Pessimists, like myself, reserved judgment. Why does it feel so lousy to find out you were right, that the habit of war would not die easy? At any rate, it was no time to think of the Ganef and his peculiar personal trauma . . . And he, out of mind, vanished again, for a further five years. Returned to whatever shadowland he had chosen until he popped up as his own death mask in the Edenvale Hotel . . . Whither have you been leading me, Thief? I can't hear your message! Can you speak up? Can you enunciate a little? What was the dream you were pursuing, and what turned it into my nightmare?

Half an hour had passed, and no more cockroaches. Disconnected fragments danced through my brain. Anxieties, fears, mixed with prison movie scenes. Searches for a silver lining. At least I had eaten well this evening (how many years ago?). I would not have to cast beady eyes on the roach corpses, like Steve McQueen in *Papillon*. And more thoughts of Anat. Surely Halabi's old-fashioned chauvinism should land her a better deal than this ... I Was the World's Number One Idiot. A fitting title for an old 'fifties film ... My brain, continuing its decomposition. Incredibly, I fell asleep. It was probably the clammy heat that zapped me. At any rate, this was the dream:

I was in a pub, in London, somewhere off an arterial road. It was crowded, mainly with young people making merry, exercising their rights, as the ads have it. Conversation flowed, buzzed. I had ordered a pint of bitter, as there was no Löwenbrau. Suddenly several Polish men entered, disguised with obviously false beards. Their leader banged with a saucepan held in his hand upon the nearest table. Everyone fell silent. He began reading names from a notebook held in his other hand. The other men moved to close off the exits, but I happened to be standing close to the main door. I darted out swiftly, and ran down the road, traffic beeping all about me. It was night, and the headlights sheered the pitch darkness like observation flares. I ran about three hundred metres before I stopped short, feeling shocked and guilty. I stopped a taxi and, standing on its running board, guided it back down the road. "Police! Police!" I shouted. Two London bobbies swerved towards me. They had the doleful faces of the Ulsterman and the silent Cockney slob. I led them into the pub, through the saloon bar doors. The Polish men with false beards were all sitting there. They looked up at us, with sheepish Halabi eyes. There was no sign of any other patrons. The man with the saucepan lounged against the bar. "What's the problem, officers?" he inquired. "There has been an incident!" I insisted. But the bearded men laughed. "Look upstairs," I suggested to the policemen, "you'll find the evidence up there." "There is nothing up there," said the man with the saucepan. But, from the ceiling, blood trickled. My policemen surged forward. The bearded men resisted. A vicious struggle ensued. Police whistles blew. Reinforcements poured in, in long blue coats and helmets. I grabbed at the beards, tearing them off the faces. Of course, they were all familiar ... Gingi, Meisinger, Lauterman, Doormat Menahem, all flashing their boy scout insignia, sports' badges, Isracards, TB Twenties ... I shouted, as the bobbies overpowered them: "You will all die as old men, rotting in jail, like Rudolph Hess ..." And then the saucepan struck me on the head.

The cell door opened.

"All right, Dekel. Your time's up."

"Not all of life's cream and blintzes."

Jews. They are always moralising. Even with a stick up your arse. The gorillas hauled me to my feet. One flicked a roach off my shoulder. "Let's go." They marched me into the corridor, up the basement stairs, to the ground floor. Here it comes, I thought, show-down time, the Iranian-trained Poles, with electrodes. My brain was about ripe for science. They stopped me in front of a door. They giggled. They unbolted the door and shoved me through.

"Goodbye, Shitface. See you soon."

The door was slammed behind me. I was out in the street. It was shrouded in clammy darkness. I leaned groggily against a bulbless lamppost. Running footsteps sounded. I turned, ready for nothing. It was Anat. She leapt on me. I fell to the ground.

"Joe! You lunatic! Are you all right?"

Perfectly safe, my dear, apart from the saucepan ...

We rose to our feet. I looked at my watch. It indicated four-thirty. I had barely been four hours inside. But it had seemed to dwarf Moishe's half decade. With Anat's arms around me, I staggered down the narrow pavement, round the corner to a courtyard. It was the frontage of the police station. Twenty metres off its neon sign glowed. The building, however, looked deserted. There were several vehicles parked in the yard. Among them, "Alexander", loaded up with our bags, which we had last seen at our mosque turret hostel, pre kebab, pre the dead Doormat, Halabi threats and roaches. "This is madness," I said. A trite observation. Not one to win the bedroom suite.

The neon "Police" sign winked at us. I felt no desire to be enticed. The smell of piss I could produce any time. We climbed into the car.

"What happened in there?" Anat asked. "I'm not sure I know," I said. "What about you?"

"They gave me a cup of tea and a bun," she said, "and stuck me alone in a room with very bizarre grafitti and a huge pile of back issues of the *Police News*."

A friend of mine edits that rag, can you believe it? There could be no response to that but silence. Some people just get by. We sat, slumped, gazing at our surroundings. We were way up the mountain. The streets of Tiberias stretched below us like the aftermath of the neutron bomb. Sporadic street lights looked on pre dawn. Not a cat, mule or bicyclist. The vagaries: one moment the Disappeared, the next, the only sentients in town. Far below, unstirring shadows of palm trees, waiting for a breath off the invisible lake, black vanished into the blackness. Somewhere to our left, the old Soldiers' Hostel, with a new anonymous clerk, no doubt, working in half light, choking on Lysol fumes and loneliness.

"Where do you want to go now?" I asked Anat, emptily.

"Anywhere. Out of this town."

I gunned the motor, easing us on to the road, following the mountain's contour. Looking back briefly at the looming police station, half expecting it to spew fire and brimstone. Not a sausage.

"I'm sorry, my love," I said, "I've been an idiot. I think I've got us into big trouble."

"We are all idiots," Anat said, "we should never have left the stetl."

We headed down, towards the water. At the Gdud Barak junction I put the brakes on and idled. North or south? Home and video-cassette immersion, or more pigheaded brinkmanship?

"Surrender?" I asked.

"Not yet," said Anat.

We headed north, parked in a layby and curled up, entwined, till daybreak. The sun was heralded by a spectacular display of deep blue and threads of gold and scarlet. It was a hard act to follow. Nevertheless, we are a stiff-necked people. We pressed on into central Galilee.

22

Safad. A poignant point of reference. Scene of the first Joe-Anat bout. No falls, no submissions, but, as it turned out, a double knock-out. The year was 1972. Golden days of post '67 hubris. Nixon was our father. Golda Meir our mother. We wished we could all become orphans. Anat and I had each, separately, been attending one of the left's periodic heart-bleeds: the solidarity sit-in with the Arab villagers of Ikrit and Bir'am in the northern Galilee. They were Maronite Christians, who had been evacuated from their homes in 1948 and never allowed to return, despite the fact that they had taken the Jewish side in the Independence War. We all gathered, the conscience-stricken Jewish liberals, assorted leftists and Communist Party members, on the site of the villagers' destroyed homes. A hullabaloo of protest placards echoing familiar angsts: "Let my People Go – to Bir'am"; "Cry the Beloved Country"; "If I Forget Thee, O Bir'am, may My right Hand Forget Its Cunning". Halcyon days. Arabs and Jews together. Of course, it was a complete failure. Nevertheless, for me, a net gain, as, pessimistically out of tune as always, I found myself sharing a back seat in a car returning south loaded with T-n Café comrades – Red Arieh, Green Barenboim, Black Ben and The Shogun, with a feisty, raven-haired, hazel-eyed girl I had not met before. I allowed my petit-bourgeois scepticism to show and, stopping at Safad, at a Viennese Pastry shop, she let me have it good and proper. It was people like me who, etcetera, were holding back the march of progress. She did not mention my hattie, but was glancing at it as if it were the horns of the devil.

"Remember?" I said, as we sat in the same place, Slovetski's, at the very same table. They had now extended the panoramic window that took in the majestic wooded hills. Balm of the clean sharp mountain air, the sweet warm smell of cakes and pastries. There are virtues, too, in this cocktail. "You accused me of being a fifth columnist of the clerical-reaction."

"Not at all," she said, "it's your imagination. I was the ranking moderate of The Tendency. It was you who were having delusions about the skull-capped masses repenting the errors of their chauvinist ways."

"I have had no delusions," I protested, "since I won the kohlrabi by mistake in the school agricultural competition."

A lie. It's true, I do not like to remember my own entrance on to the dissident stage: bearing, as I thought in my newly found self-righteousness, the gifts of my inside knowledge. Three years behind the scenes of the nation's affairs, but no one was bowled over. Red Arieh had been a captain in Field Security, Green Barenboim had fought in the crack "Chestnut" Commando, and The Shogun had even been a clerk with SHABAK, before handing in his notice. In this half-pint of a country there is no fringe. Everyone has been a scoundrel. Except perhaps the women, who could look on from the sidelines, like Anat, pushing a pen in Soldiers' Hostels, clocking us poor sods in and out ...

"Delusions are your stock in trade, Joe." Behold, the woman I live and love with. We do not seem to have stopped arguing since that first scorching July day. Why then, have we stayed together? The clichés apart: love, habit, time taking its course with the both of us ... I know what pulls me to her still waters, but what ties her to me, delusional Joe, the unreconstructed porcine male? It's true, I do clean the toilet, on occasion, and I buy the groceries, when I dare exit the door. But is this enough? Probably not. The fact is, there was so little choice, once one had quit the main consensus. A few dozen of us misfits against three million. We had to form our own little kingdoms out of the causes that moulded our post-army identities, when we emerged from the mass: Solidarity between former enemies, Peace now, yesterday, tomorrow evening ... Class, not Religion or Nation, a Socialist Middle East, with room for all. The 1973 war tore the heart from all that. There is nothing more depressing than the failure of an idea whose time has come ... Anat, I suppose, retains a part of the core, with her sponsorship of the "arts". I sold my soul for a mess of *Dallas* potage, and consoled myself by raving in private. The iniquitous mark of the Jewish heritage – they can make us feel guilty for anything ... And now, multiple deaths weighing upon me, friends' corpses, nudging me with their toes ... And Anat, chipping in with the strength of ideals that might still power her will?

Friday noon, approach of the Sabbath. In Safad, it is almost tangible. This old town is steeped in mysticism and wrapped in the cobwebs of the Kabbalah. The grandmasters Cordovero and Isaac Luria (The "Ari") settled here and studied. Then their disciples, weaving on the fabric of their esoteric searches. The famous book of Jewish rules, the *Shulkhan Arukh*, was written here in the 1550s. In 1833 the Druze sacked the town. In 1837 an earthquake flattened it. In 1975 the first MacBurger was opened. Who says there is no progress?

We had taken a room in a small pension, Masaryk's, not far from the town centre. We had stayed here before, returning twice to Safad, to the Viennese pastries. Whether it could hold up as an escape route now was another question. Departing cataclysmically from tradition, Anat joined me for the afternoon atavism. "A special case. Don't get your hopes up," she said, "I don't think I should let you out of my sight." We had stocked up our kitchenette for the weekend, so in some balance we ambled forth. Down, from the "citadel" in the direction of the ancient hillside cemetery. (Chockful of righteous men and scholars, no vacancy, hopefully, for Dekel.) Old men and women tottering down steep stairways, winding alleys, stone-arched passageways. I followed some faces that took my fancy to one of the synagogues tucked in a lane. It was a Sephardi congregation, all brown-skinned and grizzled, with laughing eyes I could not fathom. What was the joke? Perhaps existence itself. We followed them into their prayer house.

It was not much more than a large room, candlelit from strange lamps that looked like salvage from a Roger Corman Poe movie. Low roof beams, benches of faded wood, rough-hewn as their regular occupants. More candles on the stone sills of small arched windows flickered on rusty iron bars. I had not brought my toolkit, from Jerusalem, and the synagogue clerk handed me a prayer book that appeared so old it might have survived Shabetai Zvi. It was clear strangers rarely joined this congregation. Like me, it was a closed system.

To my right, in a recess, I could see Anat, oddly in place among a handful of stout Sephardi mamas, wearing coloured print dresses, looking strangely bereft without their dozen each shopping bags. One of them had adopted Anat and was thrusting her prayer book at her. I did not watch the outcome of this titanic struggle, focusing on the familiar text in my hand. The living past of the yellowing pages, the odd sensuousness of the printface. The daily liturgy, afternoon service for the Eve of Sabbath:

"Give thanks to the Lord for He is good, His mercy will endure forever . . . Let the redeemed of the Lord speak, for He has delivered them from the oppressor. He has gathered them from the lands of east and west, north and ocean. They were lost in the desert, on an abandoned road, they did not find an inhabited town . . ."

What on earth harnessed me to all this? It is a complete mystery. Perhaps the very fact that my father, believing in a break from the past, sent me to the secular school, where I was brought up to believe in the kibbutz, the work ethic and growing kohlrabis. All this in urban Jerusalem. No wonder our brains were addled. We were the golden children of the Zionist future. So, perversely, I returned to the past. My friends in the left never understood this syndrome, and berated me for my contradictions. They were just like my brother-in-law Elisha: "Joe, how can you wear that thing and spout Marx?" Marx was a scion of Rabbis, I said, he had so much hair you missed the hattie. But I saw no problem in reconciling the past with the search for a future. Still intrigued by the ghettoes from whence I came, the hook-nosed figures and their strange deals with God. We'll do your bidding, Lord, and you'll do what *you* want. There was the nub of the question. For if not for some sort of gain, then Why? What kept the whole *shtik* going? Habit, abstract Truth, a social glue that came unstuck in the age of science, and has become shriller as the decades pass? Something that so many rush to replace with new adhesives, like State and Nation ...? Or Class ...?

"Happy are those who dwell in thy house ... Happy the people that this is their lot ... Happy the people whose God is the Lord."

Who knows. Who knows. Who knows.

Safad Sabbath. Hiding out at the Pension Masaryk, avoiding the risk of coming across the one or two people Anat knows in the town's "Art Colony". Picking up a crumpled copy of the weekend rag from Mrs Masaryk in person. The usual stew: "LIKUD CANDIDATES FOR KNESSET CHOSEN". "TWENTY-NINE PARTIES REGISTERED SO FAR". "INSTANT DIVORCE FOR MENTAL PATIENT". "RED DANNY COHN-BENDIT TURNS GREEN". Not a whiff of the case of dead Doormat Menahem in a Tiberias fleapit. Nor "TV CRITIC ON THE RUN; PUBLIC ENEMY NUMBER ONE, POLICE SAY". Was it all a private grand guignol for Joe Dekel's benefit? What are they expecting next? Perhaps Nahum Lauterman is back from Cairo. Luckily, the phone would be *verboten* for the next twenty-four hours.

I spent fourteen of them unconscious. Not a whiff of a dream. Brunched with Anat on pittas and yoghourt. Risked an exit – walked off a short distance into the hills, gawping at Mount Canaan. The peaks of Meiron to the north, a buffer between us and Lebanon. The brownness of the hills. The dark green of the pines. The bracing air, good for asthma, but still not a cure for asphyxiation. Back to the yoghourt dregs.

Twilight looming, I decided to undergo a final dose of the Safad synagogue. Anat, lulled by security, passed and stayed behind. I descended the worn steps alone, arriving in the middle of Psalm 91: He who dwells in the Highest Secret . . . "Fear not the terror of the night, nor the arrow that flies by day; nor the pestilence stalking in darkness, nor the destruction that ravages noon . . . Though a thousand fall by your side, and ten thousand at your right, it shall not approach thee . . ." Amen, Amen, Selah. As we mumbled through the remainder I noticed I was not the only latecomer present. Several other men, I counted five, had appeared like wraiths here and there. They wore the black homburg hats of the practising orthodox, and were young, though suitably bearded. Their cheeks, where visible, were smooth, their foreheads like that of the unlamented Major Kazaz. They all wore identical thin dark jackets. They looked identical, period. And they did not leave when the congregation filed out, but closed in silently around me. I attached myself to the tail of the commune, but the smoothies cut off my exit.

"A good week, a good week," a spokesman said politely. "We have a friend who wants a few words with you." He handed me a thin sealed brown envelope. I opened it. End of Sabbath meditation. My private masque reasserted: inside, a postcard, a reduction of the 1939 *Wizard of Oz* film poster. The Tin Man, the Scarecrow, the Cowardly Lion. And Judy Garland in pigtails. Very appropriate. The flip side was blank. "Please," the spokesman said, pressing my shoulder.

"Is there a choice?" I asked.

He shook his head. "All right," I said, "I'll take the vanilla."

They shepherded me, politely but firmly, out into the darkened lane. The congregants threw me silent glances, like a mass of Bert Lahrs, dipping their tails, recognising my submission. I was enveloped, like the centre of a five-rayed star, expecting the saline drip any moment. Down three flights of stone stairs, into the quarter I knew as the Art Colony. Perhaps I was going to be offered the latest Holzman, a bargain, on ten days' approval. Or an elaborate revenge by some client of Anat's, whose work she might have hung upside down by mistake, sometime in the early 'seventies. My guides were not giving out the patter. In fact I barely heard them breathe. They were professionals, probably rehearsing defence against a binary nerve gas attack. We passed reconstructed stone fences, red lanterns, an ersatz Japanese rock garden, a replica liberty bell. Finally I was turned in at a blue wrought-iron gate, lazily latched, to a crazy paved courtyard crammed with bric-à-brac: sculptures, *à la* rejects from Henry Moore's garbage, hanging figures made of piano wire. Little piles that looked like robots' doodies, coloured balls dangling from metal scaffolds. And everywhere, those delicate Japanese tinklers, tinkling in the breeze. Coloured lights, from a wooden trellis, lit up this weird melange. And in the centre of the maelstrom, three pretty metal chairs set round a matching table. It was early 'fifties gunge. Perhaps Moishe-Ganef's blue period. On the table, however, an 'eighties plastic coffeepot, two cups and a pack of Hadar biscuits. Sitting on one of the chairs, the nation's carbuncle. My Karla. The elusive arsehole-picker.

"Howdie, Dorothy," he said smoothly. "Amazing, isn't it, what one finds at the end of the yellow brick road."

"Fuck your mother, Meisinger," I replied.

Re-establishing an old rapport.

23

"So you're the cuddly old professor with the puffs of smoke," I said, "please spare me your old tin medals."

"Ah, but you want to return to Kansas!" he guessed. "For this you need my magic balloon."

He certainly looked the part. Shabby jacket, with elbow patches. Crumpled trousers. The thin wispy hair, above that buzzard's beak, the sunken quiet eyes, the pencil-line eyebrows. The narrow sloping forehead giving no sign of that idiot savant memory. Still, I am told human beings can get by with a brain the size of a pea, if absolutely necessary. His moral sense needed no accommodation, residing as it probably did in the cuffs of his trousers, along with the dust, grime and fallen half-shekel coins.

I took my seat before him. The orthodox garbed minders took up discreet positions, well clear of the Japanese tinklers.

"Planning your retirement here?" I waved casually around. "Anat is the person you should consult. I can see you in the catalogue: The Kinetic Man. Fresh from his world-renowned 'Still Life at the Chatilla Gallery'."

"I was off the duty roster at that incident," he said, "and none of this is mine. This place has been borrowed briefly in the owner's absence."

"Not my style," I had to tell him.

"Mine neither," he said, "but the owner does well out of Americans."

"Don't we all," I said. The conversation was wilting before it had even begun.

Meisinger poured the coffee and offered the biscuit pack. Spurned the bikkies. Sipped the coffee. I remembered he always conjured a mean brew. He would have to, these long lonely nights at the pinnacle, counting the mass graves. He chewed thoughtfully. What was there to say? They really called him Concentration Camp Erhard.

Fed up, I broke the masticatory silence, snapping it over my knee. "It was your frame up, wasn't it," I said, "at Tiberias and Nablus. Bomber Kazaz, that poor whoever-he-was priest, the Jerusalem copper and Nice-Man Halabi."

"Halabi is an animal," he said, "a plodder. But he's good with a ring through his nose. I am sure *my* men were not rough with you. You'll notice we waited till the Sabbath's end."

"Pass the Kleenex," I said. "I am prostrate."

"I warned you, Joe, to keep your nose clean. I've done what I had to do. I wasn't obliged to reveal myself to you then, even over the phone. But I thought I'd give you the benefit of the doubt, purely for old times' sake. But no, you had to go on poking about in the kitchen. You always had to know what's cooking."

"I am particular about what I eat. Shit is for the flies, Meisinger."

"'I cater for diets, but not for fads.' Renoir: *Rules of the Game*. Remember the end of that film? The gamekeeper shot the famous aviator. He was cheating with his friend's wife. Who are you cheating with nowadays, Joe?"

"I am sure you have it all, in Polaroids."

"Always the old Joe. I admire that. But one has to know one's limitations. You can't take on the whole world and its uncle. Sooner or later you get the invoice."

"Invoices I refer to my accountant."

"All right, Joe. Let's talk turkey." He put down the packet of biscuits. This was going to be serious. He would be using both hands. "You should have taken my advice, Joe." he said. "You did not and you have become involved. Welcome back to The Family. You have reported for Reserve Duty, and your girlfriend, too. I will now inform you of your assignments."

"I have been invalided out," I said. "I have the documents. Psychological incompatibility."

"Is this where I put on the false moustache? There is a case against you, Joe. Double murder, no less. Shady political motives. An ex-Intelligence officer, who became a café leftist. Who knows what team you might be playing on now? I would say it ranks an in-camera trial, just like our old buddy Moishe. Remember? We could even bring your pal Lauterman into it. Kill two plump birds with one stone. The charming Anat Levy, too, as an accomplice. That's not so bad. Five years at Tirzah prison. A doddle. You I can't promise green fields though. Treason turns our judges purple."

"OK, Beria," I said, "so you're Ming the Merciless. Why don't you just poison my grog?"

"Because I want you to work in my laboratory, Doctor Zarkoff. I so value your contribution. Aren't you the national asset, Joe, the scourge of the eight-thirty news? Don't insult me and play the innocent. Your life is an open book to me. Ever since you got off the London plane you've been broadcasting on every possible channel. Meeting with Fatah agents in cafés. Plotting with liberal clowns. Rushing off to Tiberias, after a dead priest, following a secret message. For what purpose, Joe? A born-again baptism?"

"It's my sciatica," I said. "May's a bad month for it. I was heading for the sulphur hot springs."

"Not funny."

"They can't all be good."

"You're right. We're all growing older."

"Who killed the priest? Did you kill the Gingi? And what about Moishe Sherman?"

"You really think I'm a monster, don't you? I don't kill old comrades."

"Strangers only." The old difference between homicide and warfare. "All right, Meisinger," I said, "let's stop the games. Isn't there enough blood on the floor? What is it you want? What brings you out of your bunker to breathe air with us lumpens? What is this service you're trying to trap me into? What is the boon you crave from my soul?"

"You know what I want. I want Moishe-Ganef. Fried, and with sauté potatoes. And you know the reason too. He stole vital State property, and is using it for his private ends. The Gingi was sure you were in contact with him. And then he, too, fades from vision. Too many convenient disappearances. And guess who is left, threshing about? Who but our dear old Joe? Now it's possible you really are an idiot, Dorothy, stomping in a high moral tantrum. But, intentional or not, the threads are there. I can feel them, tangibly stretching. Things happen around you, Joe, which are no coincidence. You are a magnet for trouble. Our mission now is to use these seductive qualities to lure the monkey into the cage. I have several proposals, but point number one is to establish lines of communication. Obviously there will be other teams in the field, rivals, enemies, so-called allies. But I will handle that. I'll be your Good Witch of the East. I can tell you one thing, though: your life is guaranteed as long as people believe you can lead them to our naughty Moishe. So drop the innocent act before somebody decides you're just fodder for the knacker's yard. Do you understand me, Joe?"

I looked good and hard at him. He was enjoying the moment. A sweet revenge, no doubt, for the night I buried his trousers at KAMAN passing-out parade, the evening I walked off with black-eyed Ruthie, the Women's Corps Sergeant, and countless other slights I had forgotten but elephants and Meisinger do not. Café leftism indeed! But behind the power play there was a familiar nervousness. The ground is shifting, even under the Wise Son, Lord of the earth and all he surveys. The occupational neurosis of the Intelligence Family – not so much their desire for evil as their capacity to conjure endless phantoms out of their own suspicions. Even paranoids have enemies. They stream out on the assembly line.

"If I promised you anything," I said, "would you believe me?"

But he was given no time to savour fully the moment of my capitulation. Saved literally by the bell, for somewhere inside the house a burglar alarm erupted. It sounded like a giant computer in agony. The whole chessboard was overthrown. Meisinger's minders leapt out of the shadows, grabbing him by his jacket. They literally yanked him over the table, overturning it, coffee, biscuits and all. All the coloured lights in the junkyard went out.

It's a hard life, nursing a carbuncle. Two of the bodyguards lunged towards me, but I skipped away, behind what appeared to be an enactment in bronze of cold *tshoolent*. "Leave him! We'll get to him later!" Meisinger's voice came from the phalange. I had not understood the phrase "greased lightning" until I saw that unit rush up the road. One moment they were there, the next, not, as the alarm still blasted and lights began coming on in the houses along the alley. There were other sounds too, the crackle of firearms, from away down the hillside. If this was the target area, lingering was not called for. I rushed out into the alley. From over the city a helicopter, as is their wont, clattered into eye and earshot. Flares shot ahead of it, lighting the mountain, the woodland and the whole Goddamn town. Someone, evidently, approaching from southwards, had activated a warning. Tripwires, infra-red, heat- and breath-sensors, you name it, we probably mass-produce it, for sale to the highest bidder.

Now there were explosions down the valley. People ran out of their homes. The nation's artists, in shorts and pyjamas. One or two were holding pistols. Vigilantism – the national pastime. Perhaps they thought it was an art critics' raid. I ducked into a side lane, found another stairway, climbed rapidly towards the main road. Around me the population panicked. Staggering old men, nosy old women, frightened children, concussed Hassidim. High-pitched roll-calls of misplaced offspring. Hysterical bellows of soldiers home on leave to their loved ones to keep calm. The flares lit the quarter with a ghostly whitewash, picking out the quarried stone bricks, the tiled roofs, the webs of laundry lines, with limp upper and lower empty casements of people agitated in the commotion. Ambulance sirens now joined the riot. A second chopper thundered above. Flames shot from its flanks, it was rocketing the hills. This would not please the Safad Forestry Department.

I have heard of the town swinging on Saturday night, but this was ridiculous. The main road, when I reached it, was seething. I never knew Safad had masses, but here they were, pushing, shoving and gesticulating wildly. Police vehicles had arrived, with loudhailers. "Please clear the streets completely!" they cried. "There is no cause for alarm! Anyone not on official business is required to remain indoors!"

Ever obedient, I headed for shelter, the Pension Masaryk and Anat. The inhabitants of the hotel were all out in the street, craning their necks and chattering. I rushed up to our room. There was no sign of Anat, nor of our meagre baggage. God, not Halabi time again . . . Had Meisinger's minions been here, collecting their Dekel insurance? Or had she finally decided enough was enough, vibes of the noble past or not, and gone home to eat mama's kugel?

I rushed round the back of the hotel, where we had left "Alexander". The buggy was there, and our bags were on it. *Déjà vu,* but still no hint of Anat. "Anat!" I called. There was a pause, then she walked out, from the shadow of the building.

She was not alone. The man emerged, prodding her before him, at outstretched gun-arm length. At least it looked like a gun, and this was not a scenario I wished to call into question. "Sorry, Joe," said Anat, "he didn't knock on the door." This did not at all surprise me. For even without the flash of the flare lighting his face I recognised this further golem of my recent past by the cut of his stature. A brief acquaintance, in another country, that I could have well done without. The Tiddly Crumb. London dustbin fodder. Messenger boy to Gingi Arse-Face.

"Get in the car," he said. "You will drive. And can the wit and repartee."

24

Don't try to analyse, Joe. Just let the waggon roll.

"Seen any dead bodies in hotels lately?"

Driving east from Safad. Back the way we had come, past Mount Canaan. Post-midnight blues on the winding mountain road, rushing on the outskirts of Rosh Pinna. All that's swinging now is the Sonol sign at the closed petrol station. Rosh Pinna was the first new Jewish settlement in the Galilee, founded in 1882. Now it is full of more of Anat's daubers, old lefties who have just discovered God and vegetarianism, and cultivators of marijuana. None of this was impressing itself upon The Crumb, who, having admirably kept his Trappist vow for the last half hour, suddenly blew his verbal sphincters.

"Damn you, Dekel, you fucking turncoat! Or were you one of theirs from the start? He had faith in you, but you let him down, you bastard, and now you just dance on his grave! I'll dance on yours, don't worry about that." It was going to be a regular ballet. "He used to tell me how close you had both been, in the army, and that you were in the heart a Family man. Whatever his politics, I can trust Joe, he said. He was a totally honest man."

"I don't remember a Jesus Christ in my platoon," I mused. "Was he the tall blond with the halo?"

"I cried when he died," the geyser continued, "the tears stood in my eyes. I had only left him for an hour and there he was on the carpet. Such a cruel death – the garrotte, with piano wire. It cuts right through to the bone, you bastard. I barely had time to organise the wrap up – the funeral hearse, the shroud, the cleaners. No publicity, that was his watchword. A very private affair. And with the drunk Arabs upstairs. But you know all that, you shit. It was hell."

"It turned out a neat job," I reassured him. "He is probably proud of you, up there."

"You are a cynical piece of horse dung, Dekel. You wouldn't even bury your mother."

"No, not unless she were dead," I agreed. He made a sound like a throttled turkey.

"He was a modest man, the Gingi," he spewed, "and not even a State burial! Everything secret. Remember the Plan! But who recognises true qualities? Some people make a tower of Babel of their every fart, but the Gingi worked on the Foundations. Don't think because he's fallen in the line of duty there aren't others who can pick up his burden! You can't kill or buy us all."

"I had no intention to," I said.

"Shut up and drive," he said. "You talk too much."

I shut up and drove down from the mountain. What a vista would have spread before us were it day! What a balm it would have been had this Crumb been strangled at birth! What a relief to have had some vague idea what the hell he was doing here or what he was babbling about. I drowned in the nostalgia of my ifs. "Are you awake, Joe? Are you OK?" asked Anat, digging me in the ribs. Unanswerable questions. As the junction approached I looked up questioningly into the rearview mirror.

"Turn right, towards Tiberias."

"*Plus ça change, plus c'est la même chose.*"

"And cut out the fancy talk." He geysered again. "You people think you have it made. Just leave the dirty work to the blacks. I like music and good food, as well as the next man. You think I don't have a soul?" If you prick us, do we not bleed? If you tickle us, do we not laugh? Not bloody likely. "I tell you, it makes your blood boil. It's your people, not mine, who have fucked up this country – all you Poles, Russians and Americans."

"Pardon me," I said, "*ich bin ein Berliner.*"

"Shut your face! There you go again. Fancy education! Peres, Begin, Sharon! All of you are the same."

"What about the Gingi? He wasn't from Casablanca."

"He never read a book, I can tell you."

The conversation died. We left its corpse at the crossing and rattled on towards the lake. My watch told me it was one forty-five. The brisk mountain air had given way to the clammy closeness of the valley, Halabi odour. Just drift with the tide, Joe. Anything Can Happen and It Probably Will. Wasn't that an old Hollywood song? Anat rubbed my thigh with her knee. We exchanged glances and minute shrugs. Tiberias? Tiberias. What can we do? I put my mind in neutral.

Just before the lake, at the turn-off to Tabgha, something shimmered in the headlights ahead of us. What I had been expecting all night – a police roadblock: railing barricades, spikes strung across one lane, a jeep, a uniformed man with a lantern. A routine vision of our land, post-occupation – cop thrusts lantern in car window, scanning faces. Every constable a Lombroso. "Any Arabs in here?" "*La, habibi.*" "Pass friend." Or, alternatively: "Spread your legs, Fatah scum."

"Stop," said The Crumb. "Brake and reverse. We are getting out of here."

"In my arse," I said. This had gone far enough. I slowed, preparing to play the honest citizen as the man with the lantern ambled forward.

"You won't have an arse much longer," said The Crumb, his gun poking at the base of my spine. "Reverse, and fast, unless you want to spend the rest of your life shitting out of your ears."

That would interfere with one's hearing. Certainly with one's enjoyment of Beethoven. I pressed hard on the brakes. By the jeep at the barrier there was a sudden movement. Someone ran across the road. Then another someone. And a third. "Shit!" hissed The Crumb. "Move, Dekel, or I'll blow your guts out!" We had been seeing the same movies. I yanked the gears and reversed rapidly. The man with the lantern leapt off the road. Behind us, a red flare shot upwards. There were moving shapes off the roadside. Fifty metres in the direction I was reversing a half track lumbered on to the road. It had a mounted machine gun. I slammed the brakes again.

"Out! Out! Out!" yelled The Crumb.

"Are you crazy?" I cried. "Just keep cool!"

Submachine-gun fire opened up from somewhere. Our headlights splintered and went out. "Fucking shit, Joe!" said Anat. This was evidently serious. Not a time for *sang-froid.* The dawning week was promising to be at least as tumultuous as the week that had just clapped out in Safad. We scrambled, hitting the tarmac. The windscreen shattered over our heads. The flare faded. "Run!" The Crumb shouted. Anat and I dived for the roadside. We crashed through trees and bushes, slamming our faces in thorns. Behind us there was an explosion. I peeked, to see "Alexander" burning.

"Poor old Joe," Anat, beside me, murmured. I nearly climbed on the road. Me friend! Bala! Bala! Klaatu barada nikto! But Anat hauled me down. This was no time to wave one's identity card, army exemption, medical certificates. We bit the brambles again, crawling through underbrush, throwing ourselves into a culvert. The water was just deep enough for immersion. Amphibiously, we dragged ourselves under the roadway and leaned against the culvert arch. Booted feet clomped above us. Orders were barked. Anat threw her forearm over my throat.

"Sssh!" she whispered. "Did you hear that, Joe? Those people are not speaking Hebrew!"

Utter paranoia. Dementia praecox. An open-and-shut case. The feet faded. Automatic fire continued, in bursts, up the road. The heavier chatter of the machine gun, thank God, not in our direction. The Crumb, vanished in the gloom. A heroic decoy, or the usual bungle? Another flare lit the fields to north-west. The chase was definitely on away from us. Anat pulled me by the arm. We ran, south-east of the road, traversing a botanical gauntlet. Bushes and thorns ripped our clothes. My private parts were in danger. My beautiful "Alexander" demolished! Don't they teach respect for property in schools any more? The entire fucking country is gun mad.

"I know this area ..." Anat breathed, "we've been here before ... right on this hill, remember, last Thursday?"

Thursday, shmursday, my faithful beach buggy! Paid for out of German translations ... my soul sold for a Frankfurt publisher's conscience money ... a ball of flame on the Hula Valley road. Machine-gun fire behind us as we ran, flayed by the colossal barbs. The slings and arrows ... Above, inevitably, a helicopter rising over the lake. A searchlight, God help us, raking the fields. Passing north and ahead of us, towards the road, illuminating the slopes of the Mount of Beatitudes and the Multiplication Church.

"The Cave of Job!" said Anat, triumphantly. Where I wilt and bleed to death, she blooms. We ran on, to the foot of the hill where the Nazarene was supposed to have blessed the meek. South-westwards, the rumble of a convoy of trucks and jeeps in urgent quest of action. We reached a dirt path, and a set of signposts, barely readable in the moonlight. Ten minutes on, an abandoned guard's hut, and the notice we had encountered ten thousand years ago, last Thursday: "Closed For Renovation. Positively No Admittance. Department of Antiquities and Conservation". We bypassed the guard's hut, scrambled over the low, straggly fencing and crawled into the eponymous grotto.

At the oddest moments - sleep. When we awoke, the sun was already high. It was an unlikely survival. All night there had been sounds of clanking and clinking, far-off cries and static crackle. Several times the helicopter thundered over. But no one had breached our secret. Perhaps it did not occur to them someone might dare disobey the Department of Antiquities. Or maybe the old codger himself, Mister Bad Luck, shooed them away with his vibes. Poor Job, the real wizard of Uz, who feared God and eschewed evil. His substance was seven thousand sheep. Mine, one pathetic beach buggy, atomised. Naked came I out of my mother's womb, and naked I shall return thither. In all this Job sinned not, nor charged God foolishly.

We tumbled out into the sun. To our north, the Beatitudes. To our south, the gravel path to the lake. The cool water versus the valley heat. The valley would win by a knock-out. We examined each other. We looked like two pensioners caught in the old age home's mangle. Anat discarded her shredded sweater. I cut my torn jeans into shorts with a penknife we found in the guard's hut along with two bars of Lieber chocolate and an old rucksack. My shirt was torn too, I stripped to my waist and tied the corpse of it around my forehead. We were now the perfect 'sixties era tourists, Nashville fodder lost in desert pastures. Finally finding our destinies, perhaps, the roles we were both made for. Loading the rucksack with the penknife and the remainder of our *schmutters*, venturing out into the world.

It was seven-thirty. Very calm and peaceful. The world as God might have intended. The birds doing their thing, a hare darting to leeward, bees buzzing after the whiff of our Lieber. Soon, though, the buses would be hurtling down the road, heading for Capernaum. Ancient columns and the footprint of Jesus, kissed by the pilgrim Pope. Hand in hand we trudged in the opposite direction. In an hour we reached the main road. We walked along it warily, but all appeared "normal". The mockery of hallucination? One kilometre on, however, we found the evidence: burnt bushes, still smouldering, a black patch on the road, with metal debris. Minute memories of "Alexander". The whole wreck must have been scooped off and away. No guard of honour or barricade to mark the spot. No trace of our baggage anywhere. Our spare knickers taken to be pawed by experts, along with the automobile post-mortem: Pass the spanner, Doctor. This vehicle has been suffering a corroded chassis for the past five years.

What was Anat's strange paranoia of last night? Those people, Joe, they're not speaking Hebrew . . . "I'm sure it was Arabic," she had said in the cave. Not the place for more bad news . . .

We were walking instinctively north, up the main road, avoiding Halabian Tiberias. Truly aimless, the strengthening sun toasting what was left of our brains. Cars passed us sporadically, honking at Anat's shapely T-shirted figure. Not, I can lose no bets on this, at mine. Business as usual, they seemed to have noticed nothing. What's a burnt-out patch on the road? "Terrorist" attacks, searches, attempted assassinations, it's here today and here tomorrow.

A bus passed us, honking, and fifteen minutes later we saw it drawn up at the roadside. A ramshackle kiosk, with a Coca Cola sign, an icon of valley salvation. The passengers were crowded round the altar, their voices borne on the heatwaves towards us. Adults squabbling, children demanding. I want, I want, I want. As we drew nearer we could make out the telltale symptoms of my brethren in the faith – the knitted skullcaps, the beards, the properly covered and amply coiffed women. Intestine-churning signals to me, usually, but I was beyond caring. The magic American potion drew us. Luckily I had preserved my wallet in my back pocket through the mayhem of the last night. Anat and I were as one, at last ideally united, as we surged forward blindly towards the shimmering bottles, the pop and fizzle of caps snapping with the firm flip of the vendor's wrist . . .

And then, inevitably, the booming voice:

"Joe, sweetie! So you've decided to join us!"

There is no escape. The traps are everywhere. The umbilical cords of the tribe. Eyes bulging, beard wagging, my Old Man of the Sea, brother-in-law Elisha, throwing his arm about my shoulder. Bellowing delightedly at the sight of Anat, turning to announce to his flock:

"Hey, comrades! My brother-in-law Dekel and wife! Zip your mouths up. The media are here!"

Should one announce penicillin at a bacterium convention? Nevertheless they clustered round, braying. "It's about time!" "Welcome to the rhinocerous club!" "Show us his teeth!" "Moo! Moo!" And demands for journalistic information: "What's going on with that terrorist raid in Safad? They're still tracking them in the hills, I hear . . ." "It's so terrible . . ." "It'll never end . . ." "They should bring back the death penalty . . ."

I denied all knowledge. "We're just on holiday . . ." I said, "I don't know anything, I'm just a TV critic . . ." The patter sounding distinctly off. They introduced themselves, with formal handshakes. "Atzmon, of Kiryat Arba." "Giora Stern, Shomronia." "Albaz, of Alkayam." "A bit of a hippie, my brother-in-law, is he not?" said Elisha, "but it's not the clothes which make the Jew. Eh, Anat? You will enjoy this ceremony. We'll give those pioneers a rousing start!"

"OK, *hevreh,* it's time to go!" A *cri de coeur* from the bus door. "It's a long way to the north of the Golan! Take your seats or miss the show!"

"This day will change your life," said fucking Elisha, propelling us firmly forward. "It's an historic occasion. You'll be glad you decided to make this move. Nothing is lost by hearing out the other side. Oh, wait till Nehama hears about this!"

The funeral march played in my mind as the tide bore us into the bus. Elisha ushered Anat and I into two seats, suggesting, "Settle this territory now. We'll apply for land rights later." The settler delegates clambered aboard. Many were carrying guns. One even had a Kalashnikov. It was an assault course of overhanging shirts, bull thighs, bull necks, shaggy beards and hatties. Some of the women sat with their husbands and offspring. Others gathered at the back of the bus. The driver, a red-bearded centurion tank of a man, swished the door shut on the foot of a straggler and virilely gunned the motor. "Green?" he asked Elisha, in paratroop jargon. "Jump!" My brother-in-law confirmed. The bus surged forward, amid a burst of song:

> "I do Believe, with Absolute Faith,
> In the Coming of the Messiah,
> And even if He tends to be tardy,
> I shall wait for Him every day till He Comes . . ."

25

A makeshift rostrum on a mountain plateau. The national flag fluttering in the wind, from either side of the rostrum and from each of the fifteen mobile cabins housing the settlement's first fifteen families. Rows of benches, trucked in from the south, filling with guests disembarking from several buses and a small fleet of private cars drawn up on a cleared ridge of ground. At the lip of the ridge, four giant Caterpillar bulldozers, ready for new exertions. Looming ahead, the vivid bulk of the Hermon, two kilometres above sea level. The dark basalt brown of Golan. Just out of sight below the ridge - the Druze town of Majdal Shams, the northernmost centre of habitation before the decline into Syria.

A great relief to get off the bus. Hard to imagine a more loathsome journey. Three hours boxed in with my most hated enemies - land grabbers, dispossessors, colonial neo-fascist bastards, with their false Messianism, their utter distortion of everything I perceive as Judaism. In other words, I don't like them. Anat they merely give goose-pimples. Throughout the voyage, in between roundelays, they also pressed on us fattening foods, home-made cakes and dumplings, as we throbbed past Gadot, over the thin sliver of the Jordan River, up, past the Lower and Upper Customs Houses, those icons of the one-time Syrian Heights, their fortifications laid low, their Moslem in-habitants mostly chased into Syria, their ridges settled and finally annexed to the State in 1981. Menahem Begin, slipping one past the White House while General Jaruzelski zapped Poland. Bring on the next but one war ... and still the settlement movement prospers ...

> "David, King of Israel,
> Exists and Is Alive ..."

But it is not King David who descends in a thunderous roar and a cloud of dust from the skies, but the ubiquitous Minister Without Portfolio, né Minister of Defence. Mister Lebanon, 1982, fallen from grace but laden with ballast. Thrusting his great weight under the chopper's rotors, bounding ebulliently up the hill, shaking hands, returning embraces. He is the darling of the movement, its Grand protector, the man they most wish to see on the throne. His adulators surround him, clapping his vast back, strong enough to bear their burden. He is led directly to the refreshment table, handed a paper plate piled with dumplings. "Joe, pass the coffeepot," says Elisha. I am sucked into collaboration. Here I am, face to face with my devil, the sweaty red visage, panting heavily. The most dreaded moment comes: "This is my brother-in-law Dekel," says Elisha, "he's from the media." It is a truism that most murders occur within families. But the great man merely casts a rancid eye over my pathetic garments. He does not recognise me as the person who once wrote of him, apropos his TV appearances: "This home-made car bomb, this Genghis Khan of our most unholy nightmares ..." "If you were in my battalion, you would soon have been for it," he comments dryly, and guffaws. Elisha hands him his coffee, in a paper cup. He turns away, the flyswatting accomplished.

Freed at last from Elisha's vainglory, Anat and I sneaked aside, avoiding the Minister's entourage, the ex-General's tame hacks, the TV crew just scrambling out of the chopper after some reloading blunder. Dangers of recognition here, surely. Even worse, if Lauterman had made it back from Abdin Palace, an even more embarrassing contretemps, that I could well do without. My plate was piled high enough already. The sins of my past visited not only on myself, but on Anat too, whom I had drawn into my private sphere of anguish. Guilt, and the full realisation of the web wound about me by the Three Sons (of Whom the Torah Spake), Moishe-Ganef, The Gingi and Meisinger ... And I, the Fourth Son, Who Did Not Know How to Ask, was expected to produce an answer. Behind us, on the podium, the speeches began. We walked over to the edge of the escarpment. Standing on top of the world, the clear blue sky above us, flecked with soft feathery clouds. To our left the Druze town nestling in silence. Over the next hill, an erased border, the south-eastern tip of the quagmire of Lebanon. Armoured patrols in Dangerland, vulnerable every moment to the rocket grenade and the bomb. Just out of sight, never out of mind. To our right, a tented army encampment, and beyond that, the minefields, the barbed wire border and the implacable Syrian Enemy. Twenty-five kilometres north-east to Damascus, heart of our internal darkness. How far does vaulting ambition reach? The Minister had commenced his peroration. The Voice of Power rolled across the mountaintops as he stood, a home-made tank, on the podium. The wind agitating the white hair on his turret, flapping his incongruous skullcap:

" ... These brave pioneers ... Our finest sons and daughters ... the vanguard of the Nation ... obeying the dictates of their national conscience and of the Lord God of Hosts ... Laying down here, at our northernmost border, roots which will be everlasting ... The eternal task of defence ... the enemy who must be vanquished ... only last night, for example, in Safad ... a dastardly outrage ... prevented only by the vigilance of our armed forces ... Proof that our struggle is just and vital, despite the voices of weakness among us ... 'Peace Now', which is the 'peace' of the grave ... Peace with Strength will be *our* achievement ..."

Instinctively, without premeditation, Anat and I moved down the mountain. Placing physical distance between ourselves and the Voice, memories of 1982 Jerusalem, an act of mental self-preservation ...

"Now I did not come here to make an election address, but it's never wise to waste an audience ..." Scattered laughter, like caged birds expiring. I held Anat's hand. We were knee-deep in bushes. The mountainside was awash with wild flowers. The Golan in bloom, as always after a rainy winter. We had journeyed through a live palette of colours, up the western escarpment, which concealed the hundreds of thousands of land mines still remaining from 1967. But here we were mind free, an odd oasis amid the threats of war's concussion. We looked up and three herons banked past, avoiding the ridge of evil counsel. Everywhere there were cornflowers, daffodils, daisies, spectacular patches of poppies. Land of milk and honey. Perhaps it was the crumbling bones of so many previous poor soldier bastards that made this ground so lush. Ammonite grunts, foot-sloggers of Aram, groaning conscripts of Assyria, Rome. Mamelukes, Ayyubids, oodles of Turks, feuding Maronites and Druze ... The Druze, I am told, believe in reincarnation. Death, they say, is just like swapping hats. In the 1920s they fought the French in these hills. A great deal of headgear was exchanged. Moslems, too, swept down Golan to attack the Jewish settlements in the valley below. They killed Joseph Trumpeldor, who said: It is Good to Die for Our Country. The Druze and Joseph Trumpeldor were not afraid to die. But Joseph Dekel is. I am not yet ready to meet God. There are books I have not read, video-cassettes I have not screened. I have never seen Frank Zappa live. I have a month's unpaid grocery bills. Small matters, not important in the vast scheme of things. Somehow, with the fading voice of the General, they take on a new significance. I think perhaps I should marry Anat. Unless she kicks me in the balls for the nerve. I might get her to suspend her loathing of the Rabbis. I might slip something into her tea. I am tired, I wish to find a resting place, consecrated by signed guarantee. My feet are leaden, and slide over the rocks as if I had magnets in my boots. My head, on the other hand, seems to be brushing the sky. I feel elongated, like Carroll's Alice. And I have not even eaten anything marked "Eat me", apart from Gush Emunim's dumplings ... I seem to be a giant, astride of the earth. But my feet are clay, and stuck in the ground. Anat's hand is clammy in mine, but her face seems to be receding from me. A flight of strange black birds flees from a thicket, wheeling into the blue sky. They have yellow beaks, and white flecked tails. I was never good at natural history. I am a ghetto man, and should have remained in the prayer house, ruining my eyes over the ancient runes, trying to work out what on earth God had in mind ... When Jews died, they used to put twigs in their hands, so they could dig through to the Holy Land on The Day. Now they bring their caskets over on special discount charters. We have pulverised God into the ground. There is nowhere left for us to go since we have made ourselves pawns in our own cyclic games. We do no one's will, least of all our own. We have made ourselves slaves of our nightmares. We are the Ridiculous. Someone, somewhere, must be laughing. It certainly isn't me. Grass slips under my feet. I have now shrunk, and the thickets rise about me. There is movement somewhere. Anat's hand slips from mine. Somewhere I hear her cry in warning. They rise around me, the natural consequences of The Crumb, The Gingi, Kazaz, Halabi, Meisinger and his orthodox minder clones - sweaty, panting figures, dressed in leopard-spot camouflage, filthy socks, or so it seems, over their faces. Weighted down, as if to prevent their levitation, with submachine guns, rucksacks, grenades. A brief vision only, before my arms are pinioned behind me, a grimy rag fastened over my eyes. No further sound from Anat, who seems to have dropped out of my life with the suddenness of a stone plummeting away down a bottomless well. Clipped words of warning, in Arabic. A voice, in Hebrew, crooning in my ear:

"Do you hear me, Joe Dekel? This is Sami Khatib. Balata Camp. Sha'abani's café. Listen carefully: your girlfriend will be safe. We are leaving her behind. You are going to have to come with us. It will be a bit of a walk, the first part of the way. Then it will get easier. Please don't make any trouble. I want you to trust me. I assure you you are as safe as a baby."

A singular rebirth. Typhus, cholera, rickets, teething, everything to stretch again ahead of me ... I prefer just to stop. Hold this reincarnation. "Where the hell are you taking me?"

"Across the lines," says Sami, "to a magic country. Where everyone is always a stranger."

I am grabbed by the arms. My legs lose their footing. They scrabble to find it. I rise. *"Yallah! Nruh min hun!"* Like a blinded guide dog, I set out towards the unknown.

THE UNKNOWN

26

A song of degrees (a pilgrim's song):

In my distress I cried unto the Lord, and he heard me.
Deliver my soul, O Lord, from lying lips
and from a deceitful tongue.
What shall be given unto thee, and what shall it profit thee,
that false tongue?
Sharp arrows of the warrior,
with juniper coals.
Woe is me that I sojourn in Meshech,
that I dwell in the tents of Kedar.
Too long has my soul dwelt with the hater of peace.
I am for peace, but when I speak,
They are for War.

– Psalm 120, from the Jewish *Siddur*, or Prayer Book

27

Amazing, what one can become accustomed to in the iron grip of necessity: I am blindfolded in transit from one place to another. A mixed blessing. Now I can see no evil. But I can still hear and smell it:

The grunts, sighs, cries and farts of my captors as they go about their obscure business ...

The rip, scrape and clatter of their pouches and arsenals being set aside for a brief moment of rest, a cigarette break or a shit ...

The shock of a misfired bullet, or bursts of gunfire from near or far, denoting someone fallen out with someone else, or perhaps only target practice ...

The planes, passing overhead, the recognisable buzz of the robot drones, the sudden shriek of more serious hardware, the sonic boom of hi-technology. Just randomly feeling for some place to drop their bombs, or in search, ominously, of Joe Dekel? The way they hunted Yassir Arafat from building to building in besieged Beirut in 1982, rocketing apartment blocks to rubble two minutes after the Chairman had left to a new temporarily safe hiding hole? The long arm of Meisinger, pre-empting a deal? How far can paranoia stretch? Best not to answer that, in our battered part of the globe ...

The smells: indeterminate vermin dung, piss, shit, sweat of my jailors, the dry sweetness of abandoned apartment rooms, the mustiness of cellars, the pungent reek of deserted garages ... These interiors at least I am allowed to see, the blindfold removed, my starved eyes feasting on the peeling whitewash, the crumbling brickwork, the concrete reality of the whiffs of petrol fumes, motor oil and grease: broken-down chassis of jeeps, family cars whose families have been long since scattered or killed, heaps of rubber tyres, piles of rags, rusted carburettors, gearboxes and shafts. Metallic graveyards of an indeterminate Levant, with one live Jew rooting among the spark plugs. Most of these places were arms dumps, too, altars to the grim reaper: Kalashnikovs, M16s, FNs, carbines, rocket-propelled grenades, mines, machine guns, flamethrowers, fragmentation bombs, explosive caps, fuses. Not much use against the horrors dropped by Phantom or Mirage, but effective enough on the ground ... And beside the ammunition boxes, the piles of lethal ordnance – crates of Seven-up and Pepsi-Cola bottles, courtesy of the big bad wolf of Imperialism, via Syrian Ba'ath "Socialism".

(Location: Probably somewhere in the Bek'a valley, home of all that is alien: Syrians, Lybians, Iranian zealots, our own home-grown Palestinians ... Bloodthirsty terrorists of every ilk and hue, dreaming of carnage in King George Street and posthumous fame on television. Our own Orwellian room 101, the expanded, open-air, drive-in version ...)

Seven-ups apart, I was kept alive on Israeli K-rations looted from an ambushed patrol. My captors thought I might expire on the Syrian army issue they themselves viewed with extreme suspicion, as if it might be larded with special chemicals on the orders of President Assad, to turn them all into rabbits or obedient robots or annihilate their virility. Also they seemed to have taken note of my hattie, and had evidently decided to preserve my soul from hellfire by providing kosher. This must have been Sami Khatib's idea. He had adopted me as one adopts a mongrel one hasn't quite resolved to pass on to the glue factory. He even brought me a *siddur* which had been taken off a dead IDF soldier. There had been some blood on it, which Sami washed off carefully with a piece of wet, torn blanket. He himself had a copy of Menahem Begin's *The Revolt*, which he spent hours enthusing over, eager to make conversation but utterly determined not to answer any of my questions: Why? What? Where? When? "You'll find out, Dekel, just have patience ..." The book was dog-eared, its pages marked with copious underlinings and margin scribbles. "'The Historical and linguistic origins of the political term "terror" prove that it cannot be applied to a revolutionary war of liberation."' He read out to me the words of my ex-terrorist ex-PM, as I sat on my rolled mattress reluctantly shovelling Israeli army beans into my face. Seven years spent trying to avoid this menu. There are destinies one cannot escape. "'In a revolutionary war both sides use force. Tyranny is armed. Otherwise it would be liquidated overnight. Fighters for freedom must arm; otherwise they would be crushed overnight."'

"Don't blame me," I said, "I voted McGovern." But he turned out to be a *kokhelefl* par excellence and I was the original captive audience. This abandoned, locked garage must have been the fifth hiding place I'd been dumped in. Or was it the sixth? I'd lost count ... After the long blinded hike down the mountains of Golan, the nightmare at lights out, bound and gagged, not certain whether Anat was safe or not, or whether she still existed, I had been thrust, somewhere, into a vehicle and thereafter lost all sense of time ... Dragged out, a couple of centuries later, pulled past shouting Arabic voices, up several flights of stairs. Vision restored at last, in a bare room with just one decoration – a colour portrait of Ayatollah Khomeini. God! Not them! But Sami Khatib reassured me: "Don't worry about the old fart. This is only a temporary bivouac." "What is all this about?" I asked, again. "Don't worry, Dekel, just keep going." I slept on a bed, oh bliss, till night fell, which I could tell by the slatted shutters, closed but broken, over the room's only window. A bizarre slumber, levitated by the tenseness of my nerves, no dreams necessary to overlay the genuine nightmare of "reality". Then, another century later, shaken awake in darkness, blindfolded again, seated in a jeep or commandcar, jolted for an aeon over pot-holed roads to arrive at my first dumping ground, abode of machine oil, sweat, piss, Seven-up and Sami Khatib, bending my ear with Begin, reciting the names of the martyrs of the Jewish Irgun's war against the British, which he had learned from *The Revolt* by heart:

"Dov Gruner, hanged in Acre prison. Yehiel Drezner, hanged in Acre prison. Alkoshi, Kashani, Nakar, Haviv, Weiss, hanged in Acre prison. Barazani and Meir Feinstein, suicide, by grenade, in the death cell. They sang their national anthem before they died. Do you expect us to do any less?"

"No," I said, "by all means, the national anthem." But he spared me on that occasion. Not that I had any idea what the fight for freedom had to do with keeping Joe Dekel cooped up in cellars, but no one enlightened me on that score ...

My three other kidnapper-guardians were markedly less learned, though the youngest, Marwan, was no less gabby. He was a tousled-haired eighteen-year-old who had grown up within Israel in a village in the "triangle", spending his teens swabbing the floors of Jewish restaurants in Tel Aviv and Haifa. His view of Jews was somewhat like Harriet Beecher Stowe's view of Simon Legree. "Why are they always shouting?" he asked, perplexedly, "perhaps they will all die, of heart failure." I agreed that his view of the Final Solution was not utterly unlikely. He was undergoing the Levantine male obsessive phase, and spoke for hours about two Belgian sisters from Brugge he had apparently snared by his nifty broom action. When the War for the Liberation of the Homeland would be over he would marry both of them and live in Denmark where, it appeared, mixed marriages were ten a penny. For the moment they were presumably keeping vigil in Brugge while he kicked his heels in No-Man's-Valley guarding yours truly for unknown reasons. He was even more baffled than I was about the point of his duties. "Are you a nephew of Shimon Peres?" he asked me one morning. I did not speak to him for several hours. Of my other two jailors there is not much to say. Number Three, Ibrahim, a dour refugee product, spoke little, but fetched and carried. Number Four, Abbas, was a killer, with that look of someone one did not fuck with. Chicken necks, human gizzards, he could clearly wring either without a blink of that gaze. He and I maintained an unspoken agreement - to survive our forced companionship ...

What was it all in aid of? Khatib kept promising an answer

– "In due course, Dekel, just keep going." I bombarded him, whenever I could, with questions, about Meisinger, the Gingi, Father Parry. Was there really a Gingi envelope? Was it your lot who tried the Meisinger hit in Safad? But he just stroked his chin silently, fiddling with his moustache. "If this is all in aid of Moishe Sherman's mystery treasure," I informed him, "you have got hold of the wrong key." But he was not drawn even on that, and retired to do his regular push ups. He did five sessions a day, perhaps in lieu of prayer, or to keep in trim for a Begin re-read. "'There can be only one policy for an oppressed people: a struggle for liberation.'" Indeed. Just so. Myself nodding politely, burrowing through the corned beef . . .

Another night, and we were on the run again. No reason at all was given. Me, lying on my mouldy straw mattress, fingering the dead man's *siddur*. Young Marwan dozing over his AK47, dreaming of blonde Brugge pubes. Dour Ibrahim and Mad Dog Abbas burst in, spewing spit and flicking lights off. Was this the end of it all? Instructions received: waste the bugger and close the shop down? No, just the same rough ritual, tugging my arms, secuiing my blindfold which had become like Linus's blanket to me. I could go nowhere without it. I remembered West Bank nights, back in '67, watching the lines of prisoners detained for interrogation, torn shirts or rags secured round their heads, trembling in the yards of military barracks, faceless and shorn of identity. Now it was my turn. Clutching the dead man's *siddur*, ushered from darkness to darkness. Ibrahim humphing my K-rations, as was his wont, probably with bandoliers and three rifles. The fresh smell of a crisp late May night. Or was it already early June? Was there a whiff, saints above, of orange groves? The coastal plain of my long lost Homeland? No, just the mockery of the Levant, scoffing at one's deepest aspirations, debunking all one's illusions. The magic country, where everyone is a stranger, because all its natives are dead.

In my distress I cried unto the Lord, but He must have had urgent business, elsewhere.

28

Oriental disorientation continued. I tried to keep up with passing time, but in cellars I often found it difficult to distinguish a.m. from p.m. Above ground the stifling heat of the day, the cool of night, anchored me to some hint of chronology. I gave up, though, on trying to pin down the Sabbath. Still no information from Sami Khatib, apart from queries from his sacred text *ibid*. "What was the role of Eliahu Golomb, Chief of the Haganah?" Or: "Who was 'Comrade Parabellum'?"

"I am a Quaker," I said. "I am opposed to violence." But he could not find that in the index. Dour Ibrahim unbent towards me enough to share pittas, but not to make conversation. Abbas kept his discourse to the level of the apemen in the *2001* prologue. Marwan, on the other hand, became ever more friendly, and told me more sad tales of his youth. "When I was young," he said, as if referring to the Middle Ages rather than half an hour ago. Tales of tough times in his home village, its loss of lands, the reduction of its people to menial labour in the Jewish towns. "Every day I had to get up at three in the morning. The chickens had more sleep than we did." I shall cut a pound of my flesh and stick it in your palm, sweetie. Anything for a ticket home. Since he had learned I was not a relative of the Leader of the Opposition he had begun to consult me on politics. He had become disillusioned with the Communist Party in the village, he said, at the age of fourteen. One for the *Guinness*

Book of Records. "Why does Moscow accept the State of Israel?" he asked. "Is it true that Marx was a Jew?" "One of the Elders of Zion." I told him, solemnly. He left me alone for two days. The heat seemed to increase, exponentially.

And then, after twelve million years had passed, Sami brought me a Hebrew newspaper. I would have kissed his feet but, as far as I knew, he had not changed his socks since the Golan. So, there was a world, continuing out there, business as usual, in a parallel cosmos. Unbelievable joy to fondle the garbage that always made my blood boil: "STRIKES THREATEN TO PARALYSE THE ECONOMY"; "2.5 TONS OF HASHISH SIEZED". "TRIAL OF TWO 'UNDERGROUND' DEFENDANTS WHO PLEA BARGAINED: STALWART CITIZENS, SAYS RABBI"; "PERES RECEIVED WITH CREAM BUNS IN BEIT SHEMESH"; "CLOUD OF GAS OVER HERZLIYA." Ecstasy. But Sami directed my attention to the item he had thoughtfully marked for me on page four. Despite everything, he was a true sweetie pie:

> GIRLFRIEND URGES ACTION ON MISSING JOURNALIST
>
> Anat Levy, girlfriend of missing journalist Yosef Dekel, kidnapped last month by terrorists, has accused Ministers responsible of apathy and delays in the negotiations over the exchange of prisoners ... Ministers have denied allegations by fellow journalist Nahum Lauterman of ideological reluctance by the government to negotiate with Palestinian organisations holding several Israelis prisoners, some since the Lebanon War. "We never abandon a prisoner in the field," said the Deputy Minister of Defence yesterday.

No wonder there is a cloud of gas over Herzliya. At least Anat was alive and kicking. Life-enhancing thoughts flooding my mind, gladly banishing the vacuum ... I could imagine her, massaging the streets of Jerusalem, touching the stones on my behalf. Warding off the sexual overtures of the dwarf Rumachansky, not to speak of his artistic pretentions. Get a ladder, van Gogh of Lilliput! Cut his other ear off, comrades . . . ! I can see her, wrestling with the inheritance of the video-cassette collection. Having to manoeuvre among my abandoned bric-à-brac, my filing non-system that always drove her up the wall, my back issues of *Soldier of Fortune* . . . The ill-fated Luger was not there to annoy her, but there was still the US Air Force Survival Knife and the brass knuckleduster bought for a song in the Portobello Road . . . She always gave me stick for my obsessive attraction to all the things that I loathed. But what was going on out there? She must have been debriefed after the Golan, questioned ten ways to Sunday by army and SHABAK and Meisinger and his minions. She had obviously not failed to grab hold of Lauterman and squeeze him in a double nelson. Had she made the mistake of trusting the bastard? Where did all this uplift leave me?

I scanned the rest of the paper but there was not much enlightenment. A rash of election advertisements. The paper's date was June 23rd. Only one month to the ballot. Predictable balls-ache: "THE PEOPLE WANT LIKUD"; "I BELIEVE IN WEIZMAN: THE THIRD FORCE"; "LABOUR IS THE LAST HOPE"; God help us. "LYOBA ELIAV – AN HONEST MAN TO THE KNESSET". One knows a loser when one sees one. I shed a tear for the poor oaf. A positive item: my chosen party – the Jewish-Arab Progressive List for Peace, has been allowed to run despite attempts to ban it. So, for balance, has the ultra-right KACH party of Rabbi Meir Kahana. He campaigns to kick the Arabs out of the country, but he has to take his turn in the queue. Opinion polls still show the opposition Labour Party comfortably in the lead.

"What do you think?" asked Khatib.

I shook my head. "Likud again, for sure," I stated.

"You are a pessimist," he replied. That was rich. The man turns me into a lost postal item, and I am supposed to look to the future.

The election campaign this time round, according to the hacks, is a very quiet affair. None of the violence and hysteria of the last round of 1981. Some of this is due, the scribes say, to the dullness of our new PM, ex-Stern gang terrorist,

Shamir. Some to the silence of ex-PM Begin, who is still hiding in his bedroom. The man who wrote "fighters for freedom must arm" is himself completely disarmed. History repeats itself, once as tragedy, the second time as farce, the third as soap opera. I looked to the TV schedules, and had a laughing jag. The Israeli television was on strike. Eureka! The broadcasters had joined me in limbo.

I began to feel I might survive my present crisis. Not all the omens were disastrous.

That night I slept well for the first time in weeks and had a singularly angst-free dream: I was walking with Anat in the pristine snow of a midwinter Jerusalem. All the battlements of the Old City were capped white, the cupolas like children's *yarmulkas*. I had on thick boots, and three pairs of socks, and my lungs breathed in icy pure air. Anat, beside me, had a thick bright red sweater like a model in a skiing advertisement. She hugged my arm. I felt I could take on the world. An acutely romantic moment. I was carrying an old Mauser single-shot rifle, with a sniperscope attachment. We were walking down the wide swathe of the Paratroopers' Road towards the Damascus Gate. The curve of the white-carpeted Mount of Olives and Augusta Victoria, in background. On the battlements, a number of pigeons pecking in the snow for breadcrumbs. I began to pot them, one after another. They fell, flecking the road with red. A policeman, dressed in an Alaskan parka, trudged up to me in the snow. His feet made satisfying crunching sounds. He had the face of the Gingi, the snowman with German measles. "How are things, Joe?" "I can't complain." "Can you clean up the corpses?" he asked. I picked up the doves and slung them over my shoulder. He rooted about in the snow for spent cartridges. "I want them for my son," he said. "He's only five years old. He has never seen a shot fired in anger."

Anat and I continued, down the road. The snow was melting as we advanced. By the Damascus Gate it had gone completely, and our boots echoed on dry hard asphalt. The sun shone bright in a perfect sky. We entered Abu Shukri's restaurant. The waiter cheerfully bore off our doves. We sat and looked into each other's eyes. She has enigmatic eyes, Anat, you never know whether they are saying O light of my life or What am I doing here with this banana? Our fingers played tickle-me-touch-me. The smell of roast doves wafted from the kitchen.

I awoke, and I was alone in my room. No sign of my four musketeers of Palestine. As far as I could gather when I was brought here, this umpteenth hiding place was an apartment house of two or three storeys. I tested this proposition, opening an unlocked door, peering into another room. It was the first time in several weeks I was making a move without permission. Doubtless there would be consequences. This was so. In the next room there was no portrait of the Ayatollah Khomeini, but framed Koranic verses on the walls and a family picture, on a sideboard, of a smiling young man and woman. By definition, an ancient artefact. Dust everywhere. I moved on into the kitchen. No roast doves, but definitely consequences: three of my musketeers, dead as Dumas, my poor Athos, Porthos and Aramis. Killer Abbas, dour Ibrahim and the child Marwan, snuffed out while I mooned about with Anat, touching fingers at Abu Shukri's. The first two had blue-black bullet holes in their temples. The child Marwan had his throat cut. Their eyes were like painted ping-pong balls. The phrase pool of blood made manifest. No more tales of woe from the village child. One mixed marriage less, alas, in Denmark ... Anonymity preserved for the unknown soldiers, whose stories I had never known, nor wanted to know, nor could have borne the telling thereof ...

And no sign of d'Artagnan Sami, tattered copy of *The Revolt* and all. I circled the bodies and looked out of the kitchen window at a dusty, deserted street. It looked much like a suburb of Petah Tikva on a bad day in 1949. Once whitewashed walls. A dirt roadway. Two wheel-less chassis of cars. Two chickens. Some shop fronts closed with corrugated iron. A dead or sleeping dog. I looked at my watch. It had stopped. For several weeks I had rewound it religiously. Now, at the pay-off, failure.

On legs which had seen better days I wobbled out into the block's stairway. There was another door on the landing. I did not try it. I crept down to the ground floor. Empty letterboxes hanging askew by the lightswitch. Just like home, if such a thing survived. Someone obviously believed this place existed, at least on a post office grid. I poked my head out into the open. The leading chicken looked at me with infinite malice. Deciding I was not a small enough crumb it scrabbled off, clucking in frustrated fury. The air was brisk, the sun clearly low, the shadows long. Another day dawned. For some reason I thought of my old English teacher, his opening chorus: "Goood mor-ning to you . . ." Nothing looked good in this God-forgotten hellhole, which must have seen it all, and said no thank you. I stood in the apartment house doorway, looking up the length of the road. A car, a cream Mercedes, edged its way round the corner and buckled up the gravel towards me. Sinner man, where can you run to. I stood my ground and picked my nose. There were three men in the car. I recognised one of them. He poked his head out the window.

"Hallo, Joe. We meet in strange places."

"Don't worry. No one will think we're friends."

A long way from the Patisserie Valerie.

"Let's go." said Zaki Khatib.

29

We drove over the dog. If it was not dead before, it certainly was now. We headed out of the still town.

"Where is your brother?" I asked.

I should have known the answer.

"I am not my brother's keeper."

I cast my eye over my other travel companions. They were both, like him, in mufti. One was a small, bald middle-aged man who looked as if he had slept in his suit for three years. The other, a tall military type in his forties, with cheek scars and deep blue eyes. We were not introduced. I was having a surfeit, this summer, of unknown warriors. The car sped into a landscape I was seeing for the first time. It was a fertile valley, with a mountain range looming in blue haze ahead. Farmers with kaffiyehs, donkeys and sheep dotted the fields, as if nothing special was happening. But signs that things were otherwise soon obtruded: fields and trees scarred by fire, buildings collapsed or blasted. Every structure, in fact, seemed to have a piece missing, a roof, a storey, a bite of a corner, halves of balconies, shell-pitted patios. The remains of abandoned fortifications, piles of barbed wire, upended guardhouses. And everywhere, wrecked cars, jeeps and trucks in shell-craters and on burnt verges.

"I am sorry we had to leave you in that hole so long," said Zaki. "Do you mind taking that thing off your head?"

I snatched it off. We had long passed the limit but even I could see his point at this pass. We reached our first roadblock, a mêlée of half tracks, camouflage netting, armed leopard-spot soldiers. They had those strange berets reminiscent of the French army, inherited by Damascus. I shrank in my seat, deprived of my blindfold to protect me from the world. But Scarface waved a document at them. They passed it up, to the highest bidder, a captain, who raked it with his eyes, then impassively waved us on. I came up for air. We were on the road again. Khaki and ordnance at every point of the compass. Russian trucks, French cannons, West German jeeps. Hurrah for international brotherhood.

Zaki continued to speak to me in Hebrew, with a certain perverse enjoyment: "We think we are at last approaching a showdown. My poor brother has just delayed us a little. He was doing what he thought was the right thing, you know. It is difficult to clear a path in the jungle."

"Is he alive?" I asked.

"For the time being," he said. "And I hope I do not regret it."

Scarface and Baldy, in the back of the car, sighed like sated locusts settling.

"I'm lost, Zaki," I said, "I understand nothing. I am a *tabula rasa.*"

"We are all lost," he said, "we are pawns of chessplayers who are themselves blind."

Touché. We passed four more roadblocks. Scarface's document becoming visibly threadbare. I had become blasé, leaning out of the window, nodding at the khaki parade. I had never thought I could view Syrian soldiers with anything less than abject terror. The northern hordes, fodder for human wave attacks, stoned on army issue reefers. Sadistic torturers of prisoners of war, to whom human life is not worth a cow pat. All that was apparent now was how badly most of them were in need of a shave. A large number were children, and perhaps proud to maintain the first sprouting of their whiskers. But many others seemed middle-aged reservists, who had better things to do with their lives. Tend the garden, console the wife and kiddies, play backgammon in the café. We left them behind and turned off the main road, heading less conspicuously towards the mountains.

"The famous Shuf," Zaki said, proudly playing the tour guide. "We are not far from your countrymen here. If we headed south you might be getting home, but before that we would all be hamburger." Out of kindness for me, therefore, the car veered north, climbing up into the mountain. There was a palpable relaxation of tension. Even Scarface seemed to unbend, and smiled. I wondered if it was he who had slit the throat of my village child guardian. Or Baldy, while Scarface put professional bullets silently into the other two? Not that I had grown as attached to those three as to my mother, but nevertheless, a strange bond. The Stockholm Hostage Syndrome, I think they call it. One falls in love with new ways of death. And what of Sami Khatib, fading away, like the Cheshire Cat, minus the smile ...?

At the next roadblock an armed band loomed, loafing beneath a poster of a Star of David raining bombs upon a crying child. A row of portraits plastered a pillbox, of a youngish balding man with sad eyes, bulging at some nameless horror. I did not need a programme to recognise the face of Walid Jumblatt, heir apparent to this part of the world, and to realise I was among the Druze, the cheerful changers of headgear. Scarface left the car, and had a long pow-wow with the militiamen. He returned and we followed four men in a jeep up a side road to the outskirts of a village. Three-storeyed houses with red-tiled roofs set on the steep hillside. There was a great deal of untouched greenery. Children playing with car tyres, old men grouped under trees, women hanging out washing on porches. A scene of picturesque harmony, were it not for the ubiquitous khaki and military jeeps and guns. We entered a café. Humus, pittas and olives. I fell on them like a giant locust. Someone brought kebabs. I devoured them too. The militiamen stood by, smoking wryly. From the snatches of Arabic I heard they were taking bets whether I would eat the table. A legend is reinforced - the Ravenous Jew: It's true, they want to swallow all of us ...

The journey continued for over two hours. It was slow, and often interrupted. A Druze captain in a natty, ironed uniform had joined us, to see us past the mountain strongholds. His face looked as if it had been ironed too, and a crimp put in his moustache. He entertained us along the way with tales of atrocities. Women disembowelled, children beheaded or spitted on lances. "And they call themselves Christians," he said, amiably, of the perpetrators. "It is what you call food for thought." We had converted to English, since he knew my secret, but not the argot of the Enemy. Everyone knew my secret, except me. The old, old story. Laboriously, we curved about the hills and valleys, through vales of pine and scattered cedars. No sign of spitted children, but bizarre rock formations, as if the ground had given an early warning of the deformities to come. The air was a pure hit of oxygen. "We live in paradise," said the Druze captain, "and we intend to keep it this way."

No comment. I let the landscape roll. Sinking back, trying to reach Zaki by telepathic inquiry. But either the atmosphere was not propitious or he was blocking my barbs. He still looked like a prosperous kebab merchant, but now he did have me on the skewer. I tried to empty my mind, avoiding the thought of that barbecue of my insides.

By late afternoon we had reached the western ridges, commencing to fall off towards the sea. Heavier signs of mass destruction now, large burnt spots on the hillsides, smashed armoured cars, pock-marked buildings that looked as if they had been dinner for rampaging giant woodpeckers. The outskirts of towns that had been shelled, strafed, assaulted, taken and retaken so many times in the past two years they did not concern themselves too much with Joe Dekel passing through. Shepherds with astigmatism from looking out for shellfire drove sheep across pot-holed streets. Children gambolled on piles of rubbish or in the burnt-out shells of cars. Old men wandered about with empty petrol cans, looking for some nameless provisions. Chickens, staking their claims everywhere, reluctantly let us pass. We seemed to be zig-zagging to avoid towns or villages that were controlled by the wrong side this week. Finally, as the sky began to darken, we turned off down a narrow side road flanked by olive groves, vineyards, and small allotments of fruit trees, and drove into a small town, stopping short at the inevitable roadblock. The Druze captain decamped here, and a quiet youth, dressed *à la mode* in armaments and khaki, joined and led us to a four-storey building, at the top of a hill. It had two signs - HOTEL, and PEPSI-COLA, and turned out to be full, not of Swedish and West German trippers, but of extended families encamped like bedouin in the corridors and rooms. The children's eyes monitored us curiously as we climbed to the fourth floor, entering a bare empty suite of two rooms, with three mangy mattressed beds, opening on to a concrete balcony.

"We will wait here for a while," Zaki said. "Make yourself at home. I have to try and make a telephone call."

The two silent partners stretched out on the beds. Cigarette smoke curled up in the half light. The sighs of locusts resigned to hunger. I walked out on to the balcony. It had taken its share of shot and shell, bits of stonework were chipped here and there. But this was no distraction from the panorama which stretched away below. Plunging from the mountain, in the gleam of twilight, the majesty of the city: Beirut, the sclerotic heart of our follies, blood-red in the setting sun. The killing ground, its square miles of buildings jutting like dragon's teeth. I had spent the last two years avoiding this trauma. Like the K-rations, it claims its own. From within I heard Zaki making what seemed to be doomed attempts at telecommunication. Finally I heard him say: "I'll wait for the call," and he joined me, shaking his head at the view.

"Now that used to be really something," he said, like a person discussing an old lover now dying of terminal syphilis.

"All right," I said, "we've reached the gate of the castle. Friend or foe, give me a clue. You at least know I'm completely at sea in all this. What's the name of the game, for God's sake? What is all this odyssey in aid of? Don't tell me it stems from Moishe Sherman, the little street Ganef from Jerusalem ... What makes him so important? What did he snatch that shakes the earth so?"

"Why don't you ask the man himself?" Zaki said, calmly. "We have an appointment for a meeting later tonight, down there."

30

Soon we could make out the dead apartment blocks, parted by vast piles of rubble. Disembowelled warehouses, ruptured girders twisting towards the moonlit sky. Residential buildings with every window blown out, resembling great multi-eyed skulls. Buildings smashed from above, as if by a marauding giant. Roofs tilted into the ground. The roads were pitted with craters and strewn with rubbish. Little dots of fire burned here and there. We slowed down to approach our first roadblock, a pile of sandbags with narrow eyeslits and a drooping flag poking forth, of whom or what I could not see. The bald man carefully left the car, whispering in the dark with soldiers. Soft sounds, in the pause, of the car ticking over. Metallic chinks, scrapes, low coughs and sneezes. A terminal restlessness. I thought of my ancestors, digging underground with their little twigs through to the Holy Land. The Undead, scrabbling at coffin lids. Fuses, softly being primed. Somewhere an ambulance wailed. In the distance, the ubiquitous gunfire. Or it might have been the gnats, closer by, spontaneously combusting ...

We had entered the city after a mad, high-speed run, escaping from the frying pan into the fire. Careening down the mountain slopes, touching 130 below on the wide approach road, curling south, then jack-knifing north up the highway: the airport road, alongside the ruined stadium and the ill-fated Palestinian "camps" of Chatilla and Sabra. This much at least I knew from the newspaper maps I had devoured with my war reports two years, or was it twenty decades, ago . . . ? Now and again, a burst of gunfire from darkness, spitting useless gobs of flame. Streetlamps perforated like sieves with bullet-holes, strobed past in our dimmed headlights. But none lit the way ahead. Power-cut time. Abandon hope all ye, etcetera . . .

Only a lunatic or an assassin travels the city at night. The lunatic was me, the assassins surrounded me, everything was in perfect order. They had stocked up earlier on the requisite hardware, and we now resembled a travelling arms sale. We had a Kalashnikov, an American carbine, grenades, an Uzzi and three machine pistols. We proceeded, after the roadblock, at a much reduced speed, entering the shattered labyrinth. The streets we entered now were extremely narrow, cars tightly parked on either side. The battered buildings rose about us like cliffs. I had spent weeks, two years ago, watching in long shot from my armchair as these houses were pounded by our artillery. "Light precipitation on sources of fire." I knew I could not abide close-ups . . .

We crossed the Boulevard Saeb Salaam. Or so Zaki saw fit to tell me. "We have crossed the Boulevard Saeb Salaam," he said. "Does this improve our chances?" I asked. They all laughed. There was an air of total recklessness in the car, as if we had all jumped out of a plane without parachutes, just to see what would happen. Every now and again we halted, and Baldy left the car again, vanishing into the maw of one of the silent buildings for ten minutes while we cleared our throats, sighed and spat our fear out into the pot-holed road. Other times we would halt, as footsteps crunched towards us, and the lump of a head eased through our window. Scarface, having done his piece previously, in the valley and the mountain, actually went to sleep in the back. His stentorian snores threatened to break the balance. Someone might count them as the first volley. Eventually I, too, dozed, that ridiculous half slumber of battlefield blues that fuses truth and fancy. It seemed to me we were flying over a cityscape of ruins, the black and white aerial newsreels of post-World War Berlin, the smoky shell of destroyed Warsaw. Take me to the Hitlerbunker, James. And Zaki was happy to oblige . . .

"We are almost there," Zaki said in Arabic. He was not

risking my home tongue in the lion's mouth. Baldy emitted a short prayer, then looked embarrassed and blew his nose. He dug Scarface in the ribs. The man surfaced, spluttering, reaching vaguely in his jacket. We had turned into what appeared a prosperous side street of tall apartment blocks with marble façades. There was a whiff of sea in the air. We must have been close to the hotel area and the defunct American Embassy. Where once CIA agents sat and plotted, now just a hole in the ground. Zaki drew the car up, looking relieved, passing me a sheepish smile. "We were lucky tonight," he said, "usually this is a frightful journey."

I was glad to hear it. We piled out gingerly, my nursemaid-villains hefting their hardware. They hugged a stone wall, while Zaki led me swiftly to a heavy iron door. We stood by it as he motioned me to stay calm and in place, and pressed a bell set in the wall. I had no intention of going anywhere. I did not have to wait long. The door suddenly gave, as he pushed against it. He beckoned me to follow and we stepped into an inner courtyard. My two new guardians remained outside in the street. Melted into the city ambience. I never saw them again, but they are with me, always ...

I crossed the courtyard with Zaki to a stairway and a ground-floor door with a brass plaque, which said: "GLOBAL-LIBAN". Zaki knocked on the door. Many bolts were drawn. A chink of light showed a man's face, in shadow. The face withdrew. A last bolt was opened. We entered a short corridor to an office, whose walls were plastered with tourist posters of delights no longer on offer: happy crowded beaches, skiing on water, on snow, spas on mist-wreathed mountain peaks. The ruins of Baalbek, besieged by Japanese cameras, not by IDF Phantom jets. I felt at home, among comfortable illusions. And for a moment my heart stopped, because I thought I saw Anat before me. She was sitting behind a desk, gazing softly at me round the curve of a whisky bottle. It was, however, a trick of the light, or of the astral aura. Nevertheless, I had seen this raven-haired lady before, and the whisky confirmed my memory: Lancaster Gate, the Palestinian party, dancing on the grave of Gingi Arse-Face.

"You see," she said to me in English, "I have had to bring

my own booze again."

The man with her, after embracing Zaki, turned to face me with wry amusement. He too looked at me as if he thought I should know him, but I could not place him at all. He was small and European, though strongly tanned, with a smooth face and a short brown beard. He noted my confusion and smiled smugly. "Our paths have crossed too, Mr Dekel. I have caused you some problems, but this could not be avoided. I am Father Lucien Parry."

"Ah yes," I said, "I have seen pictures of your corpse."

He laughed. "That was a fake to fool you."

So what else is new?

"You were never a corpse?"

He shook his head, deliberately, with pursed lips, as if he had weighed the options. There was no doubt, I had to reserve judgment.

"How are we for time?" asked Zaki.

"We ought to be going," said the resurrected padre. Not a sign of the wild-flower collection. I should have been flabbergasted by this development, but it seemed all of a piece with the day. Easy go, easy come, Joe. Was this the man who had once served in the Congo, and then charmed the faithful Mrs Treen? Where does he fit into my long tale of woes? How many crosses can one bear? They should supply me a pantechnicon van. I can bring my own nails.

"You missed a very good party," said the Palestinian lady, "several people were asleep for three days."

I was not surprised. She left the whisky behind, an ominous sacrifice. We ploughed our way through a dishevelled bedroom, twin beds, unmade, strewn with clothing and loose upholstery covers. The walls covered with movie posters, Guilliano Gemma, Charles Bronson, Bruce Lee. "This used to double as a film distribution company," explained Zaki, "but there is not so much cinema in Beirut now. Everything has changed to video."

"It's the same in Jerusalem," I said, "but there the problem was cockroaches, not bombs."

We exited into a dingy back yard piled with rubbish which hid the entrance to a concrete bunker. The man called Father Parry unlocked a steel door. A flight of metal stairs led down.

We entered a tunnel, flanked by old brickwork, shored up by heavy timbers.

"I call this the Waterloo Line," said Miss Whisky, "you will soon find out why."

"The Beirut subway is quite extensive," said Parry, "but like everything else here, it too is divided. The Shia have their own tunnels, the Sunni theirs, the Kurds, the Christians, and so on. We are traversing the old PLO network, which is undergoing repair."

"You cannot destroy the PLO," said Miss Whisky, "we are like moles, we see in the dark."

For the present we were seeing by the light of torches which both she and the supposed ex-priest carried. The tunnel curved into a lengthy shaft flooded ankle-deep with sewer water. It was clothes'-peg-on-the-nose time and we had no clothes' pegs. The whisky lady turned and grinned. "Waterloo, you see?" I acknowledged her wit with an unenthusiastic murmur.

She pointed and sloshed forward. On top of everything else the shit of Beirut in my shoes. I had bought this pair at Dolcis in Oxford Street. *Sic transit gloria mundi.* Sami Khatib had offered me a pair of Fatah issue boots, but like a dunce I had turned him down. I suspected it might be one more item carved off a dead Israeli. In the event it might indeed have turned out to be so, only the carcase would be me.

After about fifteen minutes we came to a "roadblock". Three tunnels connected and branched off. The usual sandbags and armed guards. More banal city routine. Teenage youths in uniform with red bands round their heads, who had seen too many Clint Eastwood movies. "Make my day!" they drawled at me in American, as Parry bade me scrape past. I manoeuvred myself, thankfully on dry land now, along rows of crates stored along the gallery, some over the height of my head. These were very professional underground workings. They had not been built in an hour. Weapons protruded from open boxes inscribed with various deceptive markings: "SEAPORT METAL TRADING", "AGRIGCO LIEGE", "HAMBURG PORCELAIN, THIS WAY UP, FRAGILE". Other crates bore all manner of far-flung designs: Chinese, Japanese, Hindi, Russian. There was also a whole section of crates of whisky, which had their own armed guard. My Palestinian lady's eyes gleamed, but Parry nudged her on. A little further, in a niche, a thing of special wonderment: a whole wall of crates marked in Hebrew. "ELYAKIM EXPORT-IMPORT", with a host of stamped numbers.

"Somebody is in business," I remarked to Zaki.

"Everybody is in business," he said.

The row of crates did not end, but our journey was cut short by a ladder leading up a dark shaftway.

"I will go first," said Parry. For a dead man he was extremely agile. And the prospect of another dead man waiting to greet us. Still no sound of divine trumpets. Miss Whisky climbed up next. I peeked up her skirts. She wagged her behind at me. One takes one's pleasures as one can. Zaki appeared very calm by my side. Perhaps he commuted thus daily. Too late I thought of a riposte to the lady: moles do not see in the dark, they are blind.

Zaki as rearguard, I clumped up the ladder. I emerged in an amusement arcade. A large video-game machine had been shunted aside to allow us to climb out of the shaft. A small dapper grey-haired man in an expensive dark suit motioned us forward with fluttering hands. *"A'ajl! A'ajl!"* Quick! Quick! *Mach schnell*, etcetera. It was a dim cavern lit by dim blue disco lights, with two rows of inert arcade game machines on either side like modern sarcophagi. I could make out the popular "Killer Gorilla", "Ant Attack", "Beach Head", "Fort Apocalypse", "Grid Trap", "Strontium Dog", "Apache Raid" "Zaxxon" and "Psi Warrior". What ailed the youth of Beirut, evidently, was a severe lack of excitement. But we were swept past all these, through to a stairway leading up two floors. There, in a corridor, two men in short-sleeved shirts with submachine guns guarded an unmarked cream door. They were as unmarked as the door, and had the same expression. They might have been from Italy or Zarkon. They were probably, like everyone else, the kids next door. The small dapper man knocked and stood back. The door was opened by another Martian. The room beyond was an office, lined with filing cabinets. A *Playboy* calendar hung on the wall and a three-quarter face view of Amin Gemayel, President of a palace to the south of the city and of precious little else. A man sat behind a bare glass-topped desk. He had a stupid smile on his face. I had seen that smile before, and I still loathed it. He simpered, like a confessed virgin. Dracula Has Risen From the Grave, truly, but the wrong Dracula, in the wrong grave.

"Hey, Joe."

I should have known it.

Gingi Arse-Face, every freckle a plague.

31

The famous sage Rabbi Hillel once saw a skull floating on the water. He said to it: "For your drowning of others, you have been drowned, and those who drowned you will be drowned."

The pillock sat, wide-eyed before me, the Simple Son, of Whom the Torah Spake. He is the one, in the Passover Haggadah, who queries: "What is all this?" To whom you should answer: "By a strong hand God brought us out of Egypt, from the house of slaves ..."

Talk about the banality of evil.

"So it was you pulling the strings all the time."

"I suppose you might say that."

"Where's your little doggie, The Crumb?"

"Oh, he's around somewhere."

"You should be proud of him. He did a good job of pretending you were dead and gone."

"It's Menashe's speciality - making people think he is as thick as a two-by-four."

Hillel also said: "In a place where there are no men, strive yourself to be a man."

The room was very quiet, apart from my companions' wheezes. Miss Whisky was having a coughing fit. The small dapper man breathed heavily. Father Parry had lazily lit a cigarette. He used the floor as an ashtray. And this was the man who reputedly collected wild flowers, and pressed them with Saint Augustine. Amin Gemayel, on the wall, said nothing. Zaki provided chairs from an adjoining office. I would have sold my mother for a coffee. She was, however, safe from bondage.

More than I could say for myself.

"Well, you've certainly made it to the top," I told the Gingi. "If you can leave this room alive."

"Poor Joe. Ever the victim of his misconceptions. I am as safe as anyone in this city. An old lady crossing the street for groceries would be in worse trouble."

Did not Hillel also declare: "There is no ignorant man who fears sin?"

"I was led to believe I was coming to meet Moishe-Ganef."

"I'm as much Moishe as you'll ever see."

I felt suddenly as weary as Methuselah when he decided to throw in the sponge. The chorus of wheezes and coughs had now ceased. I became aware of the whine of air conditioning. The building must have its own generator, or the millennium had come for the city. One's mind does not wish to engage the issue. I could make out the sound of gunfire again, faintly travelling along my neurons.

"You're telling me everyone's been chasing a shadow."

"Story of our life, dear friend."

"Moishe-Ganef is dead."

"Two and a half points, Joe."

"He has been dead since the first reel. It was really Moishe in the Edenvale Hotel."

"Correct again. Three points."

"You killed him yourself, you bastard."

"Has anyone got a cigarette?" he asked. The ex-priest shuffled forward with a Gitane. Gingi waved it away. "My lungs won't take that," he complained. Zaki passed him a Marlboro and a plastic lighter.

"How can you work with this man?" I asked the Palestinian. "He's stolen your country. He's raped your cattle. He's sold your women into slavery and he kills people in hotel rooms."

"This is the real world, Joe," said the Gingi quietly, "wise up and open your eyes. We've been killing each other for a hundred years, and who do you think is going to stop it? A hundred demonstrators, or even a hundred thousand, with placards 'Down With the Occupation?' It's sons of bitches, like me and Zaki, who have a chance to make an impact. We have a vested interest. We are involved. We're not afraid to get our hands dirty. This is the Middle East, Joe."

"So I have noticed, Gingi," I said.

Zaki gestured at him, pointing to his watch. The Gingi put his palm up, calmly, "Poor Joe," he said to Zaki, "he's been run through the mill. I think he deserves some explanation."

To be patronised by this acned nobody! It must be true, anyone can be President. If talent were the touchstone, this man would melt in front of me, like Poe's poor Monsieur Valdemar.

"I didn't kill Moishe," he said, quietly. "Menashe, your 'Crumb', killed him by mistake. He doesn't know his own strength, the *schmendrick*. We were going to knock the Ganef out and snatch him. But there was an unforeseen struggle. That's the trouble with violence, it's so unpredictable. I prefer using the grey cells."

"You should be had up in court then," I retorted, "for wilful misuse of government issue. Why involve me in your internal feuds? Couldn't you people just kill each other off, as Nahum Lauterman suggested? I presume he's one of yours."

"He played his part, though he never knew the full story. Unlike you, Nahum is civic minded."

There could be no response to that. After being arrested, threatened, framed and kidnapped. My beach buggy atomised, my Anat endangered, myself bloodied and chased, humiliated and mortified, and finally brought to this butcher's city where Jews are about as popular as hepatitis. And all this, I am to believe, in the service of the nation? The blue and white flag? The Ingathering of Exiles? The Glory of Israel and Zion?

"We ought to move," said Zaki, "or we'll be behind time."

The Arse-Face rose, his face a pock-marked apology. "I'll have to tell you the rest on the hoof, Joe. I'm just a guest here. I have to follow the schedule. A man's got to do what a man's got to do."

But a pustule should just be squashed.

We exited through the empty arcade. The blacked-out Beirut beach stretched before us. A soft sea breeze caressed our faces. Our armed guards watched our every move. We sat round a table at a deserted café. A tattered awning creaked in pain. Behind us the hulks of the great hotels, ancient ruins of a good time.

"Waiter!" I called. "One tea with *nana!*"

But there was no waiter and no tea.

32

And the waves, white tipped black, washed on to the beach, to the deserted lido.

"Once upon a time," said the Gingi, "there was a Jewish State. It was founded on high hopes and ideals, and a great deal of blood and more than a little skulduggery on the side. It was surrounded by enemies and had few friends and no precious reserves of gold or oil. What could it do? It built its military strength, taking advantage of the divisions of its enemies. Eventually, after wars and ructions, it looked around itself and Lo, it was pretty mighty, but its enemies hadn't grown puny either. It had swallowed up some extra chunks of real estate, but acquired with them a load of rowdy tenants. It had become involved in the global power game, but was just kibitzing at the table. Where should it go from here? There were several schools of thought.

"When I entered the civilian arm of The Family, back in '72, you know what the policy was, Joe. Remember that Document, in Beersheba, the one that gave us all a jolt? And, I'm sure, it also gave Moishe the idea that finally did him in ... 'Flexible Alliance Options', remember? That was the general principle: 1984. We are no longer at war with Oceania. We have always been at war with Eurasia. Iran, Pakistan, the Yanks, the Reds, why should we miss a trick? Yesterday we were virtually married to the French. Today we're in bed with the Americans, and sucking South African cock on the side. Tomorrow, who the hell knows? Does anyone really love the Jews?

"Once one starts on that train of thought, it progresses

logically, to the core: future mutual interests where, at the moment, there seems nothing but eternal conflict. This was, if anything, strengthened after the Yom Kippur War, when the limits of our power were obvious. We were that close to playing the nuclear card, and that shook up the trade, I can tell you. And as the years went by, more new shocks – OPEC, the Arab bomb, Iran. But by the time the Ayatollah took us by the goolies, The Family was having domestic trouble. Menahem Begin had come to power, and Ideology was *über alles*."

He leaned back, settling in his beach chair, sucking a Marlboro a sidekick had found him. For all the world as if this were the Tel Aviv esplanade, and an upside-down coffee imminent. My hatred for him warmed my belly. I was grateful to him for this wellbeing. The Whisky Lady and Parry slumped beside us, in neutral. The Gingi continued the lecture:

"I don't have to tell you what Faith, not Analysis, does to the Intelligence game. The machine begins to creak. It emits strange noises. Pretty soon, fuses begin to blow. Political appointments eat away at morale. Lesser lights begin to curry favour. People you shunned at the cafeteria are suddenly Heads of Department. And, before you know it, an old mutual friend, who was brilliant but considered a little warped in his judgment, basks in the warmth of real power."

"Meisinger." Against my will, I participate.

"Comrade Meisinger," he confirmed, "a great patriot. He wants our country to be strong. He wants our country, in fact, to be unstoppable, a juggernaut that cannot be touched. Like all of us, he came up from the cauliflower growing, Holocaust trauma, etcetera. You know the man, he has no moral scruples. He'll deal with the devil if need be. He's not afraid of wars, because he knows, as we do, that Israel will not lose at this stage. But what he is desperately suspicious of is a Peace that comes before its time. Peace before the fortress is completed, ramparts unshored, battlements still on the drawing board. Peace, especially, with the Palestinians, the enemy still within the walls. He prefers, therefore, an implacable enemy: wild men, hijackers, baby killers, bombers of supermarkets. To ensure there's no shortage he owns a little property out here, in Arabland. A grouplet here, a fraction there. People whose kinks can be manipulated. People who will shoot our own ambassador, for instance, in a London street, to start a war. Am I boring you, Joe?"

"No. I've read about all this, in *Newsweek* and *Ha'Olam Hazeh*."

"It's difficult to keep secrets nowadays. People have lost their innocence. But the more they read, the less they care. It's diminishing returns, comrade. I'm just trying to explain my position here. I am the Good Guy, Joe. I have been liaison to PLO Arafat for the last three years. Ever since the ceasefire everyone denied, between Us and Them, in '81. The ceasefire our patriarchs ached to shatter, with the aid of our ex-friend. And you can see the result all around us: a broken city in a battered land. Our army bogged down, our enemies laughing at us, the Pentagon convinced we've gone loopy."

"Vote for the Progressive List for Peace," I said.

"Jokers like you can dream. And this is just the beginning. Look what's happening back home: fascist undergrounds, neo-Nazi babblings, messianic conspiracies. Bad, bad vibes, Joe. You can see the need for action."

"I still don't see why you hauled me into this. Nor why you killed poor Moishe Sherman."

"I told you it was a mistake, Joe. Your Moishe was always like that little boy who was so sharp he cut himself. He had rifled Meisinger's private safe, you know. You wouldn't believe the half of his haul! Lists of agents, position papers, names of global contacts: Christian fundamentalists, Abu Nidal, KGB men, moles in Iraqi Intelligence. And the real clincher, the item that could put the noose round the bastard's neck ... I'd waited a long time for the Superbrain to make a slip, and this was a real lulu. We set up a meeting with Moishe, to discuss a sale. And we were going to snatch the *putz*, as I told you. But it went wrong, as things do in this business, and there I was, with a dead Ganef, the loot hidden God knows where, and the perfect Meisinger-trap down the toilet. But you remember 'KAMAN' Course? They taught us to improvise. There in that hotel room I had a brainwave. I knew that you were in town. I had been keeping tabs on you as a possible Moishe contact. As it was, he avoided you like the plague. But I knew your London address. I was sure you weren't involved, but what could Meisinger be led to believe? Remember, Joe, high stakes at play. War and peace. Life and death, etcetera. Old friendships aside, time is blood. You could be the ideal witness to bamboozle our colleague, to make him believe a dead, harmless Ganef was still a live threat. Despite the dead body. I knew I could count on the mistrust that prevails in this business."

"So you sent me the Tiddly Crumb, just so I'd know nothing I was shown was on the level. And then you conveniently found a dead Turkish pusher to dump there after I'd been suckered. Was he in a dustbin, or does one phone an agency?"

"He was the courier who had lead us to Moishe, but we knew he was unreliable. Expendable alive, useful dead. It's a tough business, Joe."

"And then you set the CID on to me."

"Someone had to pass the story on. I knew they wouldn't hold you. I had to exit, of course, to smooth things over, but also to leave a proper hook for Meisinger. It took me a couple of days, to fake my own funeral, and Sana here helped firm it up for you. And lo! The vanished Moishe was reborn - puppet master, master criminal. I like to feel that up there, he approves. It was the role he always wanted. He was such a schmuck alive, wasn't he? A sticky fingered smart-ass. Dead, he was helping me to snare a scoundrel. A villain who might destroy us all ... And Banzai! Meisinger took the hook. We led him on from there. I had to have a hook, Joe, you can see that? How else could I flush out a paranoid with a twenty-four-hour guard of fanatics?"

"Brunettes. He was nuts for brunettes."

"Ten a penny, Joe. Those days are over. We are all big bad boys now, covered with the muck of impossible choices. It's been clear for a long time the country's split, civil war is on the agenda. Today, Beirut, tomorrow Jerusalem? Better to fight it out in the shadows. Zaki was cleared to assist me - 'Flexible Alliance Options' - but then we made a serious error. He brought his brother Sami in on a 'need to know' basis, but brother Sami went rogue. Not having been told our Moishe really was dead, he bought the cover story at face value, and went after the Ganef's haul. Making mischief, to disrupt our communications: fingering our man in Tiberias, Parry, through you. That was a sneaky move. Our padre had to disappear at short notice, but Meisinger played it as a killing. He set his own trap, and you fell into it. I didn't think you'd be so nosy. He also killed that policeman who was snooping around. Things were getting out of hand ... Sami's attack at Safad – that was another surprise. I got Menashe to pull you out of that one. But Sami and his little gang followed – making a pass at Tiberias, tracking you to Golan, snatching you to Arabland. You might have sat there till doomsday while Sami waited for a non-existent Ganef to make contact. I have gone to a lot of trouble to get you out, Joe. I never meant you any harm, believe me. It's been a piss of a time for me too, I can tell you. These people around me are not exactly friends and this is not my idea of home comforts."

So forlorn, the prick, I felt almost sorry for him, despite that whole pack of farfel. Sorry for the downfall he represented, blighted hopes, trampled dreams of innocence. Doing the wrong things for all the right reasons. Good intentions, lousy execution. If I could believe all those Tales of Münchhausen, with their ragged ends, unanswered questions – What did you do, son of a turd, with Moishe-Ganef's body? Etcetera, etcetera ...

But before I could marshal my inner forces for the counter blitz, Zaki Khatib, down on the beach, shouted, "Boats in view!"

"Here they come!" exclaimed Father Parry. He had been scanning the sea through binoculars. We each took a peek. It was a stirring sight, without a doubt. In the moonlight, the shape of a frigate. A row of smudges, in front of it, leaping silently upon the waves, like dolphins, heading towards the beach. Commando dinghies. Our armed Martians fanned out, disappearing behind abandoned shower stalls and shuttered ice-cream kiosks. Zaki, too, melted into the darkness. The Whisky Lady swore softly. Total regret at having left the booze behind. I looked at the Gingi. He scratched his freckles.

We sat waiting at the lost café.

33

Frogmen on the beach, alas, armed from hood to flippers. From the two central dinghies five men emerged, with short black jackets and homburgs. I could see the white of their faces by the starlight, over their sleek short beards. Meisinger's minders, incongruous in Safad, strangely at home here. At this stage an invasion of pigmies would not have surprised me at all. Their leader strode forward, to stand exposed half way towards the café. He took a white handkerchief from his pocket and noisily blew his nose. Then he stood, scratching his beard. The light hiss of waves behind him.

Nothing happened. Then the Gingi clapped me on the shoulder.

"OK, Joe," he whispered, "you're on stage."

He pushed me out from under the awning.

Metallic clicks resounded from the shoreline. Meisinger's minders hunkered. The front man turned his face towards me. I stood there, the world's Number One lummox, a whale caught grazing in the Gobi. Like a proud mother, the Gingi shooed me on, making the signs that meant, Don't worry, *bubbeleh*, everything has been arranged.

I walked up to the man I had spoken to in Safad.

"Good evening, Dekel," he said quietly.

"Can you give me a lift?" I said, evenly. "I seem to have mislaid my life."

"You're welcome," he said, "but there's some business

pending with that man up there."

"He says he's a Good Guy," I said quietly, "what do you and the Mastermind think?"

"We think he's a traitor to his country," he said, "but let's not quibble over trivia. How many men has he got hiding out there?"

"Seven or eight, I think," I said.

"Heavy weapons?"

"Submachine guns, small arms. A grenade or two. Nothing to worry grown-ups."

He scratched his nose.

"You know it's not Moishe-Ganef up there," I said, "and I don't think he has the goods you're after."

"Yes, we know about our Gingi now," he said, sadly. "Every day we get older and wiser."

There was no point inquiring when enlightenment had dawned. I tried, instead, a personal query: "Is my girlfriend, Anat Levy, all right in Jerusalem?"

"She has lit a candle in the window."

"What is your assessment of our chances to live through this?"

"Who knows. Family tiffs are ticklish."

"I think the Gingi intends to kill Meisinger."

"You are a romantic, Dekel, but let's give him his chance."

He gestured with his fist, on the top of his head. A shape stood up in the central dinghy.

Whatever stands for normal service ends here. The rest is chaos and confusion. Whether the Gingi has planned it thus, or his minions mistimed it, I would never clearly know. Out of the darkness an almighty Cr-rump! sounded across the water, and the waiting frigate, delineated on the horizon, was engulfed by a fireball. Simultaneously, the whole shoreline erupted with small-arms fire and grenade blasts. The entire beach and coastline hotels were visible in the light of the explosion. Frozen gunmen by ice-cream stalls. Bodies in wet suits on the sand, dead or astonished. The front minder had slammed my face in the sand. Now we all converged on the terrace. A scene from madness, black dreams and gangster film dénouements under the abandoned café's awning: The Gingi on the ground, Father Parry standing over him with a smoking gun in his hand. The Whisky Lady thrown back in her deckchair, a jagged black hole in her forehead. And two black holes in the Gingi's face as well. A piece of brain had fallen over his eye. I am a quite observant Joe. I can see anything as close as the tip of my nose. Anything an inch further, no. And the Gingi would answer no questions now. *Après lui, la deluge.*

Homburged minders, gathering round the body, rummaging in its clothes, pockets, shoes. One of them throwing off his hat, ripping away his whiskers. And there was Meisinger, glaring at me, with a sort of baleful rapture.

"I told you, Joe. A magnet for trouble!"

"The hell with this killing, Meisinger!"

"Hare krishna, Joe. If you can find a flower, you can stick it up your backside."

"You told me you didn't kill old comrades."

"He started this. I was going to take him alive."

"That priest - he was your man all along, Meisinger! You knew his death was fake when you framed me ..."

"I could never be sure you were not part of the game, Joe. Can I be sure now?"

Puppets, dangling on crossed strings. The chief frogman rushing up, wired for radio.

"Someone detonated a limpet mine under the ship," he said briskly. "They've transmitted a Mayday."

"Remind me who's Operations Officer for this mission?"

"I am."

"Yes, I thought so."

"We can't stay here," said the killer Padre. That was fairly obvious. Firearms sounding from within the city. The trigger happy of all sects, opening up in empathy.

Meisinger said, "Alert the choppers and the standby convoy. We'll use the emergency exits."

Running, with Joe dragged along like a sack, into a nearby hotel lobby. Father Parry leading, past abandoned tennis courts, dry swimming pools, abandoned saunas. Shooting open the door into a cellar. Boots clattering down a torchlit tunnel. Not so much the Waterloo Line now, but Andrzej Wajda's *Kanal*: the chase through the Warsaw sewers. Except we were not, I would have thought, the partisans. How does it feel, Joe, to run with the Nazis? The Whisky Lady might have laughed herself sick, if she were not now food for worms ...

Pausing for breath at a familiar junction. The rows of crates along the walls. Sweaty bodies squatting, torches playing on brickwork. Meisinger snorting at my ear: "The Gingi was a fraud, Joe, right down the line. Did he give you his PLO Option spiel? The Munich Section, we called them, the Pink Appeasers. As if we would ever deal with the terrorists. Use them, yes. Kiss their arses, never. The Gingi never knew the difference. You might think he was some sort of liberal hero, but what do you think really brought him here? Cash money, Joe, not love of country. Here, let me show you something."

He shone a torch on the crates with the Hebrew markings. A minion smashed one open with an Uzzi. It was full of neatly stacked cardboard boxes. The minion ripped one of them open. I peeked in. I did not get where I am today without recognising a video-cassette recorder, even in a Beirut sewer.

"Part of the Gingi's kingdom," said Meisinger, "anything for a fast buck. Televisions, home computers, software, database fraud. And after that, stolen State secrets. The Ganef and he were running this show together. They would have tried a corner on hashish and heroin, but the government runs that here ... They fell out in the end over the loot from my safe, which the Ganef was trying to hoard. Exit dead Ganef, leaving running Gingi. It was him or me, darling. So I used his own plots, with my Padre's help, to trap him. But I swear to you, Joe, we never intended to kill him, only to bring the bastard to justice."

"You don't expect me to believe all that," I protested.

"Suit yourself, Dorothy. Things are not as they seem. You will have to find your own bearings. I tried to warn you off the minefield from the start, remember? But you have this thirst for Knowledge ..."

The luckless Operations Officer panted up. "We have a problem with the Rachidine exit. It seems there is an Amal patrol in the area. We will have to go for 'Global-Liban'. It's certified clear and there's an intact roof for the chopper to land."

Meisinger laughed. The smirking chortle. It took me back a full eighteen years. It was the sort of sound he used to make when stuck outside on manoeuvres, midnight at zero celsius, when he wanted us to feel he had chosen to be there, whereas the rest of us idiots had been diddled.

"Can you hear them, Joe? All our cousins outside! Beirut, sharpening its knives for Passover. Jewish meat, on the block! You have brought your cyanide pill, have you not?"

"No, I'll just close my eyes and enjoy it."

"You are a born guttersnipe, Joe. At last you have the guts to admit it."

Running on, down the tunnel, the frogmen now and then firing and throwing grenades into side shafts. Up the dank stairs, out of the bunker entrance to the backyard I had traversed earlier, kicking aside the stinking rubbish. Two people who had been with me then were now dead. And Zaki Khatib? Faded away, with his brother Sami, to reappear as the avenging angel? Could any assumptions be sustained now? Any truth behind the lies? We emerged under a sky streaked with flares. But no sign or sound of helicopters. A whispered conference, amid the crackle of static, the OO appearing to hold a conversation with his own pectorals.

"The convoy is just round the corner," he said.

"Bring them and fuck the chopper," said Meisinger.

We ran through the film-travel office. Water skiing, Baalbek and Bruce Lee. Through the central courtyard to the iron front gate, as vehicles rumbled outside. A small charge blasted the gate open. We rushed out into the street. A truck and a jeep were drawn up, guarded front and back by two light wheeled tanks. Men in snappy short-sleeved shirts and tight trousers darted about, giving cover. The minders, hemming in Meisinger, rushing him into the jeep. The rest of us piling in the truck in a massive rugby scrum, the truck tearing down the road. Sweat, hairy forearms, gun butts in the ribs, a pointed shoe in my nostril. The crests of apartment blocks flying past above. Yawing telephone posts. Dangling wire. Flares like comet trails in the sky. A lone siren wailing in East Beirut. The city setting up a familiar cry of pain and violation. Lurching on to a wide, empty thoroughfare, probably, if we were heading for the airport, the same road I had come up, earlier in the night, the Avenue Camille Chamoun. Except I was then still a raving innocent and now I was privy to incompatible secrets. Which version should I believe, the Gingi's or Meisinger's? Perhaps this was just another of my dreams. But everyone around me pinched me. Rising somehow to my feet, I peeped round the truck cabin: the jeep, full of bearded men with homburgs, the leading armour, with the head of a volunteer sucker warily poking from the turret ...

The dash to freedom, however, was interrupted just as we passed the looming bulk, on our left, of the shattered sports stadium. A PLO arms dump, it had been bombed so many times before and during the war it was amazing anything was left standing. The Christian Phalange used it to process men and women they had kidnapped from the adjacent slums of Sabra and Chatilla, on that cursed September weekend. Blood and spilled guts on worldwide television, and so many Pilates, rushing to the water taps ... From the shelter of a jagged lump of concrete, a streak of flame flashed across the Avenue. The lead tank exploded. The jeep veered to avoid it. A sheet of flame slashed the width of the road. Someone must have laid down a trail of petrol. The jeep was forced on to the verge. An explosion, fifty metres down the highway, brought down one of the tall lamp-posts in front of us. I was elbowed aside from the front of the truck as the frogmen opened up with everything. The truck lurched on to the roadbank. The frogmen leapt off, firing. Grabbed again, I found my face slammed in gravel. I was becoming fed up with imitating an earthworm. I rose to my feet and advanced.

Someone shoved an Uzzi into my hand. The moon was not quite full, but nevertheless, they were turning me into a werejew again. I flattened against a concrete pillar, then peeked to view the field of fire. The jeep was burning on its side. The minders and the minded, scattering. Ahead stretched a flat plain of rubble-strewn land, leading on to the dull shapes of smashed and partially rebuilt houses of the bludgeoned Palestinians. Here and there the stumps of blasted trees, burnt-out bushes, piles of rotting garbage, rat carcases. From the houses dim lights appeared briefly, then disappeared again. I just registered one glimpse of homburg-hatted silhouettes, running. There was virtually no cover. And from the shadows, dashing towards them, a singular phenomenon: a lone figure, dressed as our own frogmen, festooned with ammunition belts, manhandling an RPG launcher. Zig-zagging across the plain, as the minders and guardians all opened fire upon him, a small shape, dwarfed by his ordnance, like a malign goblin. And his ludicrous cry bellowed across the field in Hebrew, just before he was cut down by the crossfire: "LONG LIVE BARUCH GUTTENSON! LONG LIVE THE STATE OF ISRAEL!"

The Crumb – the missing link, the eternal nuisance, the zealous lackey – fresh, it was now clear, from limpet mining the mother ship – a lone, stubborn, avenging angel of his beloved Gingi ...

"Get back!" shouted the OO. "Back on to the road. I have heavy stuff approaching!" The rumble of trucks from behind the stadium. Shots, from the distant houses. The frogmen ran, in a phalanx, towards the road, the homburged minders behind them, floundering. They gathered at the truck, counting each other, gesticulating in panic. "You had him!" "No, you, you fucking idiot!" "The last thing I saw, he was running ..." A chopper, in the sky, thundered downwards, and another, right behind it, firing rockets at the stadium. A helmeted shape gestured from the first chopper, a troop-carrying Bell. "We can't leave!" shouted the front-man minder. "Number One is still out there!" "I have fourteen Number Ones to account for!" the OO yelled back at him. "Next time your boss mounts a private mission, tell him to wheel his own barrow!"

The frogmen piled aboard the chopper. Eagerly I joined them too. The plainclothes guardians clambered after. The minders stood, wild in the field. Their heads together, in a conclave, like so many groups, around my native, farce-clad neighbourhood, haggling over the latest heresy of a rival yeshiva, or whether there were enough stars in the sky to switch on the microwave. The five detached themselves and climbed on with us, two remaining behind as the choppers roared and gained altitude, casting off their homburgs and their jackets, loping off towards the houses in search of their

Mastermind. We survivors of this strange foggy night of the spirit thrashing our way over the beach and the sea towards whatever safety home can provide, while Meisinger, detached from his human shield of protection, lost in the territory of his bitterest enemies, vanished, as totally as if he never were, leaving not a carbuncle or button behind, among the refugees of Chatilla.

THE KNOWN?

34

And the City still stands, at any rate, in the same spot I left it almost two months back. Yerushalayim, Al Kuds, Citta Eterna: the battlemented walls of Sultan Suleiman, the shopping arcades of Mayor Teddy Kollek, my Discount Bank branch, my synagogue. The telepathic angst broadcasting from every street corner, the glum bus drivers swinging their doors shut on the ankle of the last embarkee, my devout co-religionists, wrapped up against the winter frost of Bialystok in a Mediterranean July. The sloppy, sweating reserve soldiers, patrolling the Old City, besieged by offers of underwear. Our Arab cousins, squeezed between Nationalism, fundamentalist sparks, and cash money ...

My family, rallying round, to close in on the ingathered exile. My father, with his sympathetic silence, my mother, with her apple strudels. My sister Sarah, the systems analyst, punching me on the arm. Sister Nehama weeping on my neck. Relations I had not seen since birth, assembling. Brother-in-law Elisha, looking guilty as he should for having hijacked me to the Occupied Golan in the first place, pumping my hand and shaking his beard in inarticulate wonder: "Joe, I really thought you were done for ... we've all heard how they treat their prisoners ... but we knew whom we could rely on in the end ... and the Lord looks after Israel ..."

The old joke: couldn't he look after somebody else for a change?

And the quotidian political storms: the continuing general election battle ... ten days to the ballot, the television no longer on strike, the grand guignol of the election ads nightly ... Twenty-six parties scratching each other's eyes out. Three parties for the abolition of income tax. Five vying for the religious vote. Two (my dilemma) supporting a dialogue with the Palestine Liberation Organisation ... Shimon Peres, for Labour, promising an end to War, Inflation, Discontent and Division. On the right flank – Rabbi Kahana, still campaigning to kick out the Arabs, outlaw miscegenation, and grant an amnesty for the Jewish underground, whose members are still awaiting trial. One defendant, who plea bargained, has been jailed for one and a half years for plotting to blow up the mosques.

There can be no doubt, I am definitely home again.

And of course, on my return – Anat ... Not at Abu Shukri's with dream roast doves, but at The Hut, Jerusalem's latest watering hole, nursing a steaming cup of Sanka. The sun beating down outside on the contours of the alley and quarried stone walls. Steps round the corner from the street of the Sand Lily, the traffic hoot of the Jaffa Road. Is there a balm? Is there salvation? Never far, however, from bad news: Nahum Lauterman, manoeuvring his perfidious podgy frame through the door and to our table.

"Hey, Joe! You're recovering nicely." Turning to Anat: "This patient will live."

She nodded thoughtfully, as if this were not quite her idea of the best outcome for this story. Since my return there has been a distance between us, a certain nip in the summer air. Our reunification has been marred by a certain sourness that it took me a little time to fathom ... Not that she has no cause, with the mortification she endured due to my leap into folly: the Galilee chase, the violence on Golan, her rescue by, of all people, brother-in-law Elisha, who found her trussed and helpless on the mountainside ... Debriefing by Meisinger minions, police and army, the separation, the wait, the fears for my safety ... But that seemed not the nub of it. After all, Anat lives here. There was something else, being held against me, but it was taking its time to emerge ... Just, at first, those frosty looks in July, as I replugged myself into my electronic orgone box, devouring the vast newspaper backlog: Iran threatens total war on Iraq. Inflation might top 800 percent. A famous pop star is busted for heroin. Menahem Begin is still locked in his bedroom, refusing even to endorse his own party. Three Israelis have been found in London in crates trying to kidnap a Nigerian exile. Make way for Joe Dekel, brother. My own re-entry to my Homeland was less spectacular, a sneaky shoe in at Sde Dov military airport ... Debriefing by strangers, thank God, no old colleagues; just go back to sleep, comrade. A footnote on page three, kidnapped journalist returned, in exchange for three crippled terrorists. (Who the hell were they? No one ever told me.) No mention of any contretemps in Arabland, exploding frigates, imploding agents. They might announce the decease of Meisinger on active service. A posthumous medal might be awarded. He served the nation. The waitress at The Hut served me another Sanka coffee.

"You were totally wrong," I told Lauterman, "there was no grand civil war in The Family. It was all a private tiff over control of the Beirut video smuggling trade."

"It's quite possible," he said, while the birds tweeted outside, and Anat remained loudly silent. "That may well have been the clinching item in the Ganef's fabulous haul. The details of Meisinger's petty larceny. That would have been his greatest secret. Making him run through hoops of fire to Lebanon, to try and safeguard his investment. Whether Gingi had those files or not - Meisinger had to make sure in person. Could he trust his minions with such dynamite? You can imagine the revelations: the presses humming, the PM's moustache turning blue: 'Video-recorders, comrade?!' Meisinger could have kissed goodbye then to the Joint Family Committee Chairmanship. It's the ridiculous that undermines power. Criminality in itself is no obstacle. Remember what sunk Nixon: burglary, tax fraud. Not mass killings in Cambodia."

"Meisinger said the videos were the Gingi's project."

"Then the Gingi wouldn't have been able to use them against Meisinger. No, the Gingi's story was true, everything points towards that. It was Meisinger who was bent as a bagel."

"Fuck them all," I said, "I believe none of them. I'm tired of living in their private nightmares."

"So the Gingi was an imperfect hero," said Lauterman, "What else can you expect nowadays? We are all floundering in the same quicksand. It's the Middle East, Joe."

The Middle East. The excuse for everything. The killing, the delusions of grandeur. The fanaticism, the corruption, confusion and false witness, the disengagement of mouth and brain. The private agonies and loose ends dangling from the ruins of my violated summer: poor Doormat Menahem Dahab, caught in Meisinger's mangle ... The vanished brothers Khatib, rival players of both ends against a non-existent middle ... (in which café would we next rendezvous to reopen the flow of reproaches?) ... The Whisky Lady, slain by the resurrected ex-priest (surely a sign there somewhere?) ... Not to speak of my slaughtered Lebanon guardians, paying the price of Levantine free enterprise – the diehard enemy, become too familiarly human when their sweat mingles with one's own ... And the Gingi himself, Abel failing to slay Cain, leaving a trail of dead near innocents. The Middle East. Futile death is so modish. Clashing visions of unreality. A multitude of ultimate truths and none. But are all our agonies the outcome of conspiracies or abysmal incompetence? Or both? Everyone has a plan, but everything goes wrong, all the way down the line ...?

Anat told me, when she unbent enough for verbal discourse: "Joe, whatever happened out there, you'll have to decide, all over again, from the start: do you want to be a player, or to abstain? I don't have a choice, as you know. I have had to be an outsider while you performed your dance of death with your three old army friends ..."

Therein lies the cause, then, of the frosty silences, the withdrawal of the touch-me fingers ... Not the physical or mental trauma of the events themselves, but the sheer idiotic extent of my plunge into everything we had decided to run from ... My total embrace of the *zeitgeist*, the ghost of the times, Reich's Modju, the Emotional Plague ... "He peeked and was stricken", goes the phrase in Hebrew. The defilement of our private sanctuary. A heavy job to be done as time passes to rebuild these shattered bridges ...

Anat is right. I have not escaped from my moulding. The male prerogative, the potential of power. I too might have been a Gingi, a Moishe, even, God help us, a Meisinger. Nourished by the same dreams, nurtured in adjoining cocoons. The Four Sons (Of Whom the Torah Spake) are within me, lodging in my intestines. And, as I once again traversed the blazing streets of my centripetal city, the hard sun, the soft brains, the heavy hearts, the venus flytrap of unyielding history, evading my duties, fighting shy of inquisitors, dodging the loudspeaker vans exhorting me to vote for this or that salvation, my thoughts kept returning to Moishe Sherman, the little Ganef of old Yellin Street. Moishe, who was going to make his mark on the world by grabbing anything that came to hand. A kindergarten comrade's toy truck, or a secret service mogul's private database ... He must have planned his coup for years, a fitting revenge for his six years' incarceration ... A sock in the eye for Meisinger who had failed to help him in his hour of need ... But behind the rationale, that old compulsion, the abstract desire incarnate: I want, I want, I want. They say it's inadequate toilet training. But I can sympathise with his manic overkill, his obsession with beating the system that doomed him to being a volitionless tool. Dying to go for the whole pot. Ending up as the sacrificial stew. And no known resting place even for his picked bones ...

I returned to my synagogue, to much handshaking, shoulder-clapping and mumbling under beards. Returned to resume my unfinished monologue with the Great Manipulator. Everyone around me singing His praises, telling Him what they expect of Him. But I remain baffled. A fearful randomness seems to rule men's affairs. Anat accepts it, happy to reflect the world about her in its cracked facets, hanging desperate daubings on walls. But I am eaten by discontent. I demand to see Justice prevail. The lion will lie down with the calf or I will bloody well know the reason why. But as Woody Allen, I think, has said, the calf will not get much sleep.

All about me the rise and fall of the litany, repetitions of the familiar. Not much cause here to wonder about Jewish undergrounds, espionage wars, general elections. Whether Labour, or Likud, or both, or neither, win or lose, this is constant. Perhaps this constancy is the straw I clutch at. The kind drowning men set faith in. Like that memory of a lost Jerusalem street, with two small boys running, screeching with delight because they have managed to snatch a giant brassière from Mrs Tischler's laundry. Raising my voice with the congregation I joined the gallop towards the end of the evening service, closing in on the mourner's Kaddish, the prayer for the departed. Climaxed by the age-old expression of hope and reinforcement:

> Be not afraid of sudden terror, nor of the storm that strikes the wicked. Form your plot – it shall fail; lay your plan, it shall not prevail. For God is with us. Even to old age I will be the same; in your grey hairs I will sustain you. It is I who made you and I who will bear you; I who will sustain and save you.

I yam what I yam. Amen, Selah.
I said Kaddish for Moishe-Ganef.

MOURNER'S KADDISH

Glorified and sanctified be the Lord's name in the world he has created as he thought fit. May his kingdom be established, salvation be hastened and his Messiah brought near, in your lifetime and in your days and in the life of the whole house of Israel, speedily and soon, and say Amen.

May the Lord's name be blessed forever and for all time.

Blessed and praised and glorified and exalted and extolled and lauded be the name of the Holy One, Blessed be He, above all blessings and hymns, praises and consolations that are uttered in the world, and say Amen.

May there be the Lord's peace from heaven, and a good life, upon us and upon all Israel, and say Amen.

He who makes peace in his heavens, he will bring peace upon us and upon all Israel, and say Amen.